THE

SIEGE

AT

SIMEON HEIGHTS

He Thought They Were Only Legend...
Until They Threatened His Family

A NOVEL

Inspired by True Accounts

KYLE STEEL

FIRST EDITION

Copyright © 2023, by Kyle Steel

ISBN: 978-1-7777784-5-3

WILD REMNANT PUBLISHING
2023

To my three beloved children:
Jason, Marissa, and *Katelyn.*

You inspire me... to keep telling stories.

"I'm a romantic. I would like Bigfoot to exist. I've met people who swear they've seen Bigfoot. I think the interesting thing is every single continent there is an equivalent of Bigfoot or Sasquatch. There's the Yeti, the Yowie in Australia, the Chinese Wildman, and on and on and on. I've heard stories from people who, you have to believe them. So, there's something. I don't know what it is."
~JANE GOODALL, world-renowned primatologist

"Given the scientific evidence that I have examined, I'm convinced there's a creature out there that is yet to be identified."
~JEFFREY MELDRUM, anthropologist and cryptozoologist

"The savage in man is never quite eradicated."
~HENRY DAVID THOREAU, naturalist & author

ACKNOWLEDGEMENTS

Writing a fiction book has proven to be more challenging and rewarding than I initially anticipated. Throughout this journey, I have come to realize that the creation of a great story involves the contributions of numerous individuals. In his book "The 17 Indisputable Laws of Teamwork," John C. Maxwell aptly states:

"As much as we admire solo achievement, the truth is that no lone individual has done anything of value. The belief that one person can do something great is a myth. There are no real Rambos who can take on a hostile army by themselves. Even the Lone Ranger wasn't really a loner. Everywhere he went, he rode with Tonto! Nothing of significance was ever achieved by an individual acting alone. Look below the surface and you will find that all seemingly solo acts are really team efforts."

This principle certainly applies to this book.

I have been passionate about Cryptid encounters for many years now. But I have never had, nor do I necessarily wish to have a personal encounter. Encounters with these creatures can be life-changing, but also quite traumatic. Instead, to gather information and truth about these creatures and their behavior, I have relied on the testimonies of others.

Therefore, as I express my gratitude to those who have assisted in the creation of this book, I first want to

extend my heartfelt appreciation to all the individuals
who have encountered Bigfoot (or other cryptids) and
have exhibited the bravery to share their experiences. To
all those who have faced fear, ridicule, or worse—thank
you for being brave and candid enough to talk about your
encounters on podcasts, videos, blogs, or in person. It
was though your testimonies that I have gained
knowledge of the creatures, and the inspiration to write
this book. I am forever in your debt. I pray God blesses
you in mighty ways.

I would also like to extend my thanks to those
who provide platforms for individuals to share their
testimonies. The bloggers, podcasters, and YouTubers
who generously invest their time and resources in this
endeavor deserve recognition and gratitude. These are
the places, podcasts especially, where I have heard burly
men, hunters, experienced outdoorsmen, and even
military men, shed tears while sharing their powerful
testimonies and reliving their horrid experiences. Many
such individuals have expressed their gratitude to the
hosts of these broadcasts, recognizing them as the closest
thing to therapy available. Moreover, these platforms
have become invaluable sources of truth and testimonies
regarding Bigfoots and other cryptids. For all this, and
more, thank you.

Finally, I must acknowledge the indispensable
role of my wife, Elisabeth, in completing this work. Her
profound knowledge of the subject matter, along with
her timely advice and unwavering support, have been
instrumental in bringing this project to fruition. Liz, I
thank God every day for your presence in my life.

CONTENTS

Prologue

Thursday, January 20th, 8:25 p.m.

It wasn't something you'd see every day, the military engaging on a private property like this. Heck, it was downright unusual for them to get mixed up in anything civilian-related out here in rural America, especially in our quiet little Pacific Northwest community.

But you know what? These folks were my neighbors, and even though we only exchanged a few words here and there, I couldn't help but be naturally curious and concerned about what was going on.

So, as I passed by their property, I hit the brakes and slowed down, hoping to catch a better glimpse of the whole commotion. But with the darkness swallowing everything up, I could barely make out anything.

All I managed to catch was a quick glimpse of Michelle and her two teenage daughters. I forget their names, sorry. But poor Michelle; she had tears streaming down her face and looked mighty distraught. And here's the kicker; her husband Kevin was nowhere in sight, and that added to my growing concern.

Now, picture this scene: military vehicles scattered all over the place, clogging up the road and their driveway. I reckon there must've been at least five of 'em—I'm not kidding! And right there on the street, you had soldiers playing traffic cops, making sure things stayed under wraps. Oh, and let's not forget the two all-black SUVs and that big black pickup truck.

But what really caught my eye was when I saw four or five soldiers loading something huge, covered in a massive tarp, into that pickup truck. It was something big, believe me.

Fast forward to the following week, and the Thompsons, our neighbors, were gone in the blink of an eye. They had only been living here a couple of years, and then poof! Just like that, they packed up and vanished without a trace. No explanations, no warnings, not even a proper goodbye. And ever since then, no news or nothing.

Now, you know how people in small towns can't resist talking, right? Well, let me tell you, we sure talked about this for a good while, and boy, were the rumors flying' left and right. Even Glenda was in on it. Cu rious about what I'd told her, she asked me to go check it out once their house stood empty. But even without her coaxing, I would have gone. Truth be told, I couldn't resist the urge to go investigate and form my own opinion on the matter. Of course, once I got there, the doors were locked up tight, courtesy of the realtor. But the back of the house told a different story.

As I made my way around the back, the signs of some kind of altercation became crystal clear. The house had taken some damage, and the large workshop out back wasn't looking so hot either. But what really caught my attention was the missing back door to the house. To keep intruders at bay, a massive plywood plank had been nailed over the entrance. Now, I could've forced my way in, but out of respect, I didn't.

That's when things clicked in my mind, and I started connecting the dots. And let me tell you, as I pieced it all together, I couldn't help but imagine the horrific nightmare this poor family had endured, and it sent shivers down my spine.

As I left the property, I was dead certain that house would be on the market for a long, long time.

Boy, was I wrong.

I

The Mourning After

Monday, June 27th, 8:21 a.m.

He had been staring out the window for over half an hour. His gaze was unfocused, lost in thought. Every so often, his eyes would flicker towards the phone, then to the alarm clock, and back out the window. The question of whether he should make the call continued to linger in his mind.

Carter Mitchell had almost grown accustomed to his nightmares by now. Almost, but not quite. The relentless recurrence of these haunting dreams had become an unfortunate part of his life, tormenting him night after night for the past eight months.

Within those nightmares, he vividly relived the traumatic experience. It was as if he were transported back to that dreadful moment with all its intensity. The overwhelming feeling of helplessness gripped him just as strongly as it had during the actual seven seconds of that horrific ordeal. He could see everything unfolding in slow motion, a whirlwind of chaos and despair. His right arm desperately extended over Vivian's torso, his sole focus on shielding her and preventing her from being ejected from the vehicle. But it was always in vain, for he could never alter the horrific outcome.

The frequency of the subconscious night terrors remained consistent; their final result unchanged—every single night.

And so, each morning, as the haze cleared from his mind and reality seeped back in, he awoke to a profound emptiness, plagued by a sense of turmoil and dejection. His once vibrant life now felt half-empty, a constant reminder of the haunting memories that refused to release their grip on him.

Ironically, as he continued his gaze outside, he couldn't help but despise the view from his apartment window. The condominium, with its functional, sleek design, possessed an aesthetic appeal, yet it was never his personal choice. Living amidst a bustling city of over 600,000 people was never his intention, either. Having grown up in the countryside, the city life was something he loathed. The sight of gray dreary streets, monotonous apartment buildings, and what he deemed to be rat-raced individuals, only worsened his persistent melancholy. However, despite his aversion to urban living, his love for Vivian surpassed all else. And since she had a fondness for the vibrant city life, the decision had been an obvious one to make. He had agreed to endure the desolate view, and sacrifice his rural roots, all for her sake.

Back when she was pregnant with their first child, they had moved there. During that time, she dedicated herself to transforming the three-bedroom condo into a comforting and welcoming home. Every detail was meticulously taken care of. The pastel decor, though simple, exuded elegance and an inviting atmosphere. Her fingerprints were all over, from the smallest trinket to the carefully selected frames on the walls. The colors throughout the apartment harmonized seamlessly, confirming her keen eye for design.

But clearly, she was no longer here, and there was no chance of her return. With her departure, the heart and soul of the apartment left alongside her, leaving behind a void that could never be filled.

Sighing deeply and mustering his courage, Carter finally picked up his phone and called.

A burly voice picked up at the other end. "McCormick's Plumbing."

"Hey, boss. It's me."

"Carter? What's going on? You should have been here an hour ago."

"Um, yeah. I know. About that... I'm sorry. I'm... gonna have to take this week off."

"Um, all right. So, more time off, huh?"

"Yeah, I guess I do. Sorry for the inconvenience," Carter said apologetically.

He had been in and out from work for months. Initially, after the accident, both his body and mind needed time to heal. But at this point, his body had recovered for well over six months. His mind was now the only thing holding him back from the job he once loved and a semblance of normalcy.

"Look, Carter, I understand. I mean, I think I do. But the thing is… I'm trying to run a business here. I…" The man sighed as he paused, "I need *reliable people,* and right now, you're not one of them." Bill paused once more, carefully mulling over his next words, understanding the delicate situation. "Look, Carter… you take some more time—unpaid, of course. However, if you don't come back full time by the first of next month, I'm… I'm gonna have to find someone who will. In the meantime, get some help, okay?"

"Yes, I understand," said Carter.

"Look, um, maybe coming in to work gradually, just a few days a week, would help you? Take your mind off things, you know? Sometimes that helps. We could set something up. Just think about it, okay?"

"Yeah, sure. I'll think about it. Um, thanks, boss."

"Sure. You take care, Carter."

"I will. Bye."

As he hung up, a deep realization settled within him. He just knew he would not be returning to work for McCormick's plumbing. Not today, and not ever.

It's not that he didn't value the job, his boss, or his co-workers. He genuinely appreciated his time there over the past few years. In fact, he found satisfaction in being a plumber. He had landed the position straight out of trade school, starting as an apprentice. Bill McCormick, the owner, was now nearing retirement age at sixty-five.

He had been in the plumbing business longer than Carter had been alive. Bill was a respected entrepreneur, an honorable man, and a fair boss who treated his employees well. And the salary, for a hired hand, was respectable too.

Carter knew he had the skills and experience to start his own plumbing business. Under Bill's guidance, he had honed his abilities and had even been encouraged by Bill himself. But he just couldn't envision himself shouldering all the responsibilities and obligations that came with running a small business—at least not yet. Besides, the mere thought of dealing with paperwork filled him with dread.

"Da-ad!" the voice of a tween girl shattered his self-absorbed thoughts and drew his attention away from the window.

Startled, he turned to face his daughter. "Hey there, sweetie, what's up?" he mumbled, trying to refocus his attention.

A pretty girl with brown hair, a ponytail, and sparkling blue eyes entered his room and plopped down on his bed beside him. Her presence suddenly brought a speck of life to the otherwise dreary space.

"Is this going to be *another* boring day?" she inquired, her voice tinged with anticipation. "Besides, it's Monday. Aren't you *late* bringing us to day camp?" she quizzed, secretly hoping her dad would take another day off from work.

Before he could respond, she continued with an air of frustration, "You know we're bored, right? We've been glued to the TV since 6:30, trying not to disturb you.

But spending the entire day cooped up in this dull apartment is *not* how I want to spend my summer."

He sighed, realizing the weight of his absence and the impact it had on his daughter's summer experience.

Despite her occasional outspokenness, Ellie had displayed a remarkable strength of character, resiliency, and maturity throughout their ordeal. She was also patient—most days. Carrying her own burden of grief, she had nonetheless persevered and successfully completed her school year. In fact, she shouldered the responsibility of looking after her five-year-old brother, Tyler, more often than she should have. Carter was acutely aware of the extent of her sacrifices, and the weight of guilt settled heavily on his heart as he reflected upon it. Despite the circumstances, he was still a parent. They still had him, at least. And he felt much guilt for not living up to this unique privilege recently.

Observing her eager expression, he responded, "You know what? You're *absolutely right*, sweetie. This weekend *was* boring. But today doesn't have to be. How about I whip up some delicious pancakes for breakfast? And later…"

"Later?" she probed, her eyes sparkling with curiosity.

"Well, later we could go… to the zoo. How does *that* sound?"

"Yesss! Hey, Tyler! Tyler! Guess what?!" she exclaimed, rushing towards the living room where her younger brother was engrossed in the TV.

With infectious excitement, Ellie shared the news, causing her little brother to burst with joyous shouts!

Carter witnessed their elation and felt a rare sense of contentment that had been elusive lately. It was a refreshing sight.

Scooping up Tyler in his arms, he looked at both of them and said, "Today, we're going to spend quality time together. You guys deserve a special treat."

"Darn straight we do," Ellie cheekily remarked without hesitation.

Carter simply chuckled at her clever response. She possessed a wit reminiscent of her mom, and he loved her for it.

———————◆◆◆◆◆———————

When seeking respite from life's troubles, the zoo offers a sanctuary like no other. Amidst its collection of exotic creatures from every corner of the globe, it's a great way to take one's mind off things. It's a welcome sensation enjoyed by children, and if adults are honest, they too succumb to its unique charm.

Carter enjoyed the temporary escape. But the best part for this 34-year-old newly single dad was to share in the joy and wonder of his two children. Like most parents, he now appreciated many experiences vicariously, through their wide-eyed perspectives.

"Daddy," Tyler chimed in, his excitement palpable. "Are we gonna see monkeys?"

Understandably, the boy's patience had already worn thin as they stood near the African wildebeests and zebras enclosure. Tyler was nothing short of adorable, his wavy dark blonde hair and expressive blue eyes mirroring his father's features.

"Of course, buddy," Carter replied with a smile. "And we'll see apes too. Do you know the difference between monkeys and apes?"

Tyler shook his head, curiosity evident in his gaze. "What's an apes, Dad?"

Carter chuckled softly. "Well, apes are like *big monkeys* without tails, and they kinda look like people."

"Really?!" the boy exclaimed, his eyes widening with wonder.

"Yeah, really," Carter affirmed, nodding. "Gorillas, chimpanzees, and orangutans; they're all apes. You've seen them on TV, right?"

"Uh-huh. Where are they, Dad? Let's go see apes," the boy urged eagerly.

"Well, according to this sign, they're just around the next bend," Carter said, pointing his son towards the anticipated encounter.

Standing just six feet away were two attractive ladies in their forties, listening in and enthralled by the endearing exchange between the boy and his dad. One of them, a blonde wearing shorts two sizes too short, was none-too-subtly eyeing Carter, who noticed the woman's flirtatious looks and smiles, among other things.

Ever since his late teens, Carter effortlessly attracted female attention. Standing at over six feet tall, with wavy dirty-blonde hair, a well-built athletic physique, captivating blue eyes, and a ruggedly handsome appearance, it was no surprise. Years of sports and physical labor had blessed him with natural fitness, strength, and a rugged charm. However, despite his magnetic appeal and popularity, he had always been a one-woman kind of man, preferring not to engage in casual relationships. This steadfast commitment to integrity was something he had learned from his father, the late John Mitchell, a faithful husband, and a man of firm principles who had dedicated himself to his family.

But, with that said, Carter wasn't blind either. Or dead.

Well, well, there are cougars at this zoo, too, he observed, musing to himself, and smiling back at the woman. Before he could indulge in further inappropriate thoughts, however, his phone rang, abruptly snapping him out of it.

"Who is it?" asked Ellie out loud, curious.

"It's Aunt Sadie. Stay here with your brother while I take this," he told her before picking up.

"Hey sis. How's it going?"

"Hi. I'm fine. I was just thinking of you guys and wanted to know how you were. Is everything okay for you and the kids?"

"Yeah, we're fine. I'm actually at the zoo with Ellie and Ty right now."

"Oh, really? That's nice. They must be thrilled! But what about you? What about work? Aren't you supposed to work today?"

"Yes, I was. But I called them. I, um, took the week off. I've got a lot on my mind. I still need to sort out some stuff."

There was a brief silence on the line. "Yeah, I know that. That's why I called. I'm... worried about you," she paused. "You know I'm always there for you if you need me, right?"

"Yeah, I know. And I really appreciate it," he said.

"And," she continued, "I was thinking, which is the *other* reason for my call... that maybe I could come over on my vacation at the end of July. I'd bring Marty along, and spend a week with you guys. Would that be okay with you?"

"Hey, if you promise to cook, I've got no problem with it," he said, chuckling.

"Of course I would cook. I don't want to subject myself or the kids to any food poisoning," she said, teasing him. "Well, I have to go. I just wanted to touch base and make sure you were all right."

"Yeah, we're good. Thanks for calling. Love you," he said.

"Bye, Aunt Sadie!" Ellie shouted, leaning over the receiver, just as her dad hung up.

As they approached the great apes' enclosure, they noticed a guided tour in progress. Leading the tour was a short, stocky man with a friendly mustache and a jovial demeanor. His voice carried with strength as he began his well-rehearsed speech, gesturing towards the chimpanzees.

"Ever since researchers sequenced the chimp genome in 2005, they have known that humans share about 99% of their DNA with chimpanzees. This makes them our closest living relatives," he told the crowd.

As the tour guide continued his lengthy discourse on the habitat, diet, and mating behaviors of the great apes, a man from the crowd couldn't contain his curiosity any longer. He raised his hand and interjected loudly, almost heckling, "Hey, what I really want to know is how strong they are?"

Pausing mid-sentence, the tour guide flashed a smile and responded, "It's funny how I get asked this question almost every single time."

Continuing his response, he then provided an astonishing revelation. "Well, if you must know, you don't want to tangle with a chimp, even the smaller ones. A chimpanzee can bench press between 1,250 to 2,000 lbs. This is about five to eight times greater than the weight a large adult man can bench-press—which is roughly 250 lbs." With an intense gaze, he directed his words at the interrupter, who happened to be a large man.

Not stopping there, the guide went on, "And that's nothing compared to orang-outangs or gorillas. A massive silverback gorilla possesses strength equivalent to fifteen regular men combined. They can easily bench around 4,000 pounds." Pausing for a moment, he let the weight of those numbers sink in. Locking eyes with the man, he concluded firmly, "I hope that sufficiently answers your question, sir."

Feeling a mix of embarrassment and amazement, the man nodded sheepishly and flashed an awkward smile. Carter, along with the rest of the crowd, stood in awe of the astonishing facts they had just heard.

As for Tyler, he was just excited about this revelation and eagerly asked his dad for a gorilla toy, "cause they're so strong," he said.

It's funny how boys are just drawn to physical strength, mused Carter, remembering his own fascination with it as a boy—and to this day. Indeed, he still enjoyed watching the occasional *World's Strongest Man* or *Mr. Olympia* competition.

After rounding up the zoo visit with majestic lions, fierce tigers, mighty bears, graceful wolves, elusive wolverines, and a gorilla toy for Ty, Carter looked at both of them and said, "All right guys, you must be starving after all this walking? How about we head on to *Burly Burgers* to finish this day off?"

"Yaayyy!!" they shouted excitedly.

"Oh, and I want a Big Burly combo, Dad! 'Cause I'm really hungry—like a tiger," exclaimed Ellie, mimicking a predator with her clawed hands and offering a playful roar.

He smiled at her, "You can have anything you want—within reason, of course."

As they made their way to Burly Burgers, Carter couldn't help but feel a mix of anticipation and nervousness. He wanted them to sit down and enjoy their favorite burgers, creating a comfortable atmosphere before sharing the important news he had been carrying. He hoped his children would understand and embrace the changes that were about to unfold.

Sluuurp, the sound of Ellie's straw vacuuming the few drops left and scraping the bottom of the soda cup broke the silence, indicating to her father that it was time to share the big news.

"So, um, you guys seemed to enjoy taking a walk on the wild side today, didn't you?" Carter began, trying to steer the conversation towards their memorable day at the zoo.

"Wild side? *Oh*, you mean *the zoo*? Sure did! I loved it! Especially the lions," Ellie replied, her attention fully focused on her dad. Meanwhile, Tyler continued to immerse himself in playing with his new gorilla toy, oblivious to the impending conversation.

Carter took a deep breath, gathering his thoughts before continuing, "You know, guys, it's been a good three months now since… since your mama, um, you know…"

The weight of his words hung in the air, and he could feel the heaviness in his heart. He realized that conveying the news to his children was going to be more challenging than he had expected.

After a pregnant pause, he continued, "I've been thinking a lot, you know. We have some good insurance money set aside now, and I know for a fact that if I sold our condo, we could really get—"

"Sell?" interrupted Ellie, her voice filled with shock. "Do you mean? Are you talking about us… *moving*?" Her face displayed a mix of fear and devastation.

Realizing the impact of his words, he tried to remain calm and reassuring. He took a deep breath before responding, "Ellie, I understand how this might be difficult for you to hear. But moving after losing a loved one is a common step for many families. Continuing to live in our apartment only makes it harder for all of us to move forward. The truth is, I constantly see your mom everywhere in our apartment—every day. It's... It's really hard. Don't you agree?"

Tears welled up in Ellie's eyes, and her voice trembled as she cried, "I see her too. But, dad, I *enjoy* seeing her everywhere! It's, like, it's all I have left of her."

Carter felt a lump forming in his throat as his daughter's heartfelt comment pierced through him.

Then, turning to her little brother and gripping his arm gently, as if to rally him to her side, she said, "Tyler... do you understand?! Dad wants us to move away! You don't want to leave our home and live somewhere else, *do you?* Dad wants to take us away from everything we know!"

Tyler, who was previously engrossed in his gorilla toy, now had tears welling up in his eyes. Clearly, the emotional weight of the conversation was beginning to affect him, too.

Sensing an urgent need for a change of setting, Carter decided it was time to leave the restaurant premises and continue the discussion in the family van. *They'll be buckled up, have nowhere to go, and hopefully I can be heard without distractions*, he thought.

As they drove home, he persisted in explaining his perspective, emphasizing how a fresh start and a new environment could be beneficial for the entire family. He shared about his own upbringing in the countryside, highlighting the benefits of fresh air, the beauty of nature, and the opportunity for a new perspective on life.

Although Ellie remained resistant and would have none of it, he knew he was getting through to Tyler. He could sense a glimmer of enthusiasm beginning to spark in his young son's eyes, as he further explained the potential for a positive change.

Either way, he had already decided. With the life insurance from Vivian, he had a solid financial cushion to take care of his family. He saw it as both a wise life decision and a smart financial move. Selling their condo would give them the opportunity to buy a spacious three-bedroom house in the countryside, complete with a generous plot of land—perhaps even over ten acres.

The ride home was long and filled with an air of sorrow. However, Carter understood the importance of discussing their future. Despite the challenges it presented, he knew it was necessary to involve his kids in important decisions.

As difficult as it was for Ellie to accept the idea of moving, he believed that in time, she would adjust to their new life. He was convinced that she would come around. To ease her worries, he made a heartfelt promise to her during the ride: she would have an amazing bedroom in their new home.

Nevertheless, he also knew that, although necessary, this would not be an easy transition. This *new* single-dad lifestyle was going to include a steep learning curve, and despite supportive individuals offering their help and words of encouragement, he couldn't escape the feeling of solitude. The persistent void, his profound sense of loneliness, and his deep melancholy were his current battles.

As he drove on, he gazed at the cloudy summer sky and the seeming unending horizon. He silently pleaded, *God, please… if you're there, give me strength.*

II

A Fresh Start

Thursday, June 30th, 2:45 p.m.

The real estate agent fixed a direct gaze upon Carter and spoke with a confident tone, saying, "Believe me, you won't come across another property in this county at such an incredible price. I've been in the real estate business in this area for over 15 years, and I can assure you of that. So, I'll give you a word of advice: this opportunity won't last long. If you're interested, I wouldn't waste any time."

But Carter wasn't born yesterday. He could see through the real estate agent's ploy to create a false sense of urgency and close the deal quickly. He knew well that the house had been on the market for well over seven months already. The main reason for its extended listing period was quite apparent: it required some serious TLC (tender loving care).

Despite being structurally sound, the house appeared rundown and neglected. The exterior walls boasted three foreboding holes, and the absence of the back door was conspicuous. To add to the disarray, a broken window on the top floor marred the overall appearance. It seemed the back door had been forcefully torn off its hinges, yet its whereabouts remained a mystery. It was nowhere to be found inside the house, on the property, in the garage, or even in the expansive workshop at the rear.

And speaking of the workshop, it held great potential for someone skilled in manual work, like Carter. However, its current state resembled that of a battleground, as if it had endured the aftermath of a violent conflict.

When confronted with inquiries about the property's history, the agent seemed evasive and ill-informed. His responses left Carter feeling uncertain and skeptical. It was unclear whether the agent genuinely lacked knowledge about the property's past, or if he was intentionally withholding information. Regardless, the absence of transparency regarding the house's previous owners or its background was far from reassuring.

Despite its clear imperfections, however, the aging house held immense potential. Its timeworn charm shone through the updates it had received, hinting at its former glory. The two-story structure boasted three upstairs bedrooms, perfectly suited for him and the kids. Downstairs, a cozy den, a spacious open-plan living room, a functional kitchen, and ample storage space awaited them. The convenience of an attached garage added to the house's appeal. Considering all it offered, the property was seriously undervalued, with an asking price that was around a third of its true market worth.

Inside, a remarkable fireplace adorned the living room, adding warmth and character to the space. From the kitchen's back patio, a breathtaking view of the surrounding woods and mountains awaited, creating a serene and picturesque atmosphere. The expansive backyard encompassed over an acre of land, while the entire lot extended even further, promising the kids an outdoor paradise to explore and revel in.

Taking everything into account, Carter wasn't overly concerned about the house's fixer-upper condition. He knew he possessed the necessary skills to handle most renovations, having always been adept with his hands. Besides, he viewed restoring the house as an exciting endeavor, especially since he had dedicated the entire summer to focus on his children and the move. With surging optimism, he saw the opportunity to turn this house into a cherished family home.

The property rested just beyond the town limits of Simeon Heights; a charming community nestled in the serene Pacific Northwest. With a population of approximately 6,250, it exuded a cozy small-town vibe while being conveniently located about an hour southeast of the bustling metropolis of Portland. What truly set this property apart was its expansive 45 acres of lush, wooded land, creating an idyllic haven for the family.

Adding to its appeal, a meandering creek flowed gracefully through the pristine acreage, teeming with trout and lending a touch of natural wonder to the surroundings. This picturesque feature was the proverbial icing on the cake for Carter, completing his lifelong vision of an ideal setting to raise his kids. The property offered a tranquil escape, removed enough from the hustle and bustle to savor peace and quiet, yet still within easy reach of schools and essential amenities. It struck the perfect balance. For a nature enthusiast, hunter, and introvert, the place held an irresistible appeal.

Looking the agent straight in the eye, he said bluntly, "It's in a sad state—especially the workshop. I'll have to think about it. But I'll let you know in 48 hours what I've decided."

The agent persisted, desperately clinging to his sales pitch, "Sad state *maybe*, but at that price... it'll probably be sold by then. You might want to make it 24 hours instead," adding, "I've got people lining up to visit it in the next two days."

"Well, you do what you gotta do. I still have to think about it." Said Carter, resolute.

He had made some hasty purchases in the past, most of which he regretted; especially that blue Ford Mustang convertible back when he was 21. Sure, the price was low, but the poor thing had been trashed so badly by its previous owner that it needed a new transmission six weeks after he bought it. And even after he'd invested a couple of thousand dollars into it, the car still had a habit of breaking down monthly. So, he didn't want to jump the gun on such a big purchase, even if the price was alluring. And maybe that was just it—it was too low, and that raised a red flag in his mind.

Amid all the uncertainties and doubts, however, he couldn't help but imagine himself and his children living in that house. The idyllic setting, with its abundance of nature, serene streams, and invigorating fresh air, resonated deeply with his own childhood memories. He cherished those childhood memories and longed for his two kids to have a taste of the same.

Later that evening, after a hectic day of errands and tasks, at around 8:30 pm, Carter thanked the babysitter and ensured the kids were settled in bed. Seeking a moment of respite, he plopped onto the couch and tried to get his mind off things while watching TV. But a subtle and unmistakable sound coming from his daughter's bedroom caught his ear.

Ellie was awake, crying in her bed.

Duty calls, he thought as he quickly rose from the comfortable couch and made his way to her bedroom. "Hey sweetie. What's wrong?" he asked, hesitantly leaning in the doorway. Ellie continued to whimper, not responding to his presence. *Well, since she's not telling me off, I'll just come right in*, he thought as he sat on her bed and placed his hand on her arm. Gently, he asked her, "What's on your mind? Why are you crying?"

"I just… really miss mom," Ellie replied, sniffling. "I really don't want to move, daddy. I like it here. This is our home. And I don't want to change school or lose my friends."

Saddened, he looked down, pondering what to say next. *Now isn't a time for me to tell her just how much I miss her mom, too. That would just make matters worse*, he thought. Gathering his thoughts, he gently took hold of Ellie's hand with both of his and said, "Ellie... do you trust me?" He paused, giving her a moment to consider his question. "Do you *trust* that I genuinely love you and care for you?"

Hesitant, she responded, "Y--yes," unsure about the loaded question and how her answer might affect things further.

"Then you'll have to give me the rest of this summer to prove to you that good things are coming, okay?" he said, hoping to provide some reassurance.

She simply looked at him, her expression waiting for further disclosure.

Observing the anticipation in her face, he proceeded, "I might have found us a new place to live." Seeing her surprised look, he quickly added, "*But* you have to trust me that everything will be okay. *Trust me* that your happiness and well-being are at the top of my list. Can you do *that*?"

No longer shedding tears, Ellie sat up in her bed and inquired, "You bought a new place?"

"No, not yet," he clarified. "But I've come across an interesting property, and I'm considering buying it."

"Where is it?" she asked, now brimming with curiosity.

"Hey, tell you what," he said. "Instead of telling you about it, how about *tomorrow* I take you guys to go see it? Would you like that?"

"Yeah!" she exclaimed, now wearing a smile.

"All right," he replied. "First thing in the morning, we'll all go see it, and then decide *together* if this is what we want."

Bending over, he kissed her forehead and tucked her in tenderly.

———————————◆◆◆◆————————————

The following day, during a thorough and extended second visit to the property, it became clear that the kids were smitten with it—particularly Tyler, who gleefully raced up and down the stairs with his toy gorilla.

Initially hesitant, Ellie's uncertainty waned as she explored the upper level and caught sight of what would be her bedroom. The room boasted a picturesque view of the spacious yard and the majestic mountains. A radiant excitement filled her eyes, and by the end of the visit, she was imagining which curtains would suit her new sanctuary.

With his children so enthralled, Carter saw this as confirmation; a blessing on the purchase and a clear sign to move forward. So, he called the agent, made arrangements, and put a conservative offer on the table. He knew it was risky to make a low offer on an already inexpensive property, and the agent warned him that the sellers might be insulted. But, despite it all, and to his surprise, the offer was accepted. *Another green light from destiny*, he thought.

Of course, such a significant move required tying up some loose ends back home. One of these tasks was to inform Bill McCormick that he was resigning and wouldn't be returning to McCormick's plumbing. Surprisingly, the big man took the news well and even admitted that he had expected it. With a sincere smile, he firmly shook Carter's hand, "I wish you all the best—you and your family. You're a good man, Carter… and a good worker. And, *take my advice*, in a small town, you should offer your services as an independent contractor."

"Well, I've been seriously thinking about it. I might just do that. Once again, thanks for everything," reciprocated Carter, shaking his hand, and even hugging the bigger man.

Tying up another loose end; the sale of the condo turned out to be a swift and seamless transaction. To Carter's delight, a young couple of Asian descent, two professionals, made a generous offer within just a few days of it being listed for sale. The deal was completed smoothly, and it brought in a significant profit. As a result, Carter's bank account had never been fatter.

These fortuitous events made it abundantly clear to the Mitchell family that their path was providentially leading them to their new destination: the charming town of Simeon Heights. And with the fresh path came a fresh start.

Still needing to inform his sister Sadie about the sudden move, Carter dreaded it. They had grown tight since her divorce five years ago, the death of their father two years ago, and even more so in the last few months, after Vivian's passing. Sadie had taken on a more active role with the kids, visiting often and often bringing home-cooked meals. The kids absolutely loved their aunt Sadie and their cousin Marty, who was three years older than Ellie.

Although he wouldn't be moving too far from Portland, Carter knew Sadie would probably give him grief about uprooting the kids and moving away. She still acted like a first-born with him, no matter what he did.

Nevertheless, he put on his big boy pants, braced himself, and made the call...

"I understand how you may be feeling about this, but... what about Ellie?" Sadie asked, foreseeing the potential impact on her niece.

"Well, she needed some reassuring, but, after one visit, she's sold on the house... *and the move*. So, it's all good," he replied.

He continued, "And I did my homework. There's a decent school in Simeon Heights that'll be perfect for her. I even found an affordable daycare for Ty."

"Okay, *fine*. I'll give you that. But what about you?" She probed. "Are you even sure this is the right decision at this time? Isn't it too hasty? You haven't exactly been the best version of yourself lately. You didn't even take my advice and meet with the grief counselor I recommended!" She said, expressing concern.

The line fell silent as he weighed her words. Deep down, he knew she was raising valid concerns. In fact, he had been grappling with the same ones and had experienced moments of intense self-doubt. Despite his outwardly rugged demeanor, Carter was a man of deep emotions who often relied on his instincts rather than strict rationality. And when it came to justifying his own decisions to others, especially under intense scrutiny, like now; he struggled to find the right words.

Regretting her previous crossness, however, Sadie composed herself and apologized, "Hey, *look...* I'm sorry."

After a sigh and a momentary pause, she continued, "I don't want to make you feel worse than you already do. I know this probably wasn't a simple decision. I'm just..." she trailed and sighed once more, "I'm just very *concerned*—about you, about the suddenness of this move, and about the kids. And, I guess... I guess I just don't want my little brother moving away."

And then, attempting to bring some levity to the situation, she remarked, "But, hey, it's not like I can't come and visit, right? I mean... it's just over an hour away, for Pete's sake!"

"Right," he responded, still processing the weight of it all.

In an effort to reconcile further, she inquired, "So, um, are we still on for the end of July? I could assist you with finishing unpacking and putting up curtains and frames. You know... give the new house a much-needed feminine touch." She chuckled, looking at the bright side.

With an inward sigh of relief, he said, "Of course you should come. The kids will be glad to see you and Marty—and so will I."

After ending the call, Carter reflected, *one good thing about Sadie is that while she's quick to anger, she's also quick to forgive.*

And with that, the hardest part of the move was dealt with.

***

"You guys stay where I can see you," Carter shouted, holding a screwdriver in his hand, as he added the final touches to the new backdoor of his house.

Ellie and Tyler explored the beautiful scenery and spacious property, clearly enjoying every moment as if it were a summer camp adventure.

Immediately after he had put in the new back door, Carter's gaze shifted to Tyler's bedroom window just above, on the second floor, reminding him it required a new one. *Yeah, definitely a fixer-upper,* he thought with a sigh.

His task-oriented train of thought was suddenly disrupted by the unmistakable sound of a vehicle making its way onto his driveway, its tires crunching against the gravel.

Following the noise, Carter turned the corner of the house and headed towards the front, where he spotted an elderly couple stepping out of a dark blue Ford pickup truck. The lady, pleasant in demeanor and her hair neatly tied in a bun, held a basket in her hands, while the man, appearing to be close to seventy, carried a large aluminum container.

"Hello there!" the woman greeted with genuine enthusiasm as she caught sight of Carter approaching them.

"Hello. Can I help you?" Said Carter, unsure of what to expect.

"We're the MacArthurs, your neighbors. I'm Glenda, and this is my husband, Henry," she introduced, pointing towards the gentleman. "We live just down the road, just over half a mile from here. We're your closest neighbors."

Carter observed how Henry appeared reluctant, as if being pulled along by his wife. He avoided making eye contact and seemed visibly uneasy. *Maybe he's just shy*, Carter mused. On the other hand, Glenda embodied the image of a picture-perfect granny, looking no more than 65, radiating cheerfulness and warmth.

"Pleased to meet you. I'm Carter Mitchell," he said, extending his hand after quickly wiping it on his jeans. Just then, Ellie and Tyler came running, drawn by the unfamiliar voices. "… And these are my two children, Ellie and Tyler," he introduced, pointing to them as they approached.

"Well, what a *lovely family!*" she exclaimed, her gaze shifting between Carter, the kids, and the front door, as if half-expecting their mother to emerge.

She then said, "I made you some lasagna, and in this basket, you'll find some fresh-baked biscuits. We know how hard it can be to have just moved, especially with young ones. Isn't that right, Henry?" she asked, looking at him with hopeful eyes, wishing for a more affable response.

He just grunted back, "Um, yeah. That's right."

"Thank you so much for this!" Carter exclaimed gratefully, reaching for the food. He added, "It's very nice of you to come here and greet us like this."

"Oh, it's no problem at all," she replied, pausing briefly before asking, "If I may ask, where did you move from?"

"We came here from Portland," he said.

"Oh, well, you'll find it much quieter here, I'm sure," she said, smiling down at both Ellie and Tyler.

Carter pondered for a moment before hesitantly speaking up, "Um, can I ask you a question?"

"Sure! Ask away, dear," Glenda replied, kindly encouraging his inquiry.

"Well, this house, as you probably know, it's in a bit of a sad state. I mean, I've been working on it non-stop for three days already," he said, pointing at it. "Believe it or not, the back door, it seems, was torn off its hinges. I couldn't even find it anywhere around the property. And the workshop seems to have gone through hell and back. The real estate agent had very little info to give me about the previous owners. So, I was wondering…" He paused, slightly uneasy, looking at both of them. "What can you tell me about them? Why was the house left in such a poor condition? Any idea?"

Now, more than ever, Henry was visibly uncomfortable. He avoided eye contact with Carter and kept glancing back at his pickup truck, as if seeking an imaginary escape route.

Glenda adopted a more serious demeanor as well. Then she responded, "Oh, well, you know… this is a small town. We hear all kinds of things all the time. Most of it is just gossip and rumors. But what I can tell you is that the last family to live here, the Thompsons, only stayed for two years. They were pretty private, so I have little information, except that they seemed like nice people. As for the damage… well, we are in the Pacific Northwest, and the house was vacant for a while. It could be wildlife, a bear, maybe? But my best guess is that it was probably the work of up-to-no-good *hooligans*." She looked at Carter, nodding with a matter-of-fact expression.

But, being familiar with the area, and being an experienced outdoorsman himself, Carter couldn't help but question the notion of black bears causing such destruction. He was well aware that these bears were not typically known for their brazen behavior. Moreover, the larger and more aggressive grizzly bear had been extinct in the region for nearly a century. And as for teenagers, the house was quite a way off from the town center. *The distance itself would be a deterrent—well, maybe*, he thought.

Seeing his visible perplexity, she then added, "But I wouldn't worry about it too much if I were you. You'll see, Simeon Heights is a wonderful little community, and the people here are very nice."

And then, looking at Ellie, she said, "And we have some good elementary schools, too. I myself am a retired teacher. I used to teach at Simeon Heights Elementary for

25 years, which is where you'll probably end up going this fall, right Ellie?"

"Um, I guess so," said Ellie, shyly.

Glenda smiled. Looking back at Carter, she said, "Well, we won't keep you any longer, darling. You must be so busy unpacking and all. We just wanted to drop by and introduce ourselves. And if you need anything, anything at all, don't be shy; we're just a holler away. Isn't that right, Henry?" She said, turning to her husband.

By the time she had finished her sentence however, Henry was already walking back to his truck. *Finally, free from this hostile social takeover,* thought Carter, slightly puzzled by his new neighbor's antisocial behavior. *Then again, who am I to call anyone antisocial?* he thought, amused by the irony.

Nevertheless, a nagging suspicion gnawed at him, suggesting that Henry knew something about his recently obtained property.

The next morning, Carter was enjoying a quiet cup of coffee after taking two Ibuprofen caplets to counter the muscle memory from yesterday's hard labor. Suddenly, he heard Tyler's unmistakable scream of pain erupt from the yard, jolting him wide-awake. Rushing to the kitchen patio door that opened onto the wooden deck in the backyard, he found Ellie running towards him, shouting, "Ty's hurt! He tripped on a big rock and hit his head!"

"Oh, *crap!*" exclaimed Carter, his heart racing as he quickly rushed towards his five-year-old. He found Tyler sitting on the ground, bawling and clutching his forehead with his right hand.

"Mamaaaa! Maaaama!!" He screamed, distressed.

"Hey, buddy, it's okay. I'm right here. Daddy's here," he reassured, his voice filled with concern.

"Mommy! Maaaamaaa!" Tyler wailed even louder, longing for his mother's comforting presence.

"Come here, buddy. Let's have a look at you," he replied, trying to soothe his son's escalating distress.

"Mammaaaaaa!"

"Mama isn't here, Ty. Let Daddy have a look at you," he said once more, his tone now filled with both urgency and growing impatience.

But the boy just kept wailing even louder, "Mammaaaaa!"

Carter's patience wore thin, and he pleaded forcefully, his tone now tinged with frustration, "she's not here! Do you understand, Ty? Mommy's not here. Remove your hand and let Daddy look at you,"

But the boy would have none of it, his cries persisting as he continued calling for his mother.

That's when the 34-year-old single father snapped.

He got up, gazing at the heavens for a moment before locking eyes with Ty. In a moment of overwhelming frustration, he yelled, "She's gone, *okay?!* Mommy's *not here!* She can't help you! She's not coming back! She's *gone!* Do you understand that?! There's only me! I'm the only one who can help you! Do you understand that?! There's only Daddy now!"

With those words hanging heavy in the air, he turned his back on Ty, his hand covering his mouth, tormented by the bitterness of his own words and the sharpness of his tone. The weight of his outburst sank in, filling him with remorse.

Just a few feet away, Ellie stood, her eyes filled with tears as she looked up at her father. In a low, bitter, and trembling voice, she uttered, "Oh… Daddy."

Carter felt the sharp disappointment in his daughter's voice, and it pierced his heart.

Ellie, sensing the weight of responsibility now resting on her shoulders, knelt before her little brother and tenderly embraced him, trying to console and calm him amid their shared turmoil.

Ty's cries had subsided to labored groans and moans, indicating a slight sense of relief. Carter, aware of the two pairs of innocent eyes fixed upon him, felt the weight of their expectations. Despite the void left by their mother's absence, his children relied on him, and in this moment, he couldn't help but feel a deep sense of inadequacy. He felt so overwhelmed by the challenges of being a single parent, working his way through unknown terrain, often feeling it's too much for him to bear.

After a prolonged silence, lost in his thoughts and gazing into the distance, he regained his composure. Turning his attention back to Ty once more, he noticed a newfound calmness in both of them. He tenderly put his hand on his son's head and said, "I'm so sorry, little buddy. Daddy's sorry, okay? Daddy wants to help you. But for that... you need to let me look at you, *okay?*"

Convinced and reassured, Tyler slowly removed his hand from his forehead, revealing a nasty bump. Carter examined the injury and said, "Well, son, I've got good news and bad news for you." He paused, allowing a subtle smile to form on his face, and continued, "The good news is that you're going to be okay. It's just a bump on the head. And the bad news is that... well, you've inherited your dad's hard-headedness." Pausing for a moment to let the remark sink in, he let out a hearty laugh.

Witnessing her father's lightened mood, Ellie couldn't help but join in, her laughter echoing in the air. The sight of both his dad and sister laughing also proved contagious for Tyler. Amidst his relief and lingering tears, he couldn't resist and began laugh-crying as well, now finding humor and relief in his circumstance.

Ellie then pointed to the rock on which Tyler had tripped and added, "There are a lot of big rocks in our yard, dad. Look around. We should get rid of them; you know, for safety."

Carter surveyed the yard and, taken aback by the observation, nodded in agreement. He hadn't realized the extent of the sizable rocks scattered across the property grounds. Varying in size from a baseball to a softball and even larger; they did pose a threat to active children.

Acknowledging her point, he turned and responded, "Yeah, you're right, Ellie. These *are* dangerous. I'll come back and throw them past the tree-line after breakfast. In the meantime, can you prepare a cold compress for Tyler and then sit him in front of the TV?"

"Sure," she answered. And, turning to her little brother, she said, "Come on Ty, let's go watch TV."

———————————●◦●◦●———————————

The grass was ankle high on the property grounds, which explained why Carter hadn't noticed the rocks before. With many pressing tasks on his mind for repairing the house, the presence of rocks in the yard had been low on his list of priorities.

For the larger rocks, he gathered them in a wheelbarrow and transported them to the outskirts of the woods, depositing them amongst the trees. As for the smaller stones, roughly the size of baseballs, he took delight in honing his baseball throw by launching them over the tree line. In those moments, memories of his glory days as a third baseman in high school flooded back, evoking a sense of nostalgic pleasure.

There must be over a hundred of these, he thought, puzzled as to why the ex-owners tolerated or even desired that.

With the task of removing the rocks complete, he grasped the handle of the wheelbarrow and began making his way back towards the workshop. However, his peaceful stride was abruptly interrupted when an object swiftly whizzed past his left ear, rebounded off the ground, and forcefully collided with the exterior wall of the workshop.

To his surprise and shock, it was a large rock, comparable in size to a softball.

Startled by the sudden and unexpected occurrence, his body jolted with a surge of adrenaline, causing his heart to race within his chest. With a mix of confusion and concern, Carter swiftly pivoted around, his eyes scanning the area from left to right, trying to discern the source of the incident. His mind raced as he wondered if this was done by the same people who had caused all the property damage, finally exposing themselves.

"Hello?!" his voice trembled with nervousness as he shouted into the silence. "Anybody out there?!"

The only response he received was the rustling of leaves in the wind, amplifying the eerie stillness that enveloped the surroundings. Frustration mixed with concern, he continued, raising his voice, "Your rock almost took my head clean off. I had no idea someone was out there. I hope my rocks didn't hit you." His words carried an apologetic tone, echoing loudly through the empty space.

Seconds stretched into an eternity as he waited, hoping for any sign of a presence. But once again, there was no reply, no sign of another soul nearby. Determined not to be ignored, he mustered all his strength and called out once more, "Hellooo!" The sound reverberated through the air, but it was met with the same profound silence. No birds chirped; no crickets chirped in response.

His voice trailed off, the frustration mounting within him. It seemed as if the stillness had swallowed his words, leaving him with nothing but an unanswered call echoing in the emptiness.

He cast one last nervous glance towards the wood line, his senses heightened by the unsettling silence. Apprehensively, he turned around, his grip tightening on the handles of the wheelbarrow, as he slowly began making his way back to the workshop, his steps more cautious than before.

And then, out of nowhere, once again shattering the tranquility that surrounded him, a massive rock crashed onto the ground just six feet ahead. *What the--!* Carter's heart skipped a beat, his mind racing to comprehend the sudden intrusion.

Now filled with a surge of anger, his frustration overshadowed any fear he might have felt. Determined not to back down, he turned around abruptly and stormed towards the wood line, his voice echoing with fury.

"Are you *insane*?!" he bellowed, his words laced with a mix of anger and indignation. "That could have ended my life! And I have kids living here, for crying out loud!" His voice reverberated through the stillness of the surroundings as he unleashed his frustration.

"Don't make me bring out my shotgun!" he warned, his tone resolute. "I'm not afraid to use it, especially on *scum like you!* Do you *hear* me? You don't want to mess with me!" Each word was punctuated with resolve, as if daring the unseen culprits to reveal themselves.

As he stood at the edge of the forest, his nostrils were suddenly assaulted by an indescribable stench. The smell was like nothing he had ever encountered before—as if the air itself had been tainted by rot and decay. It reminded him of the times he had accidentally left meat out in the sun for too long, except a hundred times worse. His eyes began to water, and his stomach churned with nausea. He doubled over, gripping his stomach tightly as his body heaved uncontrollably. The acrid taste of bile rose up his throat and spilled out of his mouth, landing in a puddle on the ground in front of him.

There goes my morning coffee, thought Carter as he wiped his mouth with his sleeve and gasped for fresh air. The stench was so intense that it seemed to cling to his clothes and hair, and he knew it would take more than a shower to make it vanish. He felt his stomach churn once more. But as he looked up, his eyes suddenly widened at the sight before him. A towering evergreen tree, at least a foot and a half across at the base, was now shaking violently, thrashing about as if in the grip of a powerful force. The branches swayed, the trunk bowed, and leaves rustled with a deafening roar. The tree looked like it was on the verge of snapping in two. He now realized that no mere hoodlums or pranksters could cause such a commotion. As he tried to peer through the dense forest, his heart raced with fear of what could be causing the violent movement.

He was no coward. He was stronger than most and he could handle himself with no problem. But, not knowing what he was up against, he felt a primal fear take a hold of him.

His heart raced as he ran for the house, making the 250-foot dash in no time, rushing in through the kitchen patio and shutting the sliding glass door tightly behind him.

Out of breath and trembling, he leaned against the patio door, trying to see his attacker. He spasmodically looked back at the yard and then at his children, who were calmly watching TV in the living room. He was afraid that a rock, maybe even a tree trunk, might smash through the glass door, breaking the distance between the kitchen and living room, and then hit them.

Noticing her father's pale stupor and odd behavior, Ellie asked, "You okay, Dad? What's wrong? Why are you out of breath?"

Still staring out the patio window and trembling, he answered, "Um, I'm, yeah, I'm fine. I just had a bit of a workout out there—you know. Those... rocks. Some were pretty heavy. Just out of breath is all."

"What are you staring at outside?" she replied.

"Nothing." He said, pausing briefly, and then turning to her. "Nothing at all, sweetie," he added, still gasping for air.

She knows I'm lying; he thought. He wished he believed his own words. And he wished he knew what had just happened out there.

Was it a bear? No. Bears can't throw rocks. Neither can moose or mountain lions. He thought. *What the heck was that?!*

He'd grown up surrounded by nature. He was an experienced outdoor enthusiast, and an avid hunter. But he had witnessed nothing like this before. No, never.

He had only one nagging suspicion left, but quickly dismissed it. *No, it can't be.* He thought.

Yet, he knew *something* was out there.

Something **BIG**.

III

Aunt Sadie

Saturday, July 23rd, 9:51 a.m.

The forecast called for rain all day—*again*. And, sure enough, it was raining—hard.

Carter was busy on his laptop, researching Simeon Heights' plumbing companies, and contemplating if he should join one or just get business cards and take the solo route. Lost in thought, he weighed the pros and cons, occasionally jotting down ideas for business cards.

Meanwhile, Ellie and Ty kept themselves occupied playing in the living room, with Ellie every now and again eagerly peeking outside. They had been cooped up indoors for three days straight because of the bad weather. And, as children do under such circumstances, they were growing restless.

But today held a special significance for them. They eagerly awaited Aunt Sadie and Cousin Marty. After the big move, this was undoubtedly the greatest event of their summer.

"Da-ad, when will they get here?" Ellie asked, her voice filled with anticipation, repeating the question for the third time that morning.

Carter let out a patient sigh, understanding her eagerness. "I've told you, Ellie, they'll arrive *after* lunch. Aunt Sadie mentioned she had some errands to run before coming. We'll just have to wait patiently for them. They'll get here when they get here, all right?" he replied, emphasizing his point with a firm tone.

He felt a mix of joy and apprehension as he anticipated his sister's visit. He wasn't too sure if she'd bring up his lack of sensibility about the move again, or question his parenting ability, or try to convince him to move back to Portland altogether. She meant no harm by any of it, of course. She was just a concerned aunt and older sister—and she missed them dearly. Carter knew that and understood.

Growing up in a similar rural environment, Sadie had shared a childhood alongside him. However, her perspective diverged from his as she grew to embrace the allure of the bustling city and all its conveniences. With a stable career as a legal secretary and a comfortable two-bedroom house in proximity to her favorite amenities, she had seamlessly transitioned into urban living. Despite the challenges of her past marriage, which ultimately ended in divorce, she had truly embraced the city lifestyle and had become a bona fide city girl.

During their teenage years, when their mother succumbed to bone cancer, Sadie, being four years older, had made earnest efforts to bridge the void in his life, assuming a role that resembled that of a surrogate mother. Carter couldn't help but notice the similarities between Ellie's nurturing nature towards Ty and how Sadie had once cared for him. *Strange*, he pondered, *this sad story has repeated itself with the next generation of Mitchells.*

Interrupting his train of thought, a small voice alongside him posed a question while tugging on his sturdy arm, "Daddy, can I have some fish crackers?" Ty inquired.

Carter glanced down at his hungry five-year-old and chuckled, "You're always hungry, aren't you?"

Ty nodded eagerly, confident that his father would grant his request.

"All right then, snack time it is. Let me get you a handful. Just give me a moment," he responded as he rose from the kitchen table, ready to fulfill his son's request.

Just then, Ellie's voice pierced through the air, filled with excitement. "They're here! They're here!"

Carter looked outside and saw Sadie's silver SUV turning onto the long gravel driveway, an hour earlier than expected.

Without a second thought, Ellie dashed out of the house and into the pouring rain, no coat or umbrella in sight, like a bat out of hell, eager to greet her aunt and older cousin.

With her mom gone, Sadie had provided even more of a motherly and nurturing presence in Ellie's life, and she was becoming a solid role model for her niece as well. Carter appreciated how this sojourn promised to be beneficial, timely, and much needed—especially for his girl.

"Hiii, sweetie pie!" exclaimed Sadie, her radiant and expressive nature shining through as she caught sight of her beloved niece through the SUV window.

It was impossible to guess any family connection between Sadie and Carter just by looking at them. The differences in their physical attributes were striking. He stood tall, athletic, and reserved, while she was petite, plump, and exuded a vivacious and outgoing energy, relishing in the presence of others. The sole striking resemblance between them resided in their eyes—a captivating shade of blue that held an unmistakable spark of intelligence. However, it was Sadie's enchanting smile that truly set her apart, capable of illuminating even the gloomiest of atmospheres.

As she warmly greeted her niece outside the car, Sadie's motherly instinct promptly took charge, and her first words to Ellie were filled with concern, "Oh, sweetheart! It's pouring out here. Hurry back inside before you get drenched. I'll join you in just a couple of minutes, okay?"

No sooner was she done speaking that Carter made his appearance and, wasting no words, said to his sister, "Hey sis, just point me to your luggage. I'll grab it and we can all hug inside."

Quietly trailing behind his mother, Marty, a tall and slender teenager with dark hair, joined the group. The recent arrival of his teen years had brought with it a certain self-consciousness and awkwardness. If he was happy to see any of them, it didn't show. But Carter had always held a soft spot for his nephew. Marty was a bright and talented young man, excelling academically and showing great potential for the future.

Upon entering the house, Carter turned to Sadie and Marty and made arrangements, saying, "You can both stay in the kids' rooms. Ellie and Ty will sleep on the hide-a-bed here in the living room."

Anticipating his sister's potential unease and objections, he swiftly added, "Don't worry, I've already set everything up for you upstairs."

"Come on, Aunt Sadie!" Ellie exclaimed with enthusiasm. "I *can't wait* to show you my room. You're going to *love* it! It has a *great* view, and my bed is incredibly comfy!"

With a smile, Sadie willingly followed her niece up the stairs, eager to see the room and share in her excitement.

After a day filled with exploring the new property, reconnecting, sharing meals, and reminiscing, the kids were finally tucked into bed, fast asleep.

Carter and Sadie found themselves in the cozy den, finally relishing a moment of peace. Sadie, visibly tired, was not as talkative as usual. Nonetheless, they sat comfortably, sipping their decaf, enjoying the tranquil atmosphere that enveloped them.

"I was thinking, maybe this week we could spend some one-on-one time with each other's kids," suggested Carter.

Sadie looked intrigued and asked, "What do you have in mind?"

He smiled and explained, "Well, I thought you could take Ellie and Ty and do something fun together, like going to see a movie or going shopping. And I could take Marty fishing. I think he might enjoy that. What do you think?"

"Well, I like your idea. I really do. But Marty is more of a *gamer* than a *fisherman*. I guess you'll have to ask him and see if he wants to go." She smiled, knowing that might be a challenge.

"I will." He added, "Hey, they say it takes a village to raise a child, right?"

"That's true." She said.

"Well, you've done *your* part, sis. Especially recently. You've been a good influence on Ellie, and, seeing how Eric now lives five states away, I thought maybe I could return the favor. Marty's a good kid. Maybe I could try to become his favorite uncle." Carter expressed, smiling warmly at her.

She nodded approvingly. "Sounds like a plan," she said. "And you *are* a good uncle—and father. And you're his *only* uncle, silly." She chuckled.

"Hey! I'm not his uncle Silly, I'm his uncle Carter!" He retorted, grinning mischievously.

She chuckled at his cornball humor. While it didn't always show, Sadie had always enjoyed her brother's sense of humor, which had almost disappeared over the last few months. She was glad to see him joking again.

This week will be pleasant, thought Carter, glad his older sister was here. Although he had always prided himself on being self-sufficient, under the circumstances, he realized he really needed her company, cheerfulness, and support.

It was a gorgeous day, and, despite his nonchalant attitude, Marty was glad to be spending some *manly* time with his uncle Carter, who, with his large bowie knife strapped to his belt, seemed just a tad overly prepared to undertake a quiet fishing excursion.

But, following what he had experienced this past week, Carter wanted to make sure he was prepared in the woods. On the other hand, he also thought if he had brought a high-powered rifle, it might be perceived as overkill and make the lad think he was nuts.

After a few minutes of prepping, Carter said, "All right, kid, you're all set up. You use that rod and reel like I showed you, and you'll surely catch something," he said, casually walking away from his nephew.

"Where are *you* going?" asked Marty, puzzled.

"Not far. I'm just going to go dip my line past those trees there." Carter said, pointing to a blind spot past some brush along the shore of the creek.

"Oh. Okay." said the teen, with a sense of unease.

To reassure the boy, Carter added, "Even if you don't see me, I'll be just 40 yards away. I'm leaving all our stuff here with you. Gimme a holler if it bites, and I'll come and help you, okay?"

"Sure." Said Marty, still not sure why they had to part ways.

But his uncle was right. After just 45 minutes of fishing, Marty was exhilarated to have three good-sized trout in his large bucket. However, nature was calling at this point.

Although he had never relieved himself for 'number two' in the woods, Marty knew he couldn't hold it in. Grabbing the toilet paper roll from the bag, he left the bank to find an adequate and sheltered place in the forest to do his business.

After uncomfortably finishing his business, Marty was taken aback by what he perceived as his own foul odor. *Could this morning's eggs and sausage be responsible for this?* He wondered, feeling both puzzled and disgusted. *Maybe it just smells this bad 'cause I'm in the woods.*

That's when he heard his uncle shout for him, his voice filled with alarm. Hastily completing his task and emerging from the woods, Marty hurried to meet Carter, who appeared disturbed.

"I just needed to go number two," Marty explained, attempting to reassure him.

"Where are your fish? Did you release them?" asked Carter.

"What?! No." Marty then looked inside his bucket, shocked. "Hey! They're gone?!"

THE SIEGE AT SIMEON HEIGHTS

Carter, recognizing the familiar ambient stench, said, "Grab your gear. We have to go." Seeing Marty standing there, he urgently shouted, "*Now!*"

Alarmed, he scanned the surroundings, as if searching for the culprit. Marty, growing more nervous by his uncle's distressing behavior, asked, "What's wrong? Why do we have to go? Who stole my fish?"

"We just have to go. Trust me," said Carter, trying to remain calm as they hurried back to the van. Puzzled, the lad struggled to keep up with his uncle's brisk pace.

The ride back home was filled with silence, as both Carter and Marty were lost in their own thoughts. Carter couldn't help but feel disappointed and berated himself. *So much for male bonding with my nephew. Way to go!*

And Marty, sitting silently beside him, mirrored his disappointment, unaware of what had just transpired.

───────●◗◖●◗◖●───────

Early the next morning, the smell of bacon cooking roused Carter from his sleep. He came downstairs, still in his pajamas. His kids were talking with their aunt Sadie while she made breakfast.

"Good morning! How'd you sleep?" Sadie melodiously asked her brother, who had just appeared from view.

"Good," he said. "How 'bout you?"

"I slept surprisingly well, considering I'm not used to a twin bed anymore," she said, laughing.

"And what's with those darn owls outside?" she asked. "I couldn't believe it! They're so loud and persistent—I had to get up and close the window. Did *you* hear them? They were making a ruckus around two in the morning."

"Owls?" Carter said, surprised. "Nah, I heard nothing. You know me, when it's lights out, I'm out."

"Well, anyway," she said, "I made us scrambled eggs and bacon—and coffee. Very important, the coffee. The kids already ate; except for Marty. He always sleeps in late. Hungry?" she asked.

"Yeah! Sounds great. Thanks," he said, beaming at the food. He then looked at Ellie and Ty and said, "So... kids, me and Aunt Sadie are going to have breakfast now. You guys ate, so you can go play outside. Stay out of trouble, stay in the yard," he said, as they were scurrying away, "... and away from the wood line!" he then added louder, making sure they heard him.

"What's wrong with the wood line? Why can't they play there?" asked Sadie, both confused and concerned.

"I don't really know," said Carter. "The other day, some... *big animal* was there. I think it might have been a bear. I just don't know. All I know is that it was BIG," he said, trying to mask the concern on his face by bringing his coffee cup to his lips.

Looking at her, he noticed she had her anxious look, so he added, "But don't worry. I wouldn't let them play in the yard at all if I believed any harm would come to them."

"I sure hope so," she said sternly. Continuing, she added, "You know, you live in the country now. Heck, more than that... you're in the freakin' boondocks! And with what you just told me now, and what you told me when you first bought the house... Maybe you should..."

She paused, gathering her thoughts; then she looked him squarely in the eye and said, "You should think about getting a dog. It would come in real handy in these parts to have a large dog looking after the kids and the property, don't you think?" she asked convincingly.

"A dog, huh?" He said, mildly amused. "You know... that's not a bad idea. Not a bad idea at all."

The children, now joined by their cousin Marty, had been immersed in their playtime in the yard for well over an hour. Marty, wielding a large stick, energetically struck it against a nearby tree, producing a resounding sound that reverberated through the air. They found great amusement in this spirited game of echo, sharing laughter as the enigmatic presence in the woods responded to them knock for knock.

Knock, knock, knock; Marty loudly beat the stick on the tree. And sure enough, echoing back from the woods, someone would "answer" in kind.

Coming over from the house with Sadie to meet them and make sure all was okay, Carter inquired, "What game are you guys playing?"

"Oh," said Ellie, "We're playing *echo* with some neighbors."

"What do you mean, neighbors? What neighbors?" Asked Carter, exchanging a puzzled look with Sadie.

"Well," said Ellie, "When Marty knocks the stick on this tree, someone in the woods does the same knocking sound." Looking over at her cousin, she said, "Show them, Marty."

Once again, Marty did the tree knock, as they all held their breath expectantly; only this time, there was no response.

"Aww!" Exclaimed Ellie. "It stopped," she added, dejected. "It's probably cause you guys are there." She said, looking at the two bewildered adults.

"Well, *anywho*," said Sadie, "We came to tell you guys to get ready to leave. We have to get some groceries in town. So, hurry on up… do your business and get to the van, okay?"

As they accompanied her back toward the house, Carter purposely lagged behind. He looked suspiciously at the wood line for a few seconds, perking up his senses. Making sure they were all out of sight, he seized the nearby stick and delivered a couple of resounding whacks on a tree trunk. He waited; his ears attuned for any response.

None came.

That same evening, late after dinner, Sadie and Carter were finishing cleaning up the kitchen, with the kids sleeping soundly in the sofa-bed in the opposite room, oblivious to the ruckus of dishes being washed.

"I'll take out the trash." Said Carter.

"You never mind that. I'll take care of it. I told you I was here to help, so you just go on and take your shower. I'll finish up here."

"I think I should have you over more often." He said teasingly.

"Don't push your luck." She replied, "Besides, I'm only suggesting this because you have a serious case of B.O." she teased back, sticking out her tongue in jest.

He chuckled before heading on upstairs to wash and get ready for bed.

After she finished the dishes, Sadie grabbed the trash bag and headed outside to bring it to the bin, which was by the side of the driveway.

It was a beautiful Pacific Northwest summer night, complemented by a light breeze, and the moon was almost full, illuminating the nocturne landscape across the foliage of the property.

Hope I won't hear those stupid owls tonight, so I can keep my window open. She thought.

As she approached the trash bin, an ambient stench hit her like a physical force, assaulting her nostrils with the odor of decay and filth. She recoiled, a hand flying to her mouth as bile rose in her throat. The fetid aroma clung to her clothes and hair, and she struggled to breathe through the putrid fog. *What on earth did he put in there? A dead possum?* She thought. She heaved the garbage bag into the bin, holding her breath as she quickly replaced the lid.

And that's when she heard it—a sharp, distinct knocking from the woods behind her.

Knock, knock, knock!

Her heart skipped a beat, and she spun around, eyes wide with fear. "Hello?! Who--Who's there?!" she queried, her voice barely above a whisper.

No reply came, only the rustling of leaves and the occasional snap of a twig. The silence was deafening, eerie in its completeness. A shiver ran down her spine, and she took a step back towards the house.

But the knocking continued, louder now, insistent.

Knock, knock, knock!

She turned, heart pounding, and looked towards the trees. There, in the darkness, she saw two sets of gleaming eyes, crimson orbs watching her with an intensity that sent a fresh wave of terror through her body.

She stumbled back, tripping on the porch steps as she fled into the house. Her hands fumbled with the knob, and she slammed the door shut, panting for breath. Her mind raced, trying to make sense of what she had seen—the eyes, the knocking, the stench. Her heart still thudded wildly in her chest, and she pressed a hand to her sternum, willing it to slow down.

She quickly crept up the stairs, her heart pounding in her chest. Careful not to wake the kids, she paused outside her brother's door and waited, listening for any sound from inside. When he emerged a moment later, she rushed towards him, her words tumbling out in a frantic whisper.

"There's *something* out there! There's *something* out there!" Her hand flew to her mouth, and she bit down hard on her lip, realizing too late that she might wake the children. Tears streamed down her face as she looked at Carter, the fear in her eyes tangible.

He caught her by the shoulders, his touch gentle but firm. "Hey, hey... what's going on? What's got you so freaked out?" His voice was low and soothing, offering a balm to her frayed nerves.

She shook her head, unable to form words at first. After a brief pause, she said to him, "I can't believe you! I can't believe you brought these poor kids all the way out here... with these, these... these *things*... right in your backyard!" The words came out as an accusation, fueled by the adrenaline coursing through her veins.

Carter frowned; confusion etched on his face. "Wait, wha--? You *saw something*? Outside? What did you see? Tell me."

"I don't know. I don't know for sure what I saw." Her voice shook, and she wiped at her tears with the back of her hand. "But these were not bears. I can tell you *this* much."

She continued, "Carter, you have to do something! These could be dangerous. You can't let these *things* get close to your kids!" Her voice rose, and she clasped her hands together, beseeching him. "You really have to get a dog... at least. Get a *big frigging dog!*"

He nodded slowly, the seriousness of the situation dawning on him. "Okay, okay. I promise. You have my word. You can rest easy. I'll do it this week. I'll get a dog, and I promise… nothing will happen to Ellie or Ty."

"A BIG dog." Her voice was insistent. She lifted her eyes to meet his gaze, her expression beseeching. "Promise me, Carter. Promise me you'll get a dog to keep watch over the kids. I can help you pay for it."

"Okay! Yeah, yeah—a BIG dog." He told her, smiling reassuringly. "But keep this to yourself. Don't tell the kids, okay? I'll try to make it a surprise."

"Sure. I won't tell them." She was calmer now as she added, "I hate when people ruin surprises for me."

Bending down slightly, he hugged her, enveloping her with his large frame. He could feel her heartbeat and her body still trembling. And he couldn't help but feel she was right.

What were these things? What had he brought his family into? How would he get rid of them?

By this time, though, he had some idea what he was dealing with. Although he didn't want to entertain the thought of it, and was afraid to even admit it to himself; deep down, he had a very strong idea of what the creatures were.

They had reached the end of an enjoyable and eventful week. Sadie and Marty were busy collecting their belongings, packing them up, and preparing to return home. Carter was grateful for his sister's loyalty in keeping quiet about the unsettling events of the previous evening.

Sadie's visit had brought many positives. It had provided him with the time needed to complete essential repairs on the house. She had brought warmth and care to Ellie and Ty, who undoubtedly benefited from it. And, thanks to her, they had also enjoyed delicious home-cooked meals throughout the week, a rarity when Carter took charge of the kitchen. Oh, his cooking skills weren't as bad as his sister claimed, but he sure was no Gordon Ramsay either.

Carter's only regret at this point was that he felt he had failed to connect with Marty. He really wished he could have done more with the lad. But, by the same token, he knew they'd have more opportunities, as they only lived an hour away.

The kids were sad to see them go, especially Ellie, who would once again be the only female in the house after her aunt left. *Shakespeare was right,* he thought, *parting is such sweet sorrow.*

As Sadie bid her farewells to everyone, she eventually approached her brother, prompting him to lean in as she embraced him tightly. With a hushed voice, she whispered into his ear, "Don't forget your promise."

"Don't worry. I won't," he whispered back with a tender smile.

A smile also graced Sadie's lips. She knew her brother was a man of his word, much like their father had been—a trustworthy individual. Though not overly concerned, she hoped he would fulfill the promise sooner rather than later.

"Oh, and don't forget to film it and send me the video," she added.

"Sure," he replied, acknowledging her request with a nod.

Ellie, witnessing the secrecy and with her curiosity now picked, asked, "Film what? What are you guys talking about?"

"Never mind." Said the two accomplices in unison, chuckling at their choreographed response.

As his sister's SUV departed from his driveway, Carter's mind buzzed with the array of tasks awaiting him in the coming week. At the top of his list was a stop by his closest neighbor, Henry, who he thought could provide answers to some pressing questions he had.

IV

Ajax

Monday, August 1st, 10:02 a.m.

As Carter's car pulled up to the MacArthur's driveway, the first thing that caught his eye was their home; a stunning display of country living. The house was surrounded by tall trees, the kind that must have been there for decades, and the landscaping was perfectly tended. He couldn't help but admire the picturesque scene, like something out of a postcard. As he stepped out of his car, the quiet surroundings served as a calming reminder to him that despite the hardships of life, peace and prosperity were still within reach.

Anticipating his knock, and not used to seeing many vehicles pull up in their driveway, Glenda opened the door as he made his way up the porch's three steps.

"Hello dear!" She said, smiling warmly. "It's so good to see you!"

"Hello Mrs. MacArthur," said Carter, a bit surprised by her enthusiasm at seeing him unannounced. "I hope you don't mind my impromptu visit. If this is a bad time, I could…"

"Oh, *nonsense*." She said, cutting him mid-sentence. "There's no such thing at our age." She added with a big smile. "Please, come in! Come in. Make yourself at home, dear," she said, as they entered the house.

"Thank you." He said, as he sat down in their gorgeous sun room.

"Where are your lovely children?" she asked.

"Oh, um, I had a few too many errands to run today, so I booked a babysitter from town. She's a college student and has access to her parent's car, so it was an easy decision."

"Oh, I see. Well, you could have brought them here, you know. We don't get to see our grandkids as often as we'd like, so it wouldn't be any problem, I assure you."

"I'll know for next time. Thanks." Said Carter.

"Would you like something to drink? Some coffee? Or iced-tea?" she asked.

"Iced-tea sounds *great*." He answered, since it was a scorching morning. He then added, "I was hoping to speak with your husband, if that's possible."

"Of course." She replied. "I gathered as much. He's in the backyard, fiddling in the shed. I'll bring him right along with your iced tea, dear."

A couple of minutes later, Henry showed up in the sunroom, carrying two glasses of iced tea. He seemed more relaxed than the first time they'd met.

"Hello neighbor," he said, kindly, after putting the iced tea on the table in front of them, extending his hand.

Carter shook the man's bony, yet firm hand.

After exchanging a few polite words about the weather, Carter got right down to business.

"I wanted to ask you a few questions, if that's okay with you."

"Sure. What's on your mind?" said Henry.

"Well, we're getting settled down pretty good at the house, which is great. But I've noticed some strange stuff around the property. And I was wondering if you've ever experienced some strange stuff around *your* property."

At these words, Henry became somewhat troubled and was quietly staring into the distance. Carter knew the old man knew something, but he didn't want to be impolite by prying too much.

"Well, yes. There have been some things throughout the years we've been here." Admitted the man.

And then, he looked at Carter, and point-blank said, "I was hoping they'd leave you and your family alone, to be honest."

Surprised by his frankness, Carter nonetheless piggybacked on it, asking, "Who? Who is 'they'?"

At this, the old man let out a deep sigh before continuing.

"Son, do you believe in the creature they call… *Bigfoot?*" he said, looking him straight in the eye for the first time since they had met.

"Bigfoot?!" said Carter, acting surprised by the straightforwardness of the question. He had suspected as much, but he just couldn't bring himself to accept it, much less say it. "To be honest, I've heard stories, but I never believed they were true."

"Yeah, well, I don't blame ya. It's hard to wrap our minds around the fact that such creatures live in our forests—or even exist," Henry said, still staring into the distance. And then he asked, "So, you didn't *see* them?"

"Um, no. Not really." Carter said. "But I smelled them, though. Boy, did I smell them! And I saw what they can do." He added.

"Oh. Such as?" Henry asked, curious.

"Well, for one, they throw rocks—big ones. Also, they're really strong. I saw a tree being shaken—a gigantic tree, and I thought it would break. And they're opportunistic, too. I think they stole our fish when I went fishing with my nephew." Carter said, spilling it out eagerly.

"Hmmm, that tree shaking; that seems like aggressive behavior to me. Did you… *provoke them* in any way?" asked the old man, with a mix of bewilderment and interest.

Carter paused for a moment. "No. Well, maybe…" he said, unsure. "But if I did, it was accidental. I was getting rid of some rocks in the yard, and…"

As he was speaking the words, Carter realized that's where things might have derailed. He continued,

"Yeah. Come to think of it; I threw some rocks into the forest. Do you..." He paused momentarily, before inquiring, "do you think they might have perceived this as... *a threat?*"

The old man looked down, visibly concerned, and shaking his head slightly, answered, "Yeah. I'd say that might have provoked them. But, mind you, I'm no expert on these *Bigfoots.*"

Growing more curious, and sightly unnerved by this answer, Carter wanted to know more, so he asked, "So, what about you? Have *you* seen them?"

"Yes, I have. A couple of times," Henry said, still staring in the distance.

"And..." pressed Carter, hoping for more details. But he saw that was as far as the conversation would go concerning Bigfoot—at least for today. Henry would not say more about his encounters, as he was visibly uncomfortable at this point.

Snapping out of it, he nonetheless turned to Carter once again and said, "You know... as a rule of thumb, if you leave *them* alone, they'll leave *you* alone. That's what I've observed. It's the best advice I can give you for now. And just wait here. I've got something else that might help you."

The old man got up and left the sunroom before returning two minutes later with a small piece of paper. Handing it to Carter, he said, "Like I said, I'm no expert on these creatures, but here's the number of someone who's pretty close to that. He doesn't live too far from here. He's had some pretty nasty encounters with these Bigfoots. He knows a lot more about them than I do. He rarely enjoys hanging around people, but he might still help. He's a friend, so you just tell him I gave you his number, Okay?"

"Um, sure. Thanks," said Carter, looking at the small piece of paper on which was shakily scribbled the name *James Walker,* along with his phone number.

Then, looking at his watch, Carter added, "Before I leave, if I may… there's something else I wanted to ask you?"

"What's that?" asked the old man.

"Where can I get a good adult guard dog in these parts?"

As he drove into Simeon Heights, Carter couldn't help but notice the quaint charm of the town. The older buildings that lined Main Street had a certain character to them that was hard to find in modern cities. The friendly people he encountered as he drove by smiled and waved, making him feel welcome in the community. The local coffee shops, bakery, and pizza joints added to the small-town vibe, making him feel like he was in a place where everyone knew each other.

As he continued down Main Street, he noticed a sizeable four-screen movie theater, banks, and three different grocery stores, each with their own unique offerings. He even saw a Mega-Mart and some other big-name store outlets on the outskirts of town, making it easy for residents to get everything they needed without leaving the area.

Despite being a small town, Simeon Heights had everything one could need, including the most popular fast-food chains and everything else the U.S. had to offer. Carter couldn't help but feel grateful for finding a place like this to call home.

Eventually, the voice of the GPS assured him they had arrived. "The destination is on your right, 134 Main Street," it said.

Right atop of the old three-story brick building, the sign read, "Simeon Heights Animal Shelter".

"Wait... *Animal Shelter?*" Ellie quizzed, looking at her dad with wide eyes. And then she exclaimed, "Oh my goodness! Dad?! Is this for real?! Are we here for what I think we're here for?!" she asked, barely able to contain herself.

"Well, *yes*, and *no*," Carter said, trying to keep her from wishing too hard for a Shi-Tsuu or Pomeranian.

"What do you mean? We're *not* here to get a dog?" she asked, unsure.

"Well, yes, we are. We're here to get a dog," Carter confirmed, smiling.

"Yayyy!" Ty and Ellie both shouted and celebrated in unison.

"But..." added Carter, "I'll be choosing it. And that is non-negotiable."

"Aww," they said. "Why can't we pick it?" asked Ellie, disenchanted.

"Because I'm looking for a *specific type* of dog... and because I'm paying, that's why. You guys are just along for the ride, okay?"

"Oh, okay," they said, looking at each other, somewhat dejected, but accepting the bitter-sweet terms put in place by their father.

Seeing their disappointment, Carter said, "Hey, guys, this is still going to be fun, *right?*" as he tried to re-spark their initial enthusiasm.

"Yes. Of course. I mean... we *are* getting a dog, right?" said Ellie, just making sure this was still happening.

"That's right," re-confirmed her father.

As they entered the building, a woman approached them. Her hair was graying, and she wore glasses. Carter guessed she was around fifty years old. She greeted them with a smile and led them towards the kennel area.

"We have just eight dogs at this time. But there are new arrivals every week. Take your time, consider them carefully. I'll be right here for your questions, okay?" she said to Carter.

"Perfect. Thanks," he said.

Carter's eyes scanned the cramped space, taking in the sight of the few dogs on display. Most were small or medium-sized breeds, yapping or whining from their cages. But as he neared the end of the row, one dog stood out from the rest. A massive Rottweiler, with a muscular build and a glossy black-and-tan coat, caught his eye. The dog's fierce barks echoed through the kennel as it paced back and forth in its small crate. Despite the animal's aggressive behavior, Carter found himself drawn to it, wondering if there was more to this dog than met the eye. "What about this one?" he asked the lady, pointing at the large dog.

"Well, I don't know, sir," she answered uneasily. "You have small children. An adult dog like this may be a bit to handle, don't you think?" she asked, trying to figure him out.

Knowing she had a point; Carter nonetheless wanted a big dog that could protect them if the need arose. After expressing his wish to the lady, she said, "You know, I think I have the perfect dog for you and your family. Follow me," she said, walking ten feet further to another crate on the left. In the enclosure was a good-sized dog, who was acting excited to see them, and seemed quite playful.

"This one here is a German Sheppard and Labrador mix." She said, smiling back at Carter and the kids. "That makes him a German-Shepprador," she kidded.

She continued, "He's a male, and he's a year old, so still very trainable." Looking straight at Carter, she continued, "Also, as you can see, he's definitely going to make a good and strong guard dog with a very respectable size of about 90 lbs."

"Oh, wow! He's *sooo* cute, dad!" said Ellie, as the dog was licking Ty's fingers across the crate bars. Seeing Ellie's excitement, and Tyler giggling at the tongue tickles, made Carter's fatherly heart melt. And he had to agree; the dog was a nice-looking fella. He was black and tan, like a German Sheppard, but slightly bulkier, with the stronger head of a Labrador. With his half-folded ears, intelligent eyes, and a friendly disposition, he was hard to resist. And Carter knew the lady was right; genetically, this dog was primed to make a great family dog and a strong watchdog.

So, smiling at her, Carter wasted no time and asked, "All right. So, where do I sign?"

True to his word, Carter prioritized filming the dog's playful interactions with the kids as soon as they arrived home. He swiftly edited the footage and sent it via email to Sadie, who eagerly awaited the promised video. Despite her somewhat irritating inquiry, "Weren't there any larger dogs?" She couldn't help but feel delighted at seeing the sheer joy radiating from Ellie and Ty. Moreover, she was reassured that her brother had acted promptly, reinforcing her faith in his reliability.

Ellie and Ty, brimming with excitement, embraced their newfound canine companion wholeheartedly. Ellie, who had been made familiar with *The Iliad* in school the year prior, decided he should be named Ajax—like the great Achaean warrior of Homer's epic.

The name fit him like a glove.

Ajax surprised Carter in many ways. He was a docile, intelligent, and obedient dog who was just wonderful with the kids, especially with Ty. This made him very much like a big nanny-dog.

However, where he surprised Carter most was as a *watchdog*. Ajax vastly surpassed expectations. He wasn't much of a barker, but whenever there were unfamiliar sounds, his ears would prop up, and then he would head on to the appropriate window, just mildly growling and adding some very low, toned-down barks to the mix—almost as if he knew that loud barks would be frowned upon in the house. And, if let out, he would eagerly and aggressively fend off any intruding racoons, foxes, or coyotes. When outside, he looked like he was always on patrol and guard duty, walking along the wood line, re-emphasizing his territory, all the while dutifully monitoring the kids.

On a nice mid-August day, Carter decided to bring Ajax along with the kids for a walk in their 45+acre backwoods. He strapped his trusty Bowie knife on his thigh, but also secretly packed and concealed his Smith & Wesson 500 in his undercoat—*just in case,* he thought.

Ellie had also carefully prepared some peanut butter & jelly sandwiches before they set out for the afternoon stroll.

Carter was determined to make the most of the remaining days before school started. He had arranged for Ellie to start at Simeon Heights Elementary and had found a reliable daycare for Ty. As a responsible parent, he wanted to ensure that his children had a smooth transition into the new school year. Besides that, he had also advertised his plumbing services in the Simeon Heights region, and had even ordered business cards.

While balancing his work and family life would not be easy, he was eager to take on the challenge. But, for now, it was still summer, and it was a nice day for a family walk in the untamed Oregon wilderness.

As they trekked through the forest, Ajax's tail wagged excitedly as he bounded ahead of the family, his nose to the ground as he sniffed out every scent in the vicinity. They all watched with amusement as Ajax darted back and forth, clearly relishing the freedom of the great outdoors. It was a joy to see the canine so in his element, and Carter couldn't help but think of how similar Ajax was to his wild wolf ancestors, running free in the woods without a care in the world.

"Ajax! Ajax, come back!" Shouted Ellie, worried her furry friend might run away for good.

"No worries, Ellie. He'll come back. He's just really enjoying this," said her dad, carrying an elated Ty on his strong shoulders.

With Ajax now a good 500 feet away, they heard him bark up the bend, but couldn't quite catch a glimpse of him.

Curiosity piqued, they quickened their pace, eager to uncover the source of Ajax's agitation. As they reached a partial clearing just off the trail, their eyes fell upon a peculiar sight. Ajax stood nervously, barking fiercely at a cluster of broken trees. He circled anxiously, fixated on the trees, his growls and barks resonating through the air, brimming with agitation.

The family inspected the trees with a mixture of awe and bewilderment. The deliberate teepee-like formations, three in all, hinted at human intervention, but fostered a deeper sense of intrigue. Were these odd structures the work of locals, or something more enigmatic? A chill crept down Carter's spine, as he couldn't shake the feeling of intruding upon something sacred or private. A disquieting unease settled in the pit of his stomach, refusing to dissipate. And then, amidst Ajax's escalating barks, a sound reached their ears.

It was unlike anything they had ever heard before—a haunting, primal scream that seemed to emerge from the depths of the underworld. The unearthly cry sent shivers down their spines, leaving them momentarily paralyzed by its otherworldly resonance. At that moment, Ajax positioned himself protectively in front of them, barking fervently in the sound's direction. Looking intently, they couldn't discern anything, however.

"What was *that*, Dad?" Ellie asked, afraid, with Ajax still barking and clearly going out of his mind.

"I think it might be a bear," Carter answered, concerned, with Ty still on his shoulders, scanning the trees left and right. But he knew full well that no bear on earth could produce the sound he'd just heard.

"You know what guys... I think that's far enough for today," he said. "Let's just go back where we came from, and head on back home," he added, visibly worried and confused about how their family excursion was brought to a halt.

They had been walking a good twenty minutes and were now a significant distance from home.

Just as they turned to retreat, the tranquil forest erupted into chaos, overwhelming the unsuspecting family. From opposite directions, an immense presence charged through the woods, emitting spine-chilling growls and eerie sounds. It crashed through the underbrush, snapping branches and toppling trees as if they were mere toothpicks.

Amid the tumult, Ajax sprang into action, his protective instincts guiding him towards the looming threat. Ellie and Ty, now engulfed in fear, cried out for their loyal four-legged companion.

Carter's heart pounded with a mix of concern for Ajax and the instinct to protect his children. Despite his desperate calls, the dog seemed swallowed by the chaos, and Carter knew it would be reckless to go in after him. *Nope*, he thought, pushing aside the notion. *Screw that. Time to make a run for it.* His kids were his top priority, and he didn't want to chance a full-frontal confrontation with these creatures using his gun.

What if I miss? What then? There are at least two; but what if there are three, four, or five of them? He reasoned to himself, wisely choosing flight over fight.

Carter's protective instincts surged as he raced through the dense forest, his heart pounding in his chest. With every desperate stride, he hoped he wouldn't be forced to engage in a lethal struggle. As the creatures pursued them, their heavy breaths echoing ominously, growing ever nearer, he pleaded silently to heaven. *I'm all they've got. Please!*

Determined not to falter, he clutched Ty tightly, carrying him like a precious cargo. The boy's sobs intermingled with the sounds of chaos. Ellie, with tears streaming down her face, strained to keep pace, her hand clutching her father's in a desperate grip. Carter's firm hold propelled her forward, lifting her from the forest floor with each stride.

Flanked on both sides, the relentless pursuit of the creatures intensified, their rampage tearing through the forest with a destructive force. The deafening cacophony of snapping branches and splintering trees reverberated through the air, echoing like the collision of runaway locomotives, piercing their very souls with terror.

During the chaos, Ajax's presence remained steadfast. His strident barks kept reminding the family of his valiant presence as he kept up with the attackers. His resiliency to defend his family-pack resonated throughout the turmoil. *God knows what they'll do to him if they get their...* **hands** *on him,* now thought Carter, fully admitting to himself that these were indeed Sasquatches—the dreaded Bigfoots of legend.

The sound of Ajax's paws beating the forest floor, and the unwavering defiance in his bark, urged him forward nonetheless, and served as a reminder that they were not alone in this harrowing ordeal.

Pushing through exhaustion and ignoring the stinging pain of scratches from branches and vegetation, Carter refused to succumb to weariness. His heart pounded in his chest, fueled by adrenaline and determination, as he continued to run with unwavering resolve. He pressed on relentlessly, driven by the instinct to protect his children and reach the sanctuary of home.

Finally, the relentless pursuit of the creatures ceased, their presence fading into the distance. Carter, though physically drained, maintained his swift pace, unwilling to let his guard down until the comforting sight of his house came into view. A surge of relief washed over him as he felt the familiarity and safety of his own surroundings envelop him like a protective shield.

Yet, amidst the triumph of their escape, a pang of sorrow gripped his heart as he realized Ajax was nowhere to be seen.

"Ajax! Ajax!" Ellie's out-of-breath voice trembled with anxiety as she called out desperately into the now eerily silent forest.

With his priority still focused on ensuring their safety, Carter placed a comforting hand on her shoulder. "Let's get inside the house, sweetie," he urged, steadying his voice despite the lingering tension. "Right now, there's nothing we can do for Ajax."

So, with heavy hearts, they turned their gaze away from the unyielding woods and headed towards the safety of their house, hoping and praying that Ajax would somehow find his way back to them.

————————— ◦◦◦◦◦ —————————

After ensuring the kids were safely inside the house, cleaned up and out of harm's way, Carter couldn't shake off the burden of self-blame for his lapse in judgment. Standing by the patio window that overlooked the yard, his gaze remained fixed on the edge of the forest, desperately hoping to catch a glimpse of Ajax emerging unscathed.

How could I have been so stupid? He thought.

I knew these things were in the woods. Why did I have to bring the kids there? Was I in disbelief and looking for some sort of sick confirmation? I knew these things were there— didn't I? That's why I brought Ajax along... and the gun, wasn't it? He thought to himself, amazed at his own lack of judgment.

Then his mind wandered to those sad stories he read about in the papers. Stories about depressed and overwhelmed parents who, driven by desperation by the weight of their responsibilities, would kill their children just before they ended their own sad life. He wondered, worriedly, if what he just did showed the same underlying psychological turmoil. The idea was almost too unbearable to consider.

Sadie's right. I need a shrink. I must be crazy to have thought I could just take an easy-going stroll through those

woods with these things living there. I'm such a freaking idiot!
He thought, severely berating himself.

In the living room, weariness enveloped Ty, who
had succumbed to sleep on the sofa, the murmurs of the
television serving as a faint lullaby. Upstairs, Ellie sought
solace in her room, her emotions still raw and tears
flowing freely, haunted by the echoes of the harrowing
ordeal they had just endured. Carter was acutely aware
that he needed to console his beloved daughter, to offer
her comfort and reassurance. However, an
overwhelming sense of guilt and anguish held him back.
He couldn't bring himself to face Ellie's tears right now.

He walked over to the kitchen's corkboard; his
gaze fixed on James Walker's number. He pondered over
the decision to call, feeling a mixture of hesitation and the
gnawing realization that he couldn't face this alone.

Independence had always been his defining trait.
He was the epitome of a man who refused to ask for
directions when lost and always opted to buy a new tool
rather than borrow one from a neighbor. Vivian had
warned him countless times that his stubborn self-
reliance would eventually catch up with him, but he had
dismissed her concerns.

Yet, confronted with the current circumstances,
Carter recognized he had reached a point where he had
no other option but to swallow his pride. He
acknowledged he was in over his head, fully aware that
he needed help to navigate through the challenges ahead.
Maybe this James guy is a God-sent, he thought.

Lost in his own thoughts, he was suddenly jolted
by a sight that was nothing short of a miracle. There,

sitting calmly on the deck and peering through the window, was Ajax, his tail wagging with unabashed joy.

"What in the--! Is that really *you*, boy?!" Carter exclaimed; his surprise mixed with sheer excitement.

"Ellie! Ty! Come quickly, you won't believe it!" he shouted, beckoning his children to join him as he rushed to open the patio door, eagerly welcoming Ajax back inside.

The kids' faces lit up with pure elation at the sight of their beloved pooch. Upon closer inspection, Carter realized that despite being a little dirty and bearing a few scratches, Ajax appeared to be unharmed.

Relief flooded over the family, with profound gratitude filling their hearts for their dog's safe return. Beholding the reunion, with Ajax excitedly licking Ellie and Ty, Carter couldn't help but smile in wonder at the scene.

Late that night, around 11:15 pm, Ellie stirred from her bed, needing to use the bathroom. As she walked past her father's bedroom, a soft glow emanated from within, accompanied by the sound of his voice. Intrigued and concerned, she approached the door, careful to remain hidden.

To her astonishment, she discovered her father wasn't simply talking; he was also crying.

"I'm sorry, Viv. I'm sorry for bringing them here, to this *godforsaken* town, in this *godforsaken* house, surrounded by these *godforsaken* creatures. It's all my fault. Please... forgive me," he confessed, his voice shaking and choked with sorrow. He knelt at the foot of his bed, a broken man burdened by loneliness, exhaustion, and despair.

"Please, help me get through this! It's just... *too hard*," he pleaded further, desperate to be heard by a higher power, his tears flowing silently.

Overwhelmed by what she saw and heard, Ellie quietly retreated to her own room, her eyes now moist with tears.

That night, like her father, she would find relief in tears, her heart heavy with distress, apprehension for the future, and an undeniable fear of the unknown lurking beyond the confines of their home. She realized her fears were not unfounded.

Indeed, out there, in the darkness of the woods, dwelled actual monsters.

V

Back to School

Wednesday, September 14, 2:05 p.m.

Crouched under the kitchen sink, with his flashlight in one hand and fiddling with a wrench in the other, Carter said, "You're going to need a new fitting for this pipe, and some welding done. But it's really no big deal. It's an easy fix."

Getting out from under the kitchen sink, he stood up, smiled, and said, "Unfortunately, my visit will cost you more than those repairs."

"That's okay," said the old lady, her voice filled with relief. "I'm just happy you'll be able to fix it." She added.

"Oh yeah. Fixing it is no problem. No problem at all," he said, his words punctuated by a brief pause.

Carter's phone rang at that very moment. Glancing at the screen, he turned to the lady and said, "It's my daughter's school. Excuse me while I take this."

"Hello?" he answered.

"Hello, is this Mr. Mitchell?" spoke a pleasant female voice from the other end.

"Yes," he confirmed, his concern growing faintly.

"Hi, we haven't officially met yet, but my name is Alexandra. I'm Ellie's fifth grade teacher," she introduced herself.

"Oh, yes. Is… everything okay with Ellie?" He asked, his concern more evident.

"Well, yes. I mean… she's fine. Don't worry." Alexandra said in a reassuring tone. "However, I was wondering if I could meet with you. There are some things that I'd like to discuss with you in person concerning Ellie. It's nothing major, mind you. But I think there are some things you should know, and I'd like to go over them with you. Would that be okay?"

"Um, yeah, sure. When would you like to meet?" He inquired, his voice filled with a mix of curiosity and willingness to accommodate.

As he hung up the phone, his mind wandered. He couldn't help but wonder what the meeting with Ellie's teacher the next day would entail. In the past, Vivian had always taken care of such matters, and he felt a twinge of inadequacy thinking about how she had handled most of the kids' needs and Ellie's education. It reminded him of the vast responsibilities he now faced as a single parent.

He knew he would eventually find his footing and learn how to navigate these challenges on his own. But for now, it was just another aspect of the steep learning curve he had embarked upon.

Unbeknownst to Ellie, the next day, at lunchtime, her dad was working his way through her school hallway to room 201, also known as her 5th grade classroom.

Carter entered the classroom, and his eyes were drawn to the woman at the front of the room. Her dark-brown hair was pulled back into a ponytail, and she wore a beige skirt complemented by a navy-blue blouse. With her back turned, she stood in front of the blackboard, writing a math lesson. As she moved, Carter's gaze was drawn to her toned legs and her shapely figure.

Ahem. He cleared his throat, hoping to grab the woman's attention. She spun around, her eyes wide with surprise. He took in her youthful appearance, guessing she couldn't be much older than thirty. Her skin was glowing with good health, and her stunning smile lit up the room. When their eyes met, he couldn't help but get lost in the depth of her piercing blue irises, and he was momentarily taken aback by her beauty.

"Ah, you must be Mr. Mitchell." She said, walking up to him, still smiling. "I'm very pleased to meet you. I'm Alexandra Walker." she added, extending her well-manicured hand in a self-assured motion.

"Walker?" Said Carter, trying to hold his mild surprise.

"Yes. Alexandra Walker." She repeated, slightly amused by his reaction. "But my friends call me Alex."

"Oh, well, you can call me Carter. And, my friends call me... uh, well, Carter." He said, smiling back. "Actually, Mr. Mitchell was the name of my father." He added, chuckling.

After inviting him to sit down, she got right down to business.

"Recently, I assigned the students with an oral presentation. The goal of this presentation was to get me and the students better acquainted—you know, sharing the basic stuff, such as where they're from, their family, and whatnot."

Looking at him in the eyes, she added, "Ellie seems like a bright girl, really. And she gave a very candid and personable presentation. However, without going into details, she did mention that her…"

Alexandra paused, knowing this was a delicate matter.

"Well… like I said, *revealing no intimate details to the class*, she did mention that her mom… passed away recently." She said, pursing her lips and looking at him sympathetically.

Rather surprised, and feeling his personal life somewhat overexposed, Carter said, "Oh, um… I see."

Alex continued, "Look, Mr. Mitchell… Carter, I understand this is a delicate matter. And believe me, I don't want to make this conversation uncomfortable. My heart goes out to Ellie and to your family. And, rest assured, the entire class was very understanding. So, the reason for this meeting is not to make you feel uneasy."

"Okay. So, what is it then? What's the reason?" Carter asked a somewhat pointedly.

Slightly taken aback, she continued regardless. "Well, I'd like to provide Ellie with all the help she can get. This is obviously a tough time for her, and I just wanted to inform you that our school does have a very qualified psychologist on staff who could help Ellie... navigate through it all. You know?"

"Oh. I see. I understand. All right, I'll... make good note of it." Carter said, defensively brushing the information aside.

And, looking at his watch, he got up and added, "Well, Alexandra, it's been a pleasure. But I do have to get back to work... and I know you do too, so... thank you..."

"Mr. Mitchell, Carter... *wait*." She entreated. "Look, I think it's safe to say that we *both* have Ellie's best interest at heart, right?" She asked tentatively.

"Of course." He answered.

"Well, then, all I ask is that you think about what I told you." She said, looking at him gently.

Softened up by her feminine charm and her genuine kindness, Carter smiled and said, "All right. I will," before taking his leave from Ellie's class and teacher.

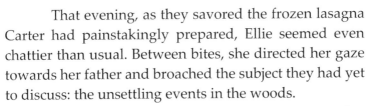

That evening, as they savored the frozen lasagna Carter had painstakingly prepared, Ellie seemed even chattier than usual. Between bites, she directed her gaze towards her father and broached the subject they had yet to discuss: the unsettling events in the woods.

"So, *dad*, you never talked to us about what happened the other day... you know, *in the woods*?" Her eyes brazenly locked onto his, as if silently urging him to provide them with an explanation. Curiosity brimming, she couldn't contain her pressing questions any longer. "So... what were those *things*, dad? Bears? Monsters? Something else?" she inquired, with an intrigued and slightly impatient tone.

Looking at her, then at Ty, and then back at her, with his grimacing face clearly indicating he preferred talking to her when they'd be alone, he nonetheless answered, "I'm not sure at this point, *Ellie*. I guess the verdict's still out on that one," he said, in an attempt to avoid the topic.

"Oh, well, that suc—"

Before she could finish saying the word, he interrupted her, "*But...* one thing I want to make clear is that you guys are to play close to the house at all times... until I figure things out. Is that clear?"

"Dad, *duh!* Do you seriously think that after what happened out there, we even *want* to go play outside anymore?" she rhetorically answered.

"Anyway," she added quickly, before he could reply. "Next Friday you have to come to my school."

"Really? Why is that?" he asked.

"Well, Miss Alexandra organized a career day. All the parents will come and speak to our class, sharing what it is they do for a living. So, Dad, I was thinking... You could come and share about your plumbing with our class. We're, like, 27 students, and everyone's parents will be there. So, you could bring some business cards. Don't you think it would be a good way to make your services known in the area?" Ellie proposed, her eyes shining with the clever idea.

Taken aback by his daughter's astute business sense, he responded, "Hmmm, well, Sure. I guess I can't argue with that." He couldn't help but admire her innovative thinking, realizing that he wouldn't have thought of such an opportunity himself.

Ellie's enthusiasm continued to bubble as she added, "Plus, you'll get to meet Miss Alexandra. You'll like her. She's *very pretty* and smart; and I think she's single, too." Her mischievous smile conveyed a hint of playful matchmaking.

Chuckling at her playful remark, he dismissively shook his head and said, "Ha-ha, very funny. Now, eat your lasagna before it gets cold."

Despite his dismissal, he appreciated her light-heartedness, ever grateful for her innate ability to bring humor into their lives—especially these days.

That night, at around 2:35 am, he heard the unmistakable voice of Ellie waking him up along with her shaking his shoulder, "Dad. Da-ad! Wake up." She whispered.

With his eyes half-opened, he made out her silhouette next to his bed and groggily asked, "Wha--whassup, sweetie? Whass wrong?"

"There's something going on in our yard." She whispered. "I think those creatures are back. I'm scared, dad. Go see outside my bedroom window. I saw something out there, near the wood line—there's more than one."

"Crap." He thought. He had hoped that the *'If you leave them alone, they'll leave you alone'* advice he'd been given would work these creatures out of his life for good.

"Where's Ajax?" he asked Ellie, surprised not to hear his dog barking up a storm at the sight of these creatures.

"I think he's hiding. I heard him whimper. He's been different ever since that day in the woods." She said. "I heard him downstairs. But I'm too scared to go, dad." She added.

"That's okay. I'll check up on him later."

Staying behind in the hallway, Ellie observed as her dad went to her bedroom window to spot the elusive creatures.

And spot them he did.

Despite the floodlights strategically positioned around the house, the creatures managed to elude them and remained concealed deep within the dark recesses of the large plot of land, their forms outlined by the gentle glow of the moonlight. Carter's eyes discerned their unmistakable colossal silhouettes—three of them. One stood out as larger than the rest, with the other two trailing closely behind. Not only could he see them, but he also detected the eerie chatter and peculiar whooping sounds that emanated from their presence.

Turning to Ellie, he said, "Stay here. I'll go and chase them off."

"Daddy, be careful!" She whispered.

He descended downstairs, where he could hear Ajax whimpering in the den. He grabbed his Remington 870 from his storage room-turned-armory, loaded it, and headed toward the kitchen.

I have to do this quickly if I'm to have the element of surprise, thought Carter, making his way to the patio door furtively.

His gaze fixed intently upon the figures in the yard, roughly 250 feet away. They lingered near the perimeter of the tree line, swaying in an unsettling rhythm and emitting their peculiar sounds. A thought gnawed at him—*Do they know I'm here watching them?* Despite his efforts to conceal himself by keeping the lights off, he couldn't shake the feeling that their eyes bore into him, seemingly challenging him to venture closer.

There he stood, in his darkened kitchen, his nerves now increasing his heartbeat, reminding him he was only human. Summoning his courage, he pumped his shotgun, quickly opened the patio door, and stepped out on the deck. Once outside, he could still see them, just standing there, their eyes locked on him, eerily still.

His voice boomed as he yelled at the creatures, "Go away! Leave us alone!" He raised his gun and pulled the trigger. The deafening blast echoed through the night sky. The creatures were startled, their wild screams mixed with roars as they quickly retreated into the forest—reminiscing wild chimpanzees in a tumult. He watched them go, relieved that his warning shot had been effective. The sound of their commotion faded away into the night as he lowered his gun and took a deep breath, hoping they wouldn't return.

Through it all, the patio door had been left ajar behind him. In a surprising turn of events, Ajax, fueled by newfound courage from his mater's gunshot, dashed outside with lightning speed. Barking ferociously, he fearlessly gave chase to the creatures, crossing the wood line, and disappearing into the depths of the forest.

"Ajax! No! Bad dog!" Shouted Carter. "Come back Ajax! *Ajax!*"

His repetitive voice echoed out into the night— but to no avail. Ajax was already far away by now.

His heart sank as he heard a piercing yelp in the distance, followed by an eerie silence that seemed to stretch on forever. His mind raced with worry and fear for his beloved Ajax, and the fate that had befallen him. The silence was only broken by the sound of his own frantic breathing and the beating of his heart, as he stood there frozen in place, waiting for some sign of what had happened to his faithful companion.

In the lingering silence, however, he knew Ajax's luck had just run out.

Carter's fists clenched tightly as he glared into the darkness of the woods. His eyes narrowed, burning with a fierce determination that bordered on folly. He could feel the anger coursing through his veins, hot and furious. As the adrenaline pumped through his body, making him feel unconquerable, he right then and there vowed to take on the creatures that had harmed his dog and threatened his family.

"You f***ing apes are gonna pay!" he roared at the top of his lungs, his voice piercing through the night. The echoes of his anger faded into the darkness. And then, internalizing his fury against them, he resolved, *I'll make you freaking pay. You just picked a fight with the wrong f***ing guy! I'll end it! One way or another; I swear I'll end it!*

By the time he returned upstairs, he found both his children tearfully huddled together in his bed. Clearly, they had heard everything. Sadly, they knew what had happened, and were mourning Ajax... all over again.

Carter, dejected, slowly approached the bed, noticing their tear-stained faces and scared expression. Ellie was holding her younger brother tightly, trying to comfort him. He could feel the anger inside him dissipating, replaced by guilt and sorrow.

"Hey, guys," he said softly, pursing his lips. "Ty, I'm sorry for waking you up. I didn't mean to scare you."

Ellie looked up at him with red, puffy eyes. "What are they, Daddy? Why won't they just leave us alone?"

Carter hesitated for a moment, not wanting to frighten his children any further. But he knew he had to tell them something. "I'm not sure, sweetie," he said, sitting down on the edge of the bed. "But," he continued, "I scared them away. They won't bother us again, okay?"

Ty sniffled and buried his face into Ellie's shoulder. "I want Mommy," he whimpered.

Carter's heart ached at the mention of their mother — again. "I know, buddy," he said, placing a hand on Ty's back. "I miss her too. But she's not here anymore. It's just us. And we're gonna be okay, I promise."

Ellie nodded, still holding her little brother close. "Can we sleep with you tonight, Daddy?" she asked.

"Of course," he said, scooting over to make room for them. "I'm right here. You're safe with me."

No question about it… they'd be sleeping in Daddy's queen bed tonight, and probably all week.

The next Friday proved to be a bustling day at Simeon Heights Elementary, with a multitude of parents attending the anticipated career day event. After the informative presentations, the adults engaged in conversations, mingling as their children proudly guided them around the classroom, showcasing their projects and schoolwork.

Amidst the lively atmosphere, Carter found himself engrossed in a friendly conversation with Alexandra near the front of the class. Ellie, intermittently glancing their way, couldn't help but observe her father's interaction with her teacher.

"You know," Alex said to him, "I'm glad to know you're a plumber. I needed some plumbing work done at my place to replace my old bathroom faucet. I had already bought the new one, but I had put off looking for a plumber to install it. Can I give you a call? Say, maybe next week, to get it done? Would that be all right?"

Alex's request gave him a valid reason to see her again, and he couldn't help but feel a surge of anticipation at the thought of it. His smile widened as he replied, "Sure. Absolutely. It'll be my pleasure."

"So, um, did you think about our last conversation? About Ellie?" asked Alex, curious.

"Yes. Yes, I did." He paused, gathering his thoughts. "And you know... I think you're right. She *should* meet with the school psychologist. I think it would probably be... a good thing." He said.

"Oh, well, that's great!" said Alex, happy about the decision. "Her name is Mrs. Cole. She's a nice lady and really has a way with children. I'm sure Ellie will love her."

"Yeah, well, I think she'll probably benefit from getting some stuff off her chest. She's been through... *a lot*. She still is going through a lot right now—still mourning, I guess," he said, thinking about Vivian, but also about Ajax's recent demise. "It's pretty tough for a girl her age to live with her silly dad, you know." He said in self-reproach, glancing downward.

"Well, I don't think you're silly. But I can relate. Believe it or not, I was raised by a single father, too." She said, smiling warmly.

On hearing this, he lifted his head, eyes wide and curious to hear more.

As she continued, Alex's face lit up with a mild chuckle, easing the mood. "And, well, if it's any reassurance to you in any way, I turned out okay; at least I think I did," she said, her hand cupped on her chin, playfully mimicking a thoughtful expression. Transitioning to a more sincere tone, she added, "But in all seriousness, I get it. And I'm sure it's not easy."

She reached out and put her hand on his forearm, her touch gentle and warm. Carter's heart skipped a beat, and for a moment, he had to remind himself of the social setting. "But I can tell Ellie loves you very much, so… you must be doing *something* right."

Looking her in the eye, he smiled, nodded lightly, and said, "Well, I better get going. I have to go pick up Ty at the daycare. You, um, have my card, so just call me when you need that faucet installed, okay?"

"Sure will." Alex replied, a warm smile gracing her crimson lips. "And thanks for coming. It definitely meant a lot… to Ellie." she said, her gaze lingering on him for a fraction of a second longer than she intended. Caught off guard by her unintentional flirtatiousness, she was surprised by her own reaction.

He smiled back, feeling a warm flush rise to his cheeks. He cleared his throat and shifted his weight before turning to leave, feeling slightly flustered by her lingering gaze.

As he walked out the door, he couldn't help but think about her touch, the way her eyes had sparkled when she smiled, and the subtle hint of flirtation in her voice. Despite his best efforts to focus on his pressing parental errands, he found his mind wandering back to Alexandra, and the unexpected chemistry he felt with her.

With Tyler safely picked up from daycare and the weekend on the horizon, Carter made a spontaneous decision to swing by *Krispy Kluckers* and treat themselves to a bucket of delicious fried chicken. The past week had been hectic, and the thought of not having to cook tonight was a welcome relief.

As he pulled into his driveway with the weekend ahead and a bucket of fried chicken on his mind, his van came to an abrupt stop.

His gasp of shock echoed through the vehicle as he muttered, "Oh...*God Almighty!* No. Oh, God, no."

Ellie and Ty, curious about their father's reaction, looked out the van window to see what had caused such dismay. Their faces quickly turned to terror as they too saw the gruesome sight: Ajax's lifeless body, brutally impaled on a large branch twenty feet above them.

Ellie's shrieks filled the air as she cried out, "... Oh, no. *Nooo!* Daddy! Noooo!"

Meanwhile, Tyler, also bawling his eyes out, asked the question that was on everyone's mind: "Why daddy?!"

It was clear to Carter that this sickening display was meant for him. He understood how the gory message was intended to rile him.

It was working as intended.

But this was more than a mere message—it was a threat. This was their retaliation for the other night. It was *them* clearly affirming, "This is what happens to anybody who threatens us. This is *our* turf."

Struggling to hold back his own tears, Carter's voice was firm nonetheless as he spoke to Ellie and Ty, urging them to get inside the house and not look at Ajax's body. His heart pounded with a mixture of grief, anger, and fear as he walked them up to the porch, trying to shield them from the gruesome sight.

As they entered the house, Carter could feel the familiar surge of anger and frustration that he had been suppressing for months. He had tried to keep his emotions in check for the sake of his children. But there was only so much he could take. The brutal and senseless killing of Ajax, and now seeing his corpse displayed in such a way, was the last straw.

He knew he couldn't let this go. He had to fight back. This was his home, his family, and he would do whatever it takes to protect them. He felt a deep-seated rage burning inside, and he knew he had to channel it into action.

Later that night, after putting the kids to bed, he walked out into his backyard with a shovel in hand, his heavy heart weighing him down. He dug a deep hole, sweat pouring down his forehead. As he worked, he could hear unnatural howls and shrieks in the distance, taunting him with each guttural yell. At this, all Carter could think was, *Oh, it's on! This means war. Challenge accepted... you bastards!*

Under the glow of the floodlights, he completed the solemn and lonely task of laying Ajax to rest, his heart heavy with grief. The taunting calls of the creatures echoed in the distance, reminding him with every shovelful of earth of the danger that lurked just beyond the tree line.

Undeterred; he would fight back. He couldn't let *them* chase him from his home. Although he didn't yet have a plan yet; he knew it wouldn't be a battle of brute strength, but a battle of wits. As his eyes locked on the darkness of the surrounding woods with fierce resolve, he now welcomed the challenge.

But he also knew he would need help.

VI

James Walker

Monday, September 26, 9:50 a.m.

As soon as Carter laid eyes on the man, he knew that his reputation as a recluse was well-deserved. With his scruffy and wild appearance, he looked like he had been living alone for quite some time. He wore jeans, a plaid green shirt, and black military style boots. His large gray mustache, messy gray hair, and black cowboy hat only added to his slightly spooky appearance.

However, once they spoke, Carter realized that there was more to James Walker than meets the eye. Despite his rugged exterior, he spoke with a sense of calmness and self-assurance that was disarming. His mid-west accent, though noticeable, was not overpowering, and his speech was well-read and intelligent. Carter guessed he was around 62 or 63 years old.

As they chatted, the man's calming presence put him at ease. He couldn't help but wonder if he was an ex-cowboy, ex-policeman, or ex-military, judging by the way he carried himself. But regardless, he knew he was in the presence of a genuine, tough-as-nails, old-school badass.

"Coffee?" Offered Carter.

"Yeah. Black." said James, with his deep husky voice. Clearly, the way he liked his coffee only added to his mystique.

"I'm sorry 'bout your dog, by the way," he said, recalling their prior phone conversation, as Carter was preparing the hot, dark brew. Then he added, "That's one thing about 'em—they don't like dogs. Even so, it's a shame when a young family loses a canine companion that way. How'r your kids takin' it?" he asked in a sincere tone.

"Pretty hard," answered Carter. "We got him about a month and a half ago. He was a great dog. Took to our family real fast, and the kids loved him. So, yeah, they're pretty rattled about the loss. To be honest… so am I."

"Yeah. That's understandable," said James, before adding, "I've heard a lot of stories of missing dogs, cats, cattle, sheep, and so on. People's first impressions don't usually go blamin' Sasquatch. They usually narrow it down to wolves, bears, or mountain lions. That's the scope of their evaluations."

"I suppose that makes sense." Said Carter.

"It does... when you don't know any better. But I tell ya... I've heard accounts of Irish Wolfhounds, Rottweilers, or even Mastiffs that were found up in a tree; some of 'em folded in half or with their necks twisted backwards—like a pretzel. Stuff of nightmares," said James.

As they sat on the deck, Carter noticed James seemed at ease in the tranquil setting. He took in the surroundings, glancing at the tall trees that surrounded the property, before turning his attention back to Carter. Unlike Henry, who often kept to himself and seemed uncomfortable in social situations, James appeared to relish the chance to have a meaningful conversation.

Carter felt a sense of relief that James had agreed to meet with him in person. It was one thing to talk on the phone, but there was something about being face-to-face that made the conversation more personal, more real. As they chatted, he observed how James was taking in his surroundings, assessing the area as he said he would. The breeze brought with it the sweet scent of flowers and fresh-cut grass, and the occasional chirping of birds added to the peaceful ambiance.

Sitting across from the seasoned man, Carter felt a renewed sense of optimism. This was a man who knew what he was talking about, and who seemed willing to help. Carter felt grateful for the opportunity to learn from him and to gain a deeper understanding of the Sasquatches that had invaded his property. He could tell that James was looking at the entire property, the land and the outbuildings, studying it, evaluating the site, and computing everything.

James took a slow sip of his coffee, his gaze fixed on the wooded area. Carter observed him, curious about what the man had to say. The sound of birds chirping and leaves rustling in the wind filled the surrounding air.

"You wanna know something interesting?" James asked, breaking the peaceful silence. Carter nodded eagerly, ready to hear what he had to share.

"Simeon Heights is a misnomer," James revealed.

Carter furrowed his brow in confusion. "What makes you say that?" he asked.

"Well, the town was founded way back in 1855," James began. "And in the official town records, you'll find that the name of this place was originally *Simian Heights*—spelled s-i-m-i-a-n. And now, most people don't know this, but, *simian* means *ape* in Latin," he explained.

Carter's eyes widened in shock. "Really?! Holy crapola!" he exclaimed.

"Yep. Really," James confirmed, taking another sip of his coffee. He paused for a moment before continuing. "And, thinking this had to be a typo, 'bout a hundred years later, they changed it to *Simeon*. But you know what...?"

"What?" Carter asked, eagerly waiting to hear James' next revelation.

"I think the town was named *Simian Heights* by its founders because during the Gold Rush days, they had seen these things, these giant ape-like creatures you're dealing with. They've been here a long time, you know. I reckon longer than we have," James speculated, his eyes still fixed on the woods as if searching for any sign of the creatures he had just mentioned.

"That's fascinating." Carter said. "So, what's been your experience with them? What more can you tell me?" he asked, curious.

"Well, we're in the Pacific Northwest, an' Bigfoot is basically like a mascot in these parts. There's a simple reason for that. And the reason is all of them sightings. But on the other hand, mascots are never really taken seriously. So, many people here don't even believe they're real."

He continued, "Personally, I've only seen Sasquatch a few times on my property—maybe four or five times while hunting, fishing, or trapping. I had no violent encounters with 'em where I live."

"Oh, I thought—"

But before Carter could finish speaking, James stopped him mid-sentence, and proceeded, adding, "*but* I've faced a bunch of 'em in battle on foreign soil."

James saw the astonishment in Carter's expression, his mouth hanging open as he listened intently. So, without missing a beat, he proceeded, "Yeah. That was back in 1991, when I was dispatched to Iraq for Operation Desert Storm."

The seasoned warrior took an instant to gather himself before continuing. "I was a first lieutenant of my team. My platoon was dispatched for a simple recon mission in the mountains of Kurdistan. I had 18 men under my command. I was about, oh 30 or 31 then, and most of 'em were much younger than me—kinda like kid brothers." He said, pausing.

As he spoke, his face showed the pain of a memory he would rather forget. He took a sip from his coffee, collecting himself further before continuing.

"Anyway… the mission was conducted at night, like most of that money-hungry and God-forsaken war. So, we had our night-vision goggles and gear handy. We were given strict orders not to engage the enemy unless fired upon. This was strictly recon, and I reminded my men. We were careful, and I wasn't expecting us to be spotted, cause the rocks and cliffs gave us some pretty decent cover. But I really didn't expect what came next."

James stopped, sighed, and staring at Carter, as if pausing for effect, he continued, "When the ambush came, it wasn't what we expected—mostly 'cause it wasn't from anything human. And it came from real close by—as if they were right next to us, blending into the landscape. To say they had the element of surprise is an understatement. Everything came at us at once. First, they threw large rocks. A couple of my men were badly injured by those. And then, they picked the rest off one by one. In record time, they took out five of my men. But we quickly rallied to fight back, with our M16's lightin' up the night sky ablaze. Even with their size and with our night vision gear, they were hard to spot. These things are elusive, strong, and fast—using the terrain to their advantage. But, from what you told me, you know that firsthand." He said matter-of-factly.

"Yeah." Acquiesced Carter, who was hanging on his every word.

Gathering his thoughts, the old soldier continued, "Despite the chaos, I could still see what we were up against. But, back then, and under those circumstances, it felt like a goddam nightmare. What I mostly had to go with was the gut-wrenching screams of my platoon comrades—not to mention these creatures' unearthly yells. I knew what to shoot at, and where to shoot, but I didn't understand what I was shooting at—know what I mean?"

"Yeah. Well, I can barely imagine, but, um, yeah." Said Carter, nodding. "Sooo, like, how *big* were they?" he asked, captivated.

"Well, like I said, although it was dark, I could still see them pretty well with night vision. I think there were five or six of 'em. They varied in size, but most of 'em were well over six feet tall, with the biggest ones around, I dunno, seven feet maybe? Not quite as big as the ones we have here in these parts. Some of 'em 'round here can reach well over nine feet tall."

"Yeah. That's my estimate of the big one I saw the other night. The other two were more like... seven footers, I guess," said Carter.

"Well, you saw three, but there might be more of 'em, you know. They live in family-tight groups. Like, like... clans." Said James.

"Anyway, all this to say that my platoon lost ten men that night. *I*... lost ten men."

"As for the rest, those of us who survived, well, you don't forget stuff like that," James said, before adding, "I still have nightmares 'bout that night in the Iraqi mountains."

Then, straightening his shoulders and slightly bending over towards Carter, he smiled and said, "I haven't told this sob story to *anyone* in a *long* time. But, with what you've been through, I figure *you get it*. I know you believe me."

"Oh, yeah. Absolutely." Said Carter, nodding vigorously.

"And I didn't tell you this to make you cry, either. I just told you this to encourage you an' make a point… an' that point is: these things are not to be trifled with, *but they can be killed*." He said with a wide and confident grin.

"Yeah, that's good. I was wondering about that, to be honest. So, how did you get to know so much about Bigfoots?" asked Carter.

"Well, after the war, when I finally came back to America, my first mistake was to seek a listening ear from family and friends. What I got instead was mockery and disbelief. Some of 'em even thought I'd lost it completely and went out of their way to shun me. You know, you can get back from a war, you can get over a war, but these experiences, *all these things*… they *stay* with you, and you just carry them inside. Few people understand this. I found out the hard way. It cost me my marriage, for one thing." James said, pensively.

He continued, "So, yeah… I haven't talked about this to nobody for, oh, just about thirty years now. But, back then, I wanted to understand my own experience, so I dug deep into researching these creatures. And that's how I found out all of this stuff."

And then, looking at Carter, he asked, "And what about you? I don't see any missus around. You divorced too?"

"Um, no, not exactly. My wife, she, um, she passed away about... well, almost a year ago." Said Carter, uneasy.

"Oh, I see. I'm sorry. That's too bad. I had no idea. I'm very sorry to hear that." Said James apologetically.

"That's okay. You didn't know." Said Carter.

Carter's mind raced as he tried to think of the best way to broach the subject he had discussed with him over the phone. He didn't want to seem rude or abrupt, but he also didn't want to lose his nerve and miss the opportunity to ask for the man's help.

Finally, he took a deep breath and cleared his throat. "James, there's actually something I wanted to ask you about," he said tentatively.

James looked at him expectantly, his brow furrowing slightly. "Sure, what's on your mind?" he asked.

"Well, when Henry gave me your number, it was implied that you could probably help me with this problem. Now, as much as I appreciate learning more about these creatures, as you know, they have been threatening my family in no uncertain terms. So, I was hoping, or rather, I'm asking... can you help me to deal with this?"

"Heh, heh, heh," chuckled the older man. "Well, I like that. You're a practical man. You're direct. I'm more talkative in my old age, but make no mistake, so am I. We're kindred spirits in that sense," he said, pausing.

He continued, "You know, there are always some rough patches on the road of life. This definitely qualifies as one for you and your family right now." He said with a sincere look in his eyes.

"Tell you what though…" he continued, "The good Lord always makes sure to send some kinda help our way through these tough patches. And it looks like He sent me here today. Anyway, that's what I believe."

He sipped the last remaining drops from his now lukewarm coffee, before adding, "Now, I can't heal no broken heart, but I sure can offer to help you take care of these overgrown apes." He said, smiling.

Carter, relieved, smiled and said, "That'd be great. I'd really appreciate that." After a brief pause, he added, "So, how do we do this?"

"Okay, so here's the deal… You're gonna need six things to get 'em off your property for good." Said James.

"Okay, sure. What are those?" asked Carter, all ears.

"*One*, some high-powered riffles, guns, and other firearms."

"Check." Answered Carter. "I'm a seasoned hunter, and I've got a decent armory."

James nodded, before continuing, "*Two*, a solid plan. Now, we'll put our heads together and I'm sure we'll come up with one."

"All right." Said Carter.

"*Three*, when we execute that plan, you have to make sure your kids are well taken care of… and not here in this house. *Catch my drift?*"

"Um, yeah. That can be arranged. Sure." Said Carter, now fully realizing the risks associated, and cashing a big reality check.

"*Four*, you're gonna need to dig deep inside your heart for *a lot* of courage."

"Check. For sure. I know that," said Carter.

"*Five*, you're gonna have to *trust me*, even when I don't seem to make any sense to you."

"I can do that. Definitely." Answered Carter.

"*Six*... you'll need to understand one thing above all others."

"Okay, what's that?" Asked Carter, eager to hear that last part.

"You see, these creatures, these... *Bigfoots*... as big and as strong as they are... they're also more intelligent than people. Do you know why?"

"Um, no. Why?" asked Carter.

"Because they fear God more than they fear man." Said James, his eyes filled with conviction.

"Um, okay." Carter's eyebrows furrowed, confused. "I don't quite understand," he admitted reluctantly.

James leaned back in his chair and took a deep breath before continuing. "Look, son, these creatures, they have a sense of awareness that we lack. They understand the natural world in ways that we can't even imagine. They know things about this earth and the creatures on it that we haven't even discovered yet. But, most importantly, they have a connection to the spiritual world that most of us humans have lost or neglected.

They understand that there are things beyond our comprehension, and that there is a Higher Power out there that we need to respect."

Carter listened intently, feeling out of his depth at the older man's words. Although raised by parents who had religious convictions, he had always been a bit of a skeptic when it came to matters of the supernatural. Hearing James talk about it with such conviction, however, made him wonder if there was more to this world than he had previously believed.

James leaned in and looked at him with a serious expression. "To win this fight, you're gonna have to fear God more than they do," he said pointedly. "And above all, you're gonna have to have more faith in the Almighty than in our plan, our guns, or our smarts. Do you *understand* me?"

Carter hesitated before nodding. "I guess," he said.

James, noticing his lack of conviction, asked, "Son, do you know the story of David versus Goliath?"

Carter nodded. "Yeah, well, the gist of it, anyway. I did go to Sunday school, you know," he said with a small chuckle.

"Well, this ain't no Sunday school," James said seriously. "And you're about to get schooled in things that'll make your head spin. So, I recommend you become *real familiar* with it, 'cause you're in a similar story now. You're gonna have to be like David. David was bold, brave, and full of faith before overwhelming odds."

Carter saw the fortitude in James's eyes and knew the old soldier wasn't kidding. So, he nodded in agreement.

James continued, "David didn't care about the size and strength of Goliath 'cause he knew the size and strength of His God. He didn't put his trust in his skill, or his plan, or the sling he carried, but in God. He had faith that *God* would deliver him, no matter what. Do you follow me?"

Carter nodded again, more confidently this time. "Yeah, I get what you're getting at. Faith. I got it," he said, determined to channel his inner David.

"Good. I'm glad we understand each other." Said James. "Now, what firepower do you carry in your inventory?" he asked, steering the conversation in more familiar territory.

As Carter gave his newfound mentor the tour of his armory, they swapped stories about their lives and interests. As they talked, James shared his knowledge about firearms, life experiences, and more of his beliefs about the supernatural.

With each passing moment, Carter felt more and more out of his depth, realizing just how much he didn't know about the world beyond his little corner of it. The older man's words made him question his own beliefs about God, faith, and the world around him.

Finally, as the conversation wound down, James rose to leave. But before they parted ways, Carter mustered up the courage to ask, "So, what about you? You told me you were married, but do you have any children?"

A small smile tugged at the corners of the older man's mouth, raising his large mustache slightly. "Yeah," he said. "Throughout this whole mess called *my life*, I was fortunate enough to get to raise a one-of-a-kind daughter."

VII

Tying Up Loose Ends

Thursday, September 29, 10:15 p.m.

"If you know the enemy and know yourself, you need not fear the result of a hundred battles. If you know yourself but not the enemy, for every victory gained, you will also suffer a defeat. If you know neither the enemy nor yourself, you will succumb in every battle."
~Sun Tzu

As he relaxed in bed, Carter had dusted off Sun Tzu's *The Art of War,* as a preparatory refresher for what lay ahead. The book had been a birthday gift from a hunting buddy of his five years ago. He had never read it cover to cover, but had skimmed through its pages once or twice. He hoped the old Chinese general's words would put him in the right mindset.

His leisurely read was disrupted when he heard little feet pitter-patter in the hallway and he saw a small silhouette appear in his doorway.

"Daddy," said Ty, "The monkey-men are back."

The trespassers on his property made sure to remind Carter of their presence. But he kept his cool.

Since he had heard nothing, he asked, "Really? Monkey-men, huh? That's what you call them?" Ty nodded. So, opening his arms wide and inviting his son, he hugged him and asked, "Did you *see* them?"

"No. But they're talking loud outside. They woke me up," said the boy.

"Hu-huh. Well, okay," said Carter, trying to remain as calm as possible not to alarm his son, "I guess we'll just have to close your window."

"I want to sleep in your bed, daddy," said Ty.

Carter sighed, smiled, and said, "All right. But just for tonight, okay?"

Ty, reassured, nodded, smiled, and then scurried under his dad's warm covers.

Carter rose from his bed and made his way to Ellie's room. As he opened the door, he could see that she was sleeping soundly. He let out a sigh of relief, but still took the time to close her slightly open window. Next, he headed to Ty's room and carefully approached the window. He paused and listened attentively to the sounds coming from outside.

Sure enough, they were out there once again— taunting him; he thought. He could hear their indistinctive primitive chatter just out back in the woods. But he couldn't see them.

He stood motionless by the window, straining to make out the incoherent sounds of the creatures lurking outside. Their language was unfamiliar to him, but it was oddly reminiscent of the ancient Samurai warriors he had seen in movies. He felt a sense of awe and disbelief wash over him as he listened to their primitive chatter. Despite his fascination, the fiery desire for revenge towards the creatures who caused him and his family so much grief remained.

As he stood listening to them, he couldn't help but think of the irony of the situation. He had been reading Sun Tzu's *The Art of War*, written by an ancient oriental warrior, as a preparation for what lay ahead, and now he was about to face off against creatures who seemed to speak that very language. The thought amused him, in a twisted sort of way.

What are these things? He pondered. Mulling over the words of Sun Tzu's, he feared he might not know enough about them to engage them successfully. Nevertheless, he took comfort in the fact that he wasn't facing this challenge alone anymore.

James knows more about them than anyone. That should tip the scales in our favor, he thought, as he kept listening outside, still trying to make sense of how he had gotten himself into such a predicament.

Lending an ear towards his moonlit yard one last time, as if to etch a recording of their voice in his mind, he finally closed the window, as their chatter faded away, before calling it a night.

As the sun rose on Saturday morning, Carter's mind buzzed with the day ahead. He mentally ticked off the places he needed to go and the people he needed to see. Rising from bed, he stretched his limbs, feeling the tension of the previous night's events still lingering in his body. He glanced at the bedside table, where *The Art of War* lay open, a keen reminder of his plans for the weekend.

Meanwhile, in the other bedrooms, Ellie and Ty prepared for their sleepover at the MacArthur's house. They packed their favorite toys and stuffed animals, and were eager to spend the night with their kindly elderly neighbors. They chattered about their plans for the day, and Carter, who overheard everything, couldn't help but smile at their enthusiasm.

He helped them finish packing and then drove them over to the MacArthur's, feeling a pang of guilt as he had lied to Glenda and the kids about his weekend plans. He hated lying. He told them he was attending a plumbing trade show in Portland. He'd never been a strong liar either, and that was the best he could come up with. *It's not like I could tell them, "Hey, I'm going to hunt Bigfoots this weekend. Please babysit my kids."* He reasoned.

As they arrived at the door, Glenda greeted them warmly and ushered them inside. Anxious, Carter was more affectionate than usual as he hugged his children tightly and reminded them to behave and listen to their hosts at all times. Ellie noticed the subtle difference in his embrace and wondered silently about it.

"I can't tell you how much I appreciate this," said Carter, looking at both Glenda and Henry.

"Oh, nonsense, dear!" replied the lady of the house. "This'll just be fun for us," she said, turning to Ellie and Ty with a complicit smile and adding, "I was going to bake my world-famous apple pies today? Would you both like to help me?"

"Apple pies! Oh, yes! Absolutely!" answered Ellie enthusiastically.

"Are they *really* world famous?" asked Ty, doubting the woman's words.

Glenda laughed at his clever suspicion, before replying, "Tell you what, Tyler... you can let me know after you taste 'em... this afternoon, with a scoop of *ice cream*. How does that sound?"

Ty's widening grin spoke volumes, and all three adults laughed heartily at the boy's reaction.

Seeing his children would be well taken care of, Carter hugged them once more, looked at both Glenda and Henry, and said, "Well, I really have to get going. Thanks again for this. We'll keep in touch. You have my cell number if anything happens."

"No worries, dear," said Glenda. "Everything will be just fine."

He watched Ellie and Ty disappear into the house, feeling a sense of relief that they would be safe here for the night.

This whole time, Henry had been his silent, withdrawn, usual self. Shaking hands with him as he departed, Carter wondered if the old man knew about the true nature of this babysitting gig.

He carefully parked his white van on the curb and double-checked the address written on the crumpled piece of paper: 255 Pine Rose Lane. Carter took a quick glance at Alexandra's house, admiring its simple elegance. The yellow siding, white window frames, and black asphalt shingles roof gave it a quaint country charm. Judging from the exterior, he guessed it was a two-bedroom home. He wondered if Ellie was right about her fifth-grade teacher being single. While the house seemed too small for a family, it seemed perfect for a couple.

As he entered her home, he was greeted by her warm smile. "Thanks so much for coming," she said, leading him toward the bathroom.

He looked around the cozy living room and kitchen area as they walked. "Nice little place you got here," he said.

"Thanks. And all of it on a teacher's salary," she jested, before asking, "You probably don't usually work Saturdays, do you?"

He chuckled. "Hey, are you kidding? You had me at home-cooked lunch," he replied, setting his tools down. "Besides, that's what we had agreed upon, right?"

"Right," she said, following him into the bathroom.

"But this is still gonna cost you, like... *a lot*," he joked, getting under the sink to start his work.

Alex raised an eyebrow. "Oh really? My cooking isn't enough to get me a freebie?" she said teasingly.

He grinned. "Well, I guess that'll depend on how good your cooking is," he said, winking at her playfully.

As he finished tightening the bolt, he wriggled out from under the cramped space and stood up, facing Alexandra. Taking a good look at her, he now fully realized how they were alone in the house, and that his previous female clients were nothing like her. They were usually married, married with children, unattractive, or just old. But Alexandra was clearly none of those things. As a result, his testosterone surged, and he felt a bit embarrassed by his own thoughts. His slightly inappropriate musings betrayed him as he spoke. "So, um, can I ask you a personal question?"

Alexandra smiled, half-suspecting where this might be going. "Sure," she said.

"Are you, like, single, or anything?" he asked.

His question made her chuckle. "Well, I don't have a boyfriend or a husband. So yeah, I'm *like, single… or anything*," she said, cleverly repeating his clumsy words, and grinning.

He smiled back, and then probed, "Why is that? I mean, not to pry, but… it's not like you're, I mean… you're not, you know."

Flattered by his awkward compliment, she answered, "Well, I guess if I'm to boil it down, I just never met the right man."

"Hmmm. And… what would *he* be like?" he asked, curious to self-evaluate how he measured up.

"That's a good question," she replied in a more serious tone. "I'm not quite the typical school teacher or girl next door, I guess. I had a *particular* upbringing."

"What do you mean?" he asked.

"Well, do you remember how I mentioned to you I was raised by a single dad?" she said.

"Yeah. I remember," he said, nodding.

"Well, while my dad is anything but perfect, I can honestly say he's a decent man. And he always taught me how to spot 'em—*the creeps*, I mean. So, as a result, I didn't date very much. It's, like, I could always tell if a guy was good, or if he had any honorable intentions at all—usually on a first date, too. And, things being the way they are today, you can imagine I didn't meet too many men I felt were worth my time," Alex said, scrutinizing the man across from her to see how he would react.

"Hmmm, that's interesting." Said Carter, reflecting on her words. "It's good, especially in today's world. I want to teach this to Ellie too," he said.

He then paused, and asked her, "So, if I may ask, your father's name… what is it?"

She cocked her head sideways. "James. Why?" she asked.

"So, James *Walker*? Right? He's your father?" he said, seeking to confirm his investigation.

"Y--yes," she said, suspiciously.

"Is he, oh, about 5'11", with a large mustache, and wears cowboy attire?" he asked, trying to confirm his suspicions.

After a slight pause, Alex, perplexed, looked at him, sighed, and said hesitantly, "Yes". And then, as if gaining confirmation, said, "So… *you are* the guy who called him concerning the…"

She seemed somewhat disconcerted. She put her palmed hand over her mouth before adding. "He had told me he was going to meet a man who'd just moved here, who lived just outside of town, and who had..." she trailed off.

Carter, slightly embarrassed, nodded, confirming her thought, as he said in a resigned tone, "It's okay. You can say it... *Bigfoot problems.*"

"Yeah. That." She said, offering an empathic look.

Not one to be pitied, he then asked her, "So, when he said that, did you suspect it was me?"

"Well, he had told me the guy lived on Simeon Road, but I was *hoping* it *wasn't* you." She admitted with a look of concern.

There was a moment of awkward silence. Carter broke it, bringing his folded finger to his chin and circling back to her father. "You know, Alex, the thought of the possibility of you two being related had crossed my mind the first time I heard your full name—on career day." He paused, before adding, "It really is a small world."

"More like a small town." She said caustically.

He laughed, shook his head, then he continued, "I still can't get over it. And, if I may; you probably look more like your mom, am I right?" he said, grinning approvingly.

She laughed, confirming the assertion, and amused at the flirtatious banter. She enjoyed it, though. After all, it had been a while since she'd received male attention that she relished. Although she barely knew him, there was just something endearing about Carter.

Conversing with him was easy and fun. He was genuine, and she felt she could trust him.

Carter further confided in Alexandra about the Sasquatch struggles on his new property. He also went into more details about meeting her dad and their plans to solve the situation tonight, God willing.

As they enjoyed the chicken pot-pie she had prepared, Alexandra opened up to Carter about her past. She confided how her mom had become a little too promiscuous after she had divorced her dad, and how, tired of it, she had asked to go live with her father at 12. She told him what it was like growing up with a conservative and God-fearing veteran. How he taught her everything he knew about boys, conspiracies, the Bible, government black ops, and, of course... *Bigfoots*.

"I was always daddy's girl," she continued, "and, with a dad like mine, I was also a bit of a tomboy growing up." She said, laughing.

"I get it, I do," Carter said, "but I still have a hard time *picturing you* as a tomboy—or a conspiracy theorist," he said, teasing her.

She played along. "Oh, but I was. Flannel shirts, hunting boots, tinfoil hats, and the whole ball of wax," she said, laughing. "I guess that was a direct result of living with a tough-as-nails army vet," she continued, "But, throughout this phase, dad always reminded me to stay feminine. He would always say, 'God made you a beautiful girl, go fishing and shoot the gun, but make sure you don't lose sight of your God given grace to become a woman.' So, eventually, I grew out of my tomboy phase," she said.

Carter had to agree, so he nodded. He could tell these were fond memories for her, and that she appreciated every bit of input her father had given her growing up.

So, Carter reciprocated as he opened up to her about his childhood, his family, growing up on a farm, his budding plumbing services in the area, briefly mentioning his mourning and the challenges of being a single dad. But then he veered the conversation back to his Sasquatch issues, wanting to probe for her opinion on the subject.

"So, um, yeah, these Sasquatches, these Bigfoots... Before I moved here, I have to confess... despite living in the Pacific Northwest... I thought they were only, like, *native folklore or legends*. I'd been in the woods a lot, hunting and all. I never saw anything. I mean, I never thought—"

"Oh yeah, they're *real* all right," she interrupted, with a tone that betrayed antipathy toward the creatures.

Surprised by her forthrightness, he asked, "So, did *you* ever, like, see one?"

"Nope," she said, "and, having heard some pretty horrific stories from my dad, I can tell you I like it that way."

"Oh," he said, pausing. "Well, I did some research online and I've found a lot of stuff, unexplained stuff, that happened right here in Oregon, or in the Pacific Northwest. For instance, have you ever heard of Ape Canyon?" he asked.

Looking up at him, she felt obligated to interrupt his enthusiastic train of thought, and said, "Carter... "

"Hmmm?" he said, sipping his ginger ale, and noticing her composure taking on a more serious nature.

"These creatures. You know they're real now. And, for sure, with what you're going through, you *need* to get informed. But..." she hesitated.

"But?" he said, eagerly itching for her two cents.

"Well... just be careful not to let it *consume you*," she sighed, looking genuinely concerned.

She continued, "My father, when he got back from the war, it was all he could think about. He put so much time and effort into researching Bigfoots that it consumed him. I mean, my mom had her faults and all, but it was *this obsession* that ultimately brought their marriage to an end. It also ostracized him from friends, family, and social settings. It caused him, and us, a lot of pain. And it wasn't until he found some balance and peace that I opted to go live with him—just so you know."

Carter looked at her, agreeing and remembering how James had told him the sad story, and feeling the need to heed the cautionary tale for himself.

"Can I be honest with you?" she then asked, looking somber.

"Sure. What's wrong?" he asked, slightly concerned.

"Well, I just wanna come clean. I kinda feigned ignorance earlier in our conversation." She paused, before adding, "Dad *had told me* he was helping the fellow who bought the property at 426 Simeon Road," she said.

"Oh, he did?" Said Carter, flustered.

Seeing his mounting embarrassment, she quickly added, "Yes. But he only disclosed the address, and nothing else. And…"

"And?" he probed, curious to know the full story.

"Well, from Ellie's coordinates, I… Let's just say I was curious, and I did a bit of homework to ease my hunch. So, bottom line, *yes*, I knew it was you… and that you had already met my dad before coming here today."

She could tell this new revelation perplexed him, so she quickly added, "But don't worry. Like I said, he never mentioned your name. He always respects people's privacy. But… I mean… everyone in our town kinda knows *that* house. After all, it had been on the market for so long, and many rumors were flying about the place."

"Rumors?!" Carter reacted, disenchanted, "Oh, okay, I see. So, everybody here knew the punchline except for me, huh?"

Feeling remorseful at his remark, she smiled gently at him. She then reached across the table, put her hand on his, and said, "Hey, listen, there was no way you could have known this, right? Now, I don't know any sane realtor who would say to a potential buyer, "Oh, and by the way, there are Bigfoots on this property.""

He sighed, snickered, and said, "Right. I guess so." Her gentle touch made him feel warm inside.

"And, I get it. I mean, every time I drove by, I thought it was a very nice property myself," she said. "And you probably got it real cheap, am I right?" she asked.

At that, he smirked slightly, before answering, "Alex… it was such a steal that I'm surprised I'm not in jail."

They both laughed.

So, trying to further lighten the mood and ease the tension, she added, "Hey, so you bought the house in *the forbidden zone*, at *Calima*. So, what? Right?"

"Um, what? I know *the forbidden zone*. But… what's *Calima*?" he asked.

She laughed, her eyes widening in surprise, and said, "Oh, you haven't seen the 2001 *Planet of the Apes* movie version, have you?"

"Um, no. Apparently, I didn't. I saw the classic one though. *Take your stinkin' paws off me, you damn dirty ape!*" he mimicked, gritting his teeth and doing his best Charlton Heston impression.

She laughed heartily.

"Tell you what," she said, "When all this is over, and you and my dad sort everything out, *because you will*, he'll see to that," she said emphatically, "Then you can come back here. I'll rent it, and we can watch it together."

"Well, *Alex*… If I didn't know any better, I'd think you're trying to bait me into coming back here. Are you proposing… a *second* date?" he said, teasing.

"Well, I don't know, *Carter Mitchell*. Are you saying that today was… *a first date?*" she said, smirking.

Clever girl, he thought, looking at her, purposefully taking his time, and slowly catching a whiff of the inebriating perfume of her long and wavy dark-

128

brown hair. Her delicate scent reminisced of vanilla-infused hyacinth.

He smiled and, although he was greatly tempted to move to first base, he felt it might push things a bit too fast.

"I would definitely like to see you again," he said. "You've made me *curious*... about the *Planet of the Apes* movie, I mean," he said, looking her in the eyes, and gently brushing her hand with his strong thumb. "And... I have to admit, this was the best chicken pot pie I've had in a long time."

Usually self-possessed, she could feel herself weakening at his gentle touch. Time slowed down as their pulses synced, and they could both feel the heat of the moment.

"You've made me curious too," she said in a whisper. "About seeing it a second time, I mean," she added, smiling at him.

But, despite the intoxicating pheromone-laden atmosphere, Carter had to go. He didn't want to, but he had to.

Before he left, she asked, "So, you're meeting my dad... *this evening*, right?"

"Yeah, that's the plan; at my place. We'll head out from there," he said.

"And your children?" she asked with a tinge of concern.

"They're spending the night at my neighbors. They live about half a mile away from my house, on

Simeon Road. You might know them... the MacArthurs," he said.

"Um, yeah. Actually, I *think* I know them. Well, that is... I know *her*. She used to teach at my school. *Glenda*, right?"

"Right." He answered.

"Well, that's good," she said, nodding approvingly. "That's good."

Taking his hand in hers, she said, "You guys will sort this out tonight, I'm sure. You're both outdoorsy types. My dad's armed to the teeth, and he's done this quite a few times, you know. He's, like, the unofficial Bigfoot-buster in these parts."

"Really?" Carter said, surprised, furrowing his brow.

"Oh, absolutely!" she confirmed. "He's helped quite a few people to reclaim their properties throughout the years." She paused, before adding reassuringly, "And you're both in my prayers."

"Well, thanks, I appreciate that," he said.

Just as he went out the door, she called out, "Carter--"

He turned around. Then she said, "Call me when it's over, okay?"

"Okay. Will do," he said.

Carter left Alex's house in the early afternoon, with his belly full... and, for the first time in months... with his heart full as well.

But his mind still weighed heavily about where he was heading to next: *Arlington Heights, Portland.*

The first thing Carter noticed when he parked his van was that the house hadn't changed since last time, and neither did the affluent neighborhood.

The Victorian style of the large five-bedroom home, combined with its double garage and beautifully manicured front and back landscaping screamed of sophistication. The entire neighborhood did.

Every single time he had been invited here, whether for Sunday dinner or special occasions, he always felt out of place—like he didn't belong.

A part of him wanted to fit in, for Vivian's sake. But another part of him struggled with impostor syndrome. He just knew this setting wasn't him. And sometimes he felt like he was cheating her out of a real chance at enjoying life's best. And yet, he fondly remembered Viv saying to him, "Yes, my parents have money—they always will. But they don't know they're bored. It's sad. I don't want their life. I want *you* in my life. We'll build our own success and happiness. Like Sinatra sang… we'll do it our way."

And, for the longest time, they did.

Ah yes, the place hadn't changed. It was still picture perfect; adorned with mature trees and pampered with the smell of money, success, sophistication… and vanity.

Carter's mind and heart were racing. He found this even more challenging than what lay ahead later tonight in the woods. With nature, the outdoors, you know what to expect: it's raw, wild, and untamed. If you're not careful, it will eat you alive. But people are different. They *seem* civilized and tame; they smile to your face; they gain your trust, and *then* they eat you alive.

Carter had always struggled with this unique aspect of human relations.

He remembered his mother's words when she used to say, "Son, one of the toughest things in life is the ability to master human relations."

This sure qualifies, he thought, as he climbed the steps. Bracing himself, he finally rang the doorbell.

A medium height, graying, and handsome gentleman opened the door. Looking at Carter with contempt, he snapped, "What are *you* doing here?"

"Hi John," said Carter, ignoring the rude comment, "I'm here 'cause we need to talk."

"I've said everything I'll ever need to say to *you*," the man replied, about to close the door in his face.

Extending his arm, Carter prevented the door from closing. "All right. Fair enough. Could you just please listen then?" he pleaded, as he saw the man's wife appear in the entryway behind him.

Esther was a pleasant-looking woman who never failed to remind Carter of Vivian whenever he saw her. Unlike her husband, John; Esther had always treated Carter like a son.

Surprised, she exclaimed, "Carter! Oh, my goodness, it's *you!*" and then, turning to her husband, she added indignantly, "Well, don't just stand there, John. Invite the man in."

Reluctantly, John obliged.

John Adams, Vivian's father, was an epitome of self-made success. His unwavering work ethic, astute investments, and an unexpected but prosperous lumber business had propelled him to great heights. However, behind his accomplishments lay a stern and all-work-and-no-play demeanor. He was a man of utmost seriousness, dedicating minimal time to frivolities or nonsense, instead prioritizing his relentless pursuit of excellence.

Although John Adams had been raised as a hard-nosed blue-collar man like Carter, he had developed a taste for the white-collar lifestyle of Portland's rich and famous. And unlike Carter, who enjoyed his blue-collar lifestyle, John preferred to put distance between his roots and his present-day status. He had raised Vivian to aspire to upper echelon living as well, encouraging her to pursue a career in law and attend an Ivy League university.

So, for Vivian, his beautiful and only daughter, to become a nurse and marry a plumber, was seen as blatant underachievement. And then he also had to deal with her untimely death. So, understandably, he carried a lot of sorrow... *and resentment.*

After sitting down in their beautiful, all whitely decorated den, and getting him a coffee, Esther eagerly inquired, "So, tell me... How are Ellie and Ty?"

"They're fine... Esther," he said, smiling gently at her. "They're both fine." He reassuringly nodded. Ty's still in daycare, and Ellie started fifth grade at her new school."

"Wh--What?! A *new* school?!" said the woman, visibly troubled by the revelation.

"Um, yeah. We moved away this summer, 'bout an hour south from here—in Simeon Heights," said Carter, uneasy.

"Oh, great!" exclaimed John, "First you prevent us from seeing our grandkids, and now you move them away from everything they've ever known! And from us."

Raising his voice back, Carter said, "Well, maybe I wouldn't have done any of this if you had been more reasonable and understanding when Vivian…"

Carter pressed his lips together and interlaced his fingers, trying to collect his thoughts before speaking. He didn't want the situation to escalate any further, so he had to choose his words carefully. The older couple looked visibly shaken by the news, and Carter knew he owed them a more detailed explanation.

"Look, the only reason I moved was to get a fresh start—a new perspective on life—on the future. It was not to cause anybody any harm or to get even with anyone," he said, staring at them.

He spoke in a calm and earnest tone, "John, Esther, please believe me when I say this; I didn't come here to argue or fight. I came to make *peace,* for Ellie and Ty's sake. They miss you both terribly. They need you in their lives. They need their family, their grandparents. And I came here to say that… well, I'm sorry for keeping them away from you all this time."

John's eyes softened somewhat. Esther now had tears running down her cheeks.

Carter continued, "Look, I was hoping we could put our differences aside and move past this for the sake of the kids… and ourselves. We've all been through so much, and I thought it was time to bury the hatchet once and for all. Don't you agree?"

"Well, yes, I'd love that. I miss them so much," said Esther emphatically.

Carter smiled compassionately at her.

John, now softened, looked down, and with trembling lips said, "I--I miss them too. Very much."

"And they miss you both very much," Carter reassured.

With that out of the way, the three of them continued to chat for a little while longer. The elderly couple asked about the kids; when they could see them again. Carter reassured them they could plan something in the next few weeks, especially for Ellie's upcoming birthday later that year.

Before leaving, Carter hesitated. He was weighing up the prospect of John and Esther becoming guardians of his children if something happened to him. He had been pondering the idea for some time and thought that this might be an appropriate moment to bring it up. However, he ultimately decided against it. This would be *too much, too soon*, he thought. He didn't want to chance saying anything that would cast a nefarious shadow on his upcoming endeavors in the woods. Instead, he held on to his mustard-seed faith and kept his peace.

After an hour of polite conversation, he took leave of his ex-in-laws, on good terms and with a clear conscience.

135

With everything now sorted out, he could enjoy the relaxing drive back home. He was relieved that the kids were in a safe environment for the weekend. He also felt a sense of closure after months of conflict with his in-laws. He enjoyed a peace of mind that he hadn't felt in a long time. He looked forward to venturing out with James, even though the nature of this particular hunt was going to be unlike anything he'd ever experienced before.

He was ready for this unique *call of the wild*.

VIII

Locked and Loaded

Saturday, October 1st, 6:25 p.m.

How do you prepare for something like this? Carter thought. He had tracked and hunted deer, moose, elk, and even black bear since youth. But he'd never gone after anything like *this*. Heck, he'd never even hunted grizzly bear. And this was like going after two, three, or more grizzlies all at once. Was he insane? Should he just give all this up, put the house back up for sale, and move elsewhere? And to top it off, he was going in there with a man he barely knew. Oh, yeah, he could feel it; he could feel the nerves creeping up on him.

That's when the doorbell rang, announcing a point of no return.

James had said he'd be there at 6:30, and true to his word, he was right on time.

Upon opening the door, Carter faced a man who was prepared—*Very prepared.*

Standing before him was not a hunter, but a soldier. Dressed in camo from head to toe, James was equipped with all kinds of gear that gave away his military past. He also carried a large U.S. Army-issued backpack he had slung over his shoulders. What caught Carter's eye and added to his sense of awe, however, was the sight of his massive pickup truck with an attached trailer carrying two four-wheelers in the driveway behind him.

"Woah! Four-wheelers, huh? That's impressive. Real nice," expressed Carter.

"Well, I don't know 'bout you, but I ain't goin' out there to fail," said James, who then began unpacking his backpack on the kitchen table. The list of equipment he displayed was both impressive and reassuring. Some of it was also foreign to Carter.

"What are those?" he asked, pointing to small lantern-looking thingies.

"Those are T238 flash grenades. They emit a loud noise and blinding light. You see, Bigfoots are mostly night creatures, so they *hate* that," assured James. And then, looking at Carter, he began singing playfully, "This little light of mine, I'm gonna let it shine… this little light of mine, I'm gonna let it shine."

Carter chuckled at the older man's sense of humor.

"Whoa! Wait, are those—" pointed Carter.

"Yep. Four-eyed night vision goggles. They're used by the marines. There's just nothing like 'em. Makes you see in the dark like it's practically high noon."

"But... how did you—"

"I still have very good contacts on the inside who, while they don't back up what I do, they see some value in it. I'll just leave it at that," said James.

Carter chuckled, "You're like... worse than Batman," he said.

"Batman's a wuss," retorted James, smirking.

Then, looking at Carter from head to toe, he smiled and said, "I can see you're pretty well prepped yourself. That's good."

Indeed, Carter was fully geared up for the expedition as well. He wore a camouflage hunting outfit and a heavy fall coat to keep warm. He carried a high-powered rifle on his shoulder, a Smith & Wesson 500 tucked securely into a conceal-carry shoulder holster. A sturdy machete hung from his right hip. He also sported two hunting knives; a Bowie on his left hip and strapped to his ankle, a dagger. He felt confident these extra precautions would provide him with extra protection if needed. His pockets were fully stocked with ammunition, including some tucked away inside and on the sides, ready for quick access. Indeed, he had prepared to take on anything that lay ahead.

"Now, look at me," said James earnestly.

Carter looked at him. James stared him right in the eye and asked him a one-word question. "Scared?"

Not to be undone, Carter took on a confident air and answered, "No."

But James knew better. He had been in combat situations with hundreds of men before—facing the threat of death multiple times. He knew the look.

He told Carter, "There's no shame in being afraid, son." And then he matter-of-factly said, "I'm scared."

"You... *are?*" said Carter, taken aback by the older man's unexpected confession.

"Of course I am. I'd be stupid not to be," he said, "And I'll tell you what else... out there, *fear* can be your friend."

"Huh? How so?" asked Carter.

Without even blinking, James answered, "*Fear* keeps you from being overconfident. It keeps you accountable. It keeps you watchful. It keeps you on your toes. You know what I'm sayin'?"

"Um, yeah. I guess I do," acknowledged Carter.

"Now, tonight, you and I are bound by the warrior's code. I ain't gonna sugar-coat it for ya. And I ain't sayin' that to sound cool or melodramatic. I'm just stating a fact. We're going out there and we don't exactly know how it's gonna go."

Carter was just listening at this point. Waiting for more intel from his more experienced comrade-in-arms.

So, the elder soldier continued, "But despite all the uncertainty we're dealin' with, I can still give you some guarantees."

"Really? What are those?" asked Carter.

"Well, number one, I *guarantee* that I've got your back… and I expect the same courtesy from you. All right?"

"Um, yeah. Sure. Absolutely." Said Carter.

"All right. Number two, I *guarantee* that I ain't leaving you behind if I can help it. Now, can you do the same for me?" asked James, looking sharply at Carter, expecting a positive response.

Carter snapped into a soldier's stance, facetiously bringing his right hand up to his temple. "100%, sir!" he declared.

James smiled, "Good." He said. "And third, I *guarantee* that I'm going to give you my best tonight; cause you know what?"

"What?"

"I really want to see you and your family find peace," said James, with a sincere, compassionate, and mustachioed smile.

This last part moved Carter. Here stood a man whom he barely knew, who was willing to go out with him in a life-or-death match with giant ape-like creatures—the legendary and mysterious Bigfoot. Would his best friend have done the same?

Even more, he thought of Alex. James, after all, was her father, and so he felt an added responsibility to look after him.

But before he could indulge further in overly sentimental musings, James got right down to more business. "Son, I told ya we'd need the help of the

141

Almighty as we head out. And I meant it. So, first things first."

He reached into his pocket and retrieved a silver cross on a chain. "Call me superstitious or sentimental, but I want you to have this," he said as he extended his hand to present the gift to Carter.

"As you can see, I'm wearing an identical one." Said James, showing off the silver cross that hung over his chest. "Now... put it around your neck." He added.

Although Carter admired the old soldier's faith, and had been brought up with Christian values too, he didn't consider himself very religious, and hesitated to accept the gift, "Geez, um, thanks, but—"

"No *buts*. I'm not asking. You just put this around your neck—for protection, okay?" Then he continued, "Hey, it never hurts to have an angel on your side, right?"

"Um, yeah. I guess so," Carter said, as he obliged his partner.

It was a nice gesture. And the cross, without being fancy, was made of sterling silver and had a stylish touch to it. For sure, it would be nice to have angelic assistance tonight, not that he put too much weight on that sort of thing.

"All right. Good," Said James, adding, "I also took the liberty of printing out for you my two favourite Psalms," he said as he handed him two pieces of folded paper. "These are Psalms 23 and 91. Put them in your jacket pocket for safekeeping. I've got my own copies here. We'll read them out loud before we head out," he said.

And they did—they read both Psalms out loud. Carter was pleasantly surprised at how good it felt to read those Scriptures. It had been a while since he had earnestly read from the Bible, and he had forgotten the sense of peace that it could bring. It reminded him of his childhood when he would recite the Lord's Prayer with his mom before bed, or read passages from Scripture in church. Without realizing it, he had missed these simple acts of faith.

"There's something else I want you to know," said James.

"Sure. What's that?" asked Carter.

"I ain't doing this to get famous."

"Um, okay." Said Carter, unsure what his older mentor was getting at.

James cleared his throat, before explaining, "To be clear, I don't hunt Bigfoot. I help people. There's a big difference. So, I ain't taking no prisoners or bringing back bodies or any such nonsense. What we kill, we leave behind and let nature take its course. I'm telling you this so that you don't get any ideas. Believe me; I've seen it before, gung-ho types trying to get smart when they kill one, and then negotiate with the media or with authorities—it *never* ends well. So, you wanna keep a low profile. You're just gonna have to trust me on that. Okay?"

Carter attempted to lighten the mood with a semi-joking question. "Um, okay. So, not even a hand or a finger?" But when he noticed James's sigh and serious expression, he immediately dropped it. This, clearly, was no laughing matter for the older man.

So, under the crisp autumn evening sky, they strode out of the warmth of the house and onto the porch, braving the chilly air. Their arms loaded with weapons, and their hearts bound by the code of the warrior, their faith, and the unbreakable bond of trust; they made their way towards the pickup truck. And then, they set out into the vast and dense Oregon woods of Simeon Heights.

———————— ●●●● ————————

Having thoroughly discussed and reviewed Carter's past encounters and sightings, James decided they should enter the woods through Old Pine Road. This was the same route that Carter took back in July, when he had gone fishing with his nephew, Marty. This reminded him of the fateful day they had to end their fishing expedition prematurely because of the disgusting smell of the repugnant creatures and the missing fish.

Nevertheless, Old Pine Road was the perfect entry point for their mission. The well-maintained gravel road was wide enough to accommodate the truck and trailer, and was secluded enough to avoid any unwanted attention. The nearest house was Carter's, which was located three miles away, making it an ideal spot for their undertaking.

After rolling on the wooded trail for about five hundred yards, James said, "That's far enough. We'll take the four-wheelers from here on."

Carter was impressed by the veteran's assuredness and readily followed his lead. When they reached the river, James asked, "Do you hear this?"

"Um, no. Hear what? I don't hear a thing," said Carter.

"Exactly," said the old soldier with a grin. "We'll set up camp here. Go gather some firewood. We'll make a fire."

———————————————————

The flame served a dual purpose for the two men. Not only did it offer warmth, but the flickering orange glow and the sound of crackling firewood brought a primal comfort to Carter. He had always found solace in a good campfire during his years of hunting elk and moose, whether with his dad or friends. It was a familiar rallying point for them in the woods and often a setting for deep, meaningful conversations. The only thing that could have made tonight better was a cold beer. This was not an option, however, given the nature of the hunt.

Remembering his earlier conversation with Alexandra, Carter was curious about James' track record. "You told me you don't consider yourself a Bigfoot hunter, but rather a *people helper*. So, um… how many have you *helped* to sort out this kind of thing?"

James laughed. "What? You don't believe me? Are you worried I'm bluffing?"

"No—no, not at all!" replied Carter, thinking he was being misunderstood.

James laughed all the more heartily at the younger man's nervous reaction. "Relax, son. I'm just yankin' yer chain." He said.

"Truth be told, I didn't really keep count of all the people I've been fortunate enough to help. There's been quite a few of them. But you're the first one I've helped who's been so actively involved. I can tell you that much." He said with an appreciative nod and a smile.

"Oh." Said Carter.

"Yeah, usually folks just prefer to let me work alone and pay me what they think the job is worth. I never charged any price up front. I always told people they could give me whatever they felt was right—once I completed the job, that is."

"That's interesting," Carter said. "And, if I may, do you have any information about my house? Was there any known previous Bigfoot activity there before I contacted you? I was always under the impression that Henry knew something about my property's past, but that he refused to talk about it." He asked, hoping to gain insight into his own situation and place of residence.

James took a moment to answer, his gaze fixed on the flickering campfire as he poked at the logs with a stick. "Well, your property seems to have a history with these creatures," he said, finally looking up at Carter. "I remember Henry telling me about it before the last owners, the Thompsons, moved out."

"The Thompsons, yeah, Glenda briefly mentioned them." Said Carter, adding, "So, what can *you* tell me about them?"

"Well, according to Henry, he thinks a Sasquatch got shot on the premises by the lady of the house, and that all hell broke loose afterward."

"Holy crap! Really?!" Reacted Carter. "Well, that would sure explain a lot," he said.

"Yeah. *Really*. Well, that's what the evidence seemed to suggest at the time, anyway. And when I say *all hell breaking loose*, I don't mean retaliation from the creatures, but rather government involvement. Again, from what Henry told me."

"Geez. So, what happened? What did the feds do?"

James sighed. "They did what they always do when Bigfoot is involved. They took the body, cleaned up everything, and probably made the Thompsons an offer that they couldn't refuse; if you know what I mean. Which would explain why they left so quickly afterward."

"Unreal." Said Carter, stunned.

"*Diabolical* is more like it," replied James. "That's why I *never* involve the authorities with what I do—no matter how bad things may get. Bigfoots are bad enough, but the feds are a level of evil I want nothing to do with. I could tell you some of the black ops stuff involving them with these creatures, *and others*, that would make your blood boil."

He stopped, pursing his lips and shaking his head, visibly troubled by some past unpleasant experiences.

"Lies, money, secrecy, and cover-ups. All of it— *damned lies*," he continued. "May they all burn in hell someday!" He said bitterly, gazing into the flames, with the reflecting orange glow dancing in his eyes.

Carter sensed James had a wealth of hidden knowledge and experience. He couldn't fathom all that the older man had been through, but he could sense the bottled-up pain and anger in him. He didn't want to stir up those emotions and make things worse. So, refocusing on the task at hand, he asked, "So, how long do we have to camp here before they make an appearance?"

"They? Oh, you mean the Sasquatches? They're already here. They've been watching us since we arrived," James replied nonchalantly.

And with that, Carter's head began to nervously shift back and forth as he scanned the surrounding trees, hoping to catch a glimpse of the elusive creatures. However, in the dim glow of the moonlight and campfire, he saw nothing. He was surprised that he hadn't picked up their smell yet, but then he wondered if perhaps they had the ability to control their odor. *Maybe they only emit the stench when they want us to know they're around*, he thought.

James, grabbing a pair of night-vision goggles, gently threw them in his direction, saying, "Put these on. Don't make any sudden moves. Act casual. There's one at your ten o'clock, and another one at twelve o'clock."

Sure enough, he was right. The assertion was even more impressive since James hadn't put on *his* pair yet.

The goggles, U.S. Navy issued and unavailable to the public, were an impressive piece of tech. They did indeed make it seem like high noon for the two men.

"So, what do we do now? Do we grab our rifles?" whispered Carter.

"First off, don't whisper," replied the veteran soldier. "Stay calm and casual. We've only spotted two, but I'm sure I heard four of 'em. And remember what we discussed back at your place. Stick to the plan, okay?"

"Y--yeah, sure." Replied Carter, trying to keep his composure.

The plan, remembered Carter, had everything to do with spotting and taking down the *alpha male*. According to James, they usually tower over nine feet tall, are massive, are masters of stealth, and are clever as hell.

Yeah, a walk in the park, thought Carter, as he kept his sight on the two he *could* see.

"I saw movement in the brush about twenty-five yards behind you. I think it's the BIG guy, but I can't confirm. What I do know is they're getting ready to get rowdy. So, you can expect crashes and projectiles, like rocks."

Indeed, the two seven-footers in Carter's sight were bobbing side-to-side, huffing. They clearly were agitated and getting ready to make a move. Perhaps they were waiting for a signal from "the BIG guy".

"So now, I've got my rifle. You've got your gun," said James. "You let me worry about the one behind you, and you go for a kill shot to the head on the ones you see. Are we clear?"

"Got it. So, what can we expect as we make our move?" asked Carter.

"Anything. So be ready. I've got your back. On my signal…"

"3-2-1, NOW!" shouted James.

As soon as the word crossed his lips, both men sprang up and executed their plan precisely.

However, what they encountered was beyond their expectations. The creatures they were facing were not only ready for the encounter, but displayed an incredible level of intelligence.

Reacting quickly, Carter reached for his powerful handgun tucked inside his vest and, holding it with two hands, aimed at the Bigfoot to his left, which was the closest one. The creature seemed to sense the threat and let out a bloodcurdling scream before charging towards him, while also hurling an enormous rock in his direction. Carter barely dodged the rock in time by leaping to his right. As the creature closed in on him, however, he regained his footing and took aim, firing a shot at the charging Bigfoot.

The bullet hit its target with perfect precision, finding its way straight into the forehead of the seven-foot-tall Sasquatch. The impact of the round made the creature fall backwards and drop heavily onto the forest floor, taking one last labored and gurgling breath before becoming still.

Yes! One shot! Die, you bastard! This one's for you, Ajax! Carter gleefully thought to himself.

Fueled by adrenaline, he wasted no time celebrating his successful shot. Instead, he swiftly redirected his attention to the other Sasquatch, which had fled in the opposite direction. Despite the challenging circumstances—the dense forest cover, the moving target, and the cumbersome night-vision goggles—he aimed his gun and fired. He knew that in the heat of the moment, taking any shot was better than not taking one at all.

Carter was surprised at himself by how much he was revelling in this entire ordeal. He screamed loudly and shouted profanities at the Bigfoots.

Despite the deep brush and the difficulty of the shot, the bullet managed to find its way smack dab into the back of the creature, and straight out through its left shoulder. He heard the Bigfoot crash, breaking branches and falling onto the forest floor while uttering a hellish pain-howl. Still very much alive, it kept on yelling and screaming, probably to alert the others of its plight. Nonetheless, it seemingly had been immobilized, and no longer posed a valid threat. This gave him the chance to turn to James and assess how he could aid his more experienced companion.

Meanwhile, James had remained focused on the creature he believed to be the alpha. It darted diagonally and swiftly through the trees behind Carter, making it a hard target to hit. Despite the deafening echoes of his AR-10, the creature had managed to evade all six shots James had fired at it. The soldier had missed shots before, but he knew that when it came to taking down Bigfoot alphas, time was of the essence. And there was nothing he liked better than a quick knockout. With each passing moment, however, the situation became increasingly precarious, which only added to the mounting pressure of the dire situation.

The two men's plan was carried out amidst a cacophony of snapping branches, eerie roars, and an array of spine-chilling screams that reverberated through the dimly lit darkness of the night.

James kept following the alpha's trajectory and movements as best he could, trying to predict its movements and anticipating its next move, hoping to get an open kill shot. But the alpha cleverly stayed out of sight, and was getting more elusive by the second. Concerned that his inability to take down the alpha would create additional risks, James quickly pivoted towards Carter and yelled, "I'll handle the alpha, keep an eye out for the hidden fourth one."

"Which hidden fou—" Carter couldn't finish his question before a large rock from behind James suddenly came hurtling towards him, crashing heavily onto the vet's left ankle and sending him into a world of excruciating pain as he tumbled to the ground. The impact of the large projectile had instantly broken his ankle. James was fully aware of it. He screamed in agony. He had suffered broken bones before, and recognized the pain. But he couldn't let this derail him.

The veteran soldier was now on all fours, wincing, groaning, and cussing up a storm; angry at his own predicament, feeling he was to blame. But he couldn't let his injury derail the mission. He crawled towards his high-powered rifle, determined to regain his advantage. He knew he couldn't afford to stay vulnerable for even a second. He couldn't let this setback push him off track. He had seen the consequences of losing focus too many times before. It was a matter of kill or be killed, and he was not about to let himself or his younger partner become the prey.

But Carter, less experienced and seeing his partner in trouble, turned to him to help him, kneeling at his side to inquire of his condition. His compassionate thoughts and naïve actions, however, were interrupted by an additional predicament. Following the rock he had just thrown, the previously hidden Bigfoot jumped straight into the fray, landing just a few feet away from the two men. There he stood, towering over them. No… it wasn't the elusive alpha. Rather, it was a bold and brazen juvenile male, standing at around 6 foot 6 inches tall—and he looked pissed.

As the Bigfoot moved assuredly towards the two sprawling men, Carter, in sheer panic, aimed and fired at the creature while on his knees. The shot was sloppy and nervous, hitting the Bigfoot in the shoulder, but it only seemed to anger it further. With a vicious gaze, the creature lifted its powerful arms in the air, attempting to gather momentum for a killing blow on the single father of two.

Just as the Bigfoot was about to strike, a sudden burst of bright lights and a deafening 170-decibel sound exploded in the six-foot gap between the creature and the two men. It was a T238 flash grenade that James had quickly retrieved from his pocket and deployed. The blinding lights and ear-splitting noise disoriented the enraged juvenile male, rendering it momentarily incapacitated and unable to attack. Carter, too, affected by the fierce noise and light discharge, couldn't focus.

With the creature now dazed, another shot thundered in the night air, this time from James' AR-10. And this time, there was no mistake.

The .475 BSM round pierced straight through the creature's left eye, exiting through the back of its head and killing it instantly. The massive creature fell backwards with a resounding thud.

"Yes! Ha-ha!" exclaimed Carter, excited. Quickly turning to his companion, he said, "Good shot! Now, let's have a look at your leg. And let's get you out of here."

"Don't, *hffffmm*, don't… celebrate too fast," advised James, huffing in pain, and knowing their potentially delicate situation all too well. Putting his finger before his lips and pointing towards the forest, he added, "*Shhh.* Listen…"

Carter strained his ears towards the direction James had pointed, where the wounded Bigfoot lay. The creature's moans and groans were still audible, but now accompanied by another sound. It was the alpha who had made his way around and had found his fallen comrade. The two men could hear the fading sounds of the large alpha male carrying his ailing companion deeper into the cover of the dark and dense Oregon woods.

After the chaos had subsided, the forest slowly returned to its usual nocturnal symphony. The eerie silence was replaced by the familiar and soothing sounds of nature. The hoots of owls, the chirping of crickets, the scampering of mice, and the croaking of frogs were once again audible, signifying that the danger had finally passed.

"Looks like we won the night. We're still, *hummff*, at the top of the food chain," James wheezed through the pain, before looking directly at Carter and urging, "Now, don't just stand there like a dork! Get me to a hospital ASAP! Can't you see I have a broken ankle?"

IX

Reprieve

Sunday, October 2nd, 1:28 a.m.

When her phone rang in the middle of the night, Alex expected it was Carter touching base, just like she'd requested. Nevertheless, having been asleep for over two hours, she was groggy when she picked up.

Carter was plagued with guilt as he dialed her number. He had known the Walkers for only a short time, yet James had already risked his life to help protect him and his family. And now, his beloved daughter was also involuntarily tangled in the ordeal.

"Hi Alex. It's me, Carter."

Clearing her throat, she replied, "Hey, um, yeah, what's up? How's everything? You guys okay?"

"Well, yeah, we're both *alive*. So, that's good news, right?" He said, nervously. "But…"

"But?" she echoed with apprehension.

Carter's voice shook slightly as he spoke. "Well, I had to take your dad to Simeon Heights General Hospital. He—"

Alarmed, she quickly cut in. "What! What happened? Is he okay?!"

"Alex, please try to stay calm," said Carter, attempting to defuse the situation. "He's okay; he's going to be all right."

"Are--are you sure? What happened? What's wrong with him?" She asked.

"Yes, I'm sure," he reassured before continuing as calmly as possible. "The thing is… his left ankle. It's… broken."

"Oh, no!" She Gasped.

"Yeah, it--it's pretty bad. But like I told you, the doc says he's going to be fine. And your dad, he's the one who asked me to call his daughter—you—and he gave me your number. I never told him I knew you."

…

"Alex? You still there?"

"Yes, I am," she responded. "Sorry, it's… *a lot* to process. But I'm relieved, I guess. Somewhat, anyway. I mean, it could have been much worse, right?"

"Oh, absolutely, yeah," he agreed.

"But, to be honest, he just drives me nuts," she said in frustration, adding, "Do you know how many times this kind of thing has happened over the years? I mean… I understand *why* he does what he does; and, don't get me wrong, I'm glad he helped you. But as his daughter, it's... it's just *really* upsetting."

"Um, yeah, I can imagine. Look, I'm really sorry. I—"

"There's no point in talking about this now. I'm getting dressed. I'll be right over. So, I'll see you there? What room did you say he was in?"

"We're in room 112."

As Alex walked into the hospital room, her father beamed with delight. "There she is! Thanks for comin', sweetie-pie. I'm sorry to have to bother you so late with this bad news," James said, his cheerful expression shifting to shame.

Carter could tell how proud the man was of his daughter; a feeling he knew well. However, he could also see that the pain medication had taken effect, making James sightly woozy.

"Oh, Daddy," Alex said sympathetically, glancing sorrily at his raised and plastered ankle.

"Aww, it's all right, pumpkin. The doctors said I'll be just fine. I told them it was a hunting accident," James said with a wink.

Then he pointed to Carter. "This is Carter. He's the guy who got me stuck in this damn hospital bed." He joked.

Carter felt a sense of embarrassment wash over him, and he couldn't help but shake his head. Alex, too, looked visibly uncomfortable with the awkward situation.

Thinking the charade had gone on long enough, Carter cleared his throat and spoke up. "Actually, we already know each other, sir," he said, trying to sound casual despite his nerves.

James looked taken aback. "You *do*? And, did you just call me 'sir'? Really?" he asked incredulously.

Then, raising an eyebrow, he looked suspiciously at the two of them. "And how, *pray tell*, do you two know each other?" he asked.

Carter and Alex both spoke up simultaneously, their words overlapping awkwardly, like a pair of rookie synchronized swimmers. "I'm her plumber," said Carter. "I'm his teacher," said Alex.

Realizing their mutual blunder, they exchanged an embarrassed glance. Alex quickly attempted to clarify, stumbling further over her words in the process. "We know each other from school. I mean, I work at the school where Ellie, Mr. Mitchell's daughter, goes. She's a really sweet girl," she said, hoping to clear up any confusion.

James, seemingly accepting her explanation, nodded slowly. "Right, right. That makes sense, I guess," he said.

And then, turning to his Bigfoot-hunting disciple, he asked, "So, Carter, oh you *plumber-of-my-daughter*... why didn't you tell me you knew Alex?"

This is beginning to sound like a cheesy sitcom, thought Carter, who, feeling cornered, answered with a lie, "Er, well, sir, you just *vaguely* told me you had a daughter. You never really disclosed her full name. I--I guess I just didn't know for sure you two were related."

"Huh-uh," said James, still incredulous. He then added edgily, "An' why the heck do you keep calling me *sir* all of a sudden?!"

Tired by the night's events, and feeling overly scrutinized, Carter was at a loss at this point, barely able to string two words together, "Er, I, um…"

"Relax chum. I'm just yankin' yer chain, as usual," interjected the tough old vet, before bursting into laughter. "How else can I get my kicks in this crappy hospital bed?"

Despite his attempt at light-heartedness, his pain was still evident as he groaned and winced. "Tell you what," he said, "I'm gonna have some shut-eye for a bit, if that's okay with both of you. You should go do the same, especially you, Carter. It's been a *long evenin'*."

"Yeah, I suppose I will," said Carter, as he moved closer and grabbed the older man's sturdy hand, "Thanks. For everything. I'll come back and check up on you as soon as I can."

"You're very welcome, young man," said James, adding, "Hey, despite the ankle, it was fun, don't you think?" he asked, a twinkle in his eye.

Carter couldn't help but shake his head and smile widely at the man's grittiness. "Yeah. I guess it was. I won't forget it anytime soon, that's for sure."

As he exited the room, Alex followed him out into the half-lit hallway.

Inching closer to Carter, she said, "I'll stay the night. It looks like I'm going to have a patient staying over at my place as soon as the docs give him his leave. He told me he'd be in this cast for 8-10 weeks, maybe longer."

She sighed, obviously strained by the night's events.

Carter felt bad. "This is my fault, Alex. Again, I'm sorry." He said, pursing his lips sympathetically. "You let me know if you need anything, okay?"

"Don't be silly, this isn't your fault," she said. "He would have gone in there by himself even if you hadn't. That's just the way he is. Even at his age, he seems to need his adrenaline fix, like a junkie."

Carter chuckled slightly.

"But he's right, you know," she continued. "You should head on home and get some sleep."

"Yeah. I'll do that," he said. "It's obvious your dad cares very much about you." Then, looking at Alex, he asked, "Um, do you think he knows, like, about *us*?"

She took a step back from him and smiled. He was a mess. Dishevelled. Smelly. Visibly exhausted. She took a hold of his coat lapels and said, smirking, "You can't hide too much from a man like my dad."

"I guess not." He agreed.

"But I can tell he likes you. He'd probably approve… that is… if there *was* an 'us' to begin with." She said, teasing, pushing him back slightly.

Carter smiled, amused by her spunk.

"Nice cross, by the way." She said, looking at the silver pendant resting on his chest. "Dad has one just like it."

"Yeah, he does. Actually, he's the one who gave me this one, too."

"Well, it suits you." She said, smiling.

Inching closer, she looked up at him, and, almost in a whisper, said, "You know… I really prayed last night, for you both. I'm relieved you're okay."

"Thanks." He smiled. "It… it's always nice to have an angel on your side," he said, as his eyes were getting lost in hers. He inched even closer to her. Their eyes locked, and their lips also found themselves on a mission to collide for the first time. But before they could… a voice coming from the nearby room interrupted the moment.

"Hey kids, *I ain't sleepin' yet*, and with the door open, I can *see* you!" James said in a sing-song tease, before adding, "Oh, and Carter, *now I know* why you kept calling me 'sir'. We're *definitely* gonna need to have a talk you and I."

Hearing the older man's morphine-infused teasing tirade, they both burst out laughing.

As Carter was about to leave, Alex said to him, "Hey… with all this craziness, I forgot to ask the most important question. Were you guys successful in handling your *situation?* I mean, is it… over?"

She asked, although she knew her dad had never failed… yet.

Carter smiled, "Yeah. Absolutely. We... um," he lowered his voice down to a whisper, not to be overheard by any hospital staff, "We killed two and severely injured a third one. We showed them who's boss. I'm pretty sure they won't be messing with me and the kids again. I'll tell you all the details later, I guess."

"Oh, that's good. I'm glad. See, I told you so." She smiled, and tippy-toing, she rose and gave him a soft peck on the cheek, "Now, go home, wash, and get some rest. You've had a long day. I'll call you later. Like, *much later*, you know... to let you sleep, like, past noon."

As he made his way back home, he couldn't help but feel a warmth on his cheek where she had just planted a sweet kiss. Even though he was covered in dirt and grime, he hated to wash it off. The memory of her lips on his cheek made him feel alive and renewed, as the exhaustion of the day had all been lifted away. He smiled to himself, replaying the moment over and over in his mind.

When he returned home, Carter took a long, hot shower in an effort to reduce the soreness of his muscles and help him unwind. But it did little to that effect.

By now, it was well past 3:00 am.

Still on edge, he found it near-impossible to fall asleep. The events of the previous night, aside from the car accident with Vivian, had been the most chaotic and disturbing experience of his life. He couldn't stop replaying the scenes in his mind. He also thought about

Alex and James, and his children who were safely sleeping at the MacArthur's house half a mile away. *I wonder how that went,* he thought, and then his stomach growled, which furthered his thought, *and I wonder if Glenda would give me one of her apple pies.*

It was nine in the morning when he finally gave up on sleep. Opting to get up, he made himself some coffee and toast before he would head out to pick up the kids.

The kitchen was filled with the gentle rays of the morning sun, and a light breeze filtered through the slightly open patio door. He gazed out at his tranquil backyard, admiring the subtly changing colors of the trees lining the property.

Despite the now-peaceful surroundings, his mind was still troubled by the events of the previous night. He couldn't shake the thought of the alpha and its wounded companion. Had they really disappeared for good? He had told Alex that it was all over, but deep down, he knew he had no way of knowing for sure.

I should have asked James more questions, he thought.

"Daddy!" Ellie and Ty both shouted in unison, as they jumped off their chair, and ran to him. Ellie, probably as a reaction to the Sugar-O's cereal box Carter spotted on the table, couldn't contain herself. "We had *sooo* much fun with Glenda and Henry, dad! She makes the best apple pies, and they have a swing set, and a full box of toys, and I made you an apple pie! Wait 'till you taste it, dad! It's amazing! And..."

Chuckling at Ellie's inexhaustible logorrhea, he told her, "Okay, okay, settle down, sweetie. I'm not going anywhere. You can tell me more at home."

Looking over at Glenda and offering his most charming grin, he asked, "Um, about that pie... is there really one for little ol' me?"

She laughed at his silliness. "Absolutely! Your daughter speaks the truth."

His grin widened as she pointed to the pie set on her kitchen counter.

Henry, who was merely a spectator so far, spoke up, asking, "So, tell us, how was the plumber's meeting in Portland?"

Carter had almost forgotten about his made-up story and was slightly taken aback. "Oh, yeah. Well, you know, it's mostly about new tools, materials, techniques. It was all right, I guess. It helps me to stay abreast of everything going on in the trade."

The old man just nodded, which made Carter wonder how much of his BS he could smell.

About to leave, he kindly thanked them both. Glenda, grabbing him aside, said to him, "Young man, you have the sweetest kids. Ellie and Tyler were both very well behaved. You know... as a single dad, you should be proud. It says a lot about you. That means you're doing *something* right." She said, smiling tenderly.

"Thanks," he replied, surprised by the compliment. "That's... *really good* to hear."

It really was. Despite his best efforts, he couldn't shake off the feeling of self-doubt that had been gnawing at him ever since Vivian's passing. He wanted nothing more than to raise his children to be good and well-rounded individuals, but he felt like he was failing at every turn. He constantly second-guessed himself, never feeling quite confident in his abilities as a single father. There were moments when he felt lost, inadequate, and incompetent. And he often blew the consequences of his parenting mistakes out of proportion in his mind, feeling like he was ruining his children's lives. In reality, he was just too hard on himself and needed to give himself a break.

Deep down, nothing gave him more satisfaction than seeing them happy. And happy they were as they returned to the more familiar setting of home.

By the time he had returned home, he felt immense relief to find Ellie and Tyler playing happily, oblivious to what had occurred during the weekend. Their innocence brought a smile to his face, and protecting it was his top priority.

The events of late made him recognize the need for better property surveillance, especially during the night. He wanted to make sure they were all out of harm's way for good.

He already had some floodlights installed all over the property, but these had proven quite useless. The creatures knew exactly where the specific trigger points were, and skillfully avoided them. To address this issue, he planned to install trail cams at different spots around the property. James had given him a couple of extra ones, and he now had four in total. He'd put one in the front, and three in the back, where most of the activity took place.

Sure, he'd read online that Bigfoots always spotted and avoided trail cams, just like they did floodlights, but he thought it was worth a shot anyway.

That afternoon, as soon as his phone rang, he knew it was Alex. He had anticipated her call, but he was surprised at *just how much*. And no, his worries about James had little to do with this.

He was genuinely beginning to fall for the lovely and somewhat unorthodox schoolteacher. He was captivated by her smarts, beauty, and independence. That she was the daughter of a valiant ex-soldier only increased her appeal and mystery to him.

Alexandra Walker may have fallen a couple of inches short of model height, but her physical appeal was nothing short of desirable. Her slim and yet curvaceous frame boasted undeniable feminine appeal. Her sharp wit, warmth, and intelligence enthralled Carter. But what he really couldn't get enough of were her piercing, deep blue eyes. In his youth, he had never been one to focus on a woman's eyes, but Alex's gaze was hypnotic. It's what he enjoyed the most about her... *at least for now*, he thought, smiling, while indulging in a few illicit thoughts about what she would look like under more intimate circumstances. His smile extended as he realized Alex was quickly becoming his favorite thing about life these days.

As he picked up his phone, however, the weightiness of her circumstances somehow snapped him back to reality.

"Hello."

"Hey, *hi*. It's *me*, Alex."

The relationship being so new, they both still felt the need to disclose their names over the phone.

"Yes, it is. Nice to hear your voice. How's everything?" He asked.

"Well, everything is pretty good, under the circumstances. The doctors gave dad the green light to go home. So, that's where I'm calling you from, believe it or not."

"Oh, well, that's good. There's nothing worse than rotting in a hospital bed. Is there anything you guys need? Any errands you'd need me to run?"

"Oh, that's really sweet of you to ask, but we're good for now. Really. I stopped at the drugstore on the way out to pick up some more pain meds for him, so we'll be okay, at least for today. He's napping right now, cause of those meds, and I'm thinking of doing the same later," she said, before asking, "So, what about *you*? Did you pick up your children?"

"Yeah, they're home. They didn't miss a beat. I wish I could say the same." He laughed.

"Yeah. It's been a rough night," she said. "Hey, I've been thinking, wondering, really... I took a leave of absence from school for a couple of weeks, to take care of dad. What would you say if I invited you and your children, say... *this Friday night,* for dinner at my place?"

"Oh, yeah. *Absolutely!* That sounds great. They'd love that!" he said.

"They?" she quizzed.

He laughed, "Yes... *and me too,* definitely! I'll be looking forward to it."

"Good. Me too." She said.

"Oh, one more thing..." He said.

"What?"

"Could you ask your dad to call me when he wakes up? I have... um, *a few questions* to ask him."

"Sure. Is... everything *okay*?"

"Yeah. But I just want to make sure it stays that way." He said matter-of-factly.

Although the requested phone conversation with James provided answers, they weren't the answers he was hoping for. Carter remained unconvinced that his house was now and always Bigfoot-proof.

The veteran soldier made it very clear to him that Sasquatches tend to hold grudges and take revenge.

Bummer, thought Carter.

James also confirmed that trail cams, although a good idea and strategically sound, are usually inefficient. "They're just too smart for those," he added.

He also told him to keep the kids inside for the next couple of weeks, and carefully monitor *everything* that goes on *outside*. Every. Single. Night.

"Eventually, you'll know," said James. "It won't just be the absence of evidence. You'll just know in your gut that your problem has gone away for good. And if they show themselves again, then we'll just go back out there you and I. So, don't worry about it."

Carter appreciated James' bravery and willingness to help him in those woods, but he doubted the older man could do so again, considering his age and current condition; not that he'd ever insinuate this to his face. Moreover, the thought of facing these creatures once again filled him with dread. He couldn't help but entertain the idea of moving to a new location to avoid any further encounters.

He also reflected on the impact of James' risky endeavors on Alex. He recognized the burden it placed on her and empathized with her perspective. As he considered the situation, he concluded James should probably retire from "helping people," for her sake.

On the other hand, James' help had been invaluable to him and his young family—and perhaps many others over the years. So, the service James provided was definitely unique and very needed. This much was undeniable.

Going through Old Pine Road and into those woods once again seemed like going back to the scene of the crime for Carter; not to mention that it stirred back some awful and way-too-recent memories. But he had agreed over the phone with James to go back and retrieve the four-wheeler they had left behind after the battle. The plan was simple: retrieve it and store it in the trailer along with the other.

Considering how much anxiety was now gripping him, however, this would be a classic case of *easier said than done.*

Of course, in the daytime, the risk was lessened, or so he told himself. Nonetheless, haunted by the lethal encounters, he took no chance, bringing a rifle and his handgun, a bowie knife, and even a flash grenade in his pocket.

I can't believe I'm back here, he thought. *I must be certifiable.*

He looked around from the cab of the large pickup truck before working up the courage to leave its relative safety. He cautiously stepped out of the vehicle and onto the forest floor. Once out, he carefully scanned his whole surroundings, making sure he heard birds chirping. He felt his heart beat faster. He couldn't help but feel like he was walking back into hell. His heart pounded in his chest as he carefully scanned the area, clinging to his rifle, keeping it at the ready. Once he heard the chirping of birds and the scurrying of other small animals, however, he was relieved. He let out a sigh, felt his nerves relax, and felt his shoulders fall back to their resting position as he advanced quickly through the forest.

Making his way towards the spot where they had set up camp, his eyes widened in shock and disbelief.

Sure, the four-wheeler was there, but it had been destroyed. The metal and plastic components of the vehicle had been twisted and shattered into hundreds of unrecognizable pieces. It was as if a massive force had ripped it apart like a cheap child's toy.

Scanning the area, it was evident that the Bigfoot's bodies and remains had disappeared. This was to be expected, however. Carter's research had taught him that Sasquatches usually bury their dead—which explains why no one ever discovers a corpse in the woods, or any kind of skeletal remains.

But what really shook him was the absence of any signs of the battle that had taken place. Not a drop of blood, no foul odor, no hair, no footprints, no spent shells or flash grenade—nothing. It was as if the entire area had been wiped clean. Even the remains of the campfire had vanished.

Carter's mind raced with possibilities and scenarios, not all of which involved Bigfoot. But he knew without a doubt that the creature had destroyed the four-wheeler. The thought of it made his adrenaline surge once more, and his heart began pumping blood in overtime. He jogged back to the truck, scanning the forest apprehensively as he went.

Once inside the truck, he shifted into gear and floored the gas pedal, leaving the area at breakneck speed. A thick cloud of dirt and dust billowed behind him as he raced down the forest road, his mind reeling with questions and fears.

———————————◆◎◆◎◆———————————

That same night, Carter walked into the forest once more. But this time, he wasn't alone. As he gazed lovingly into Vivian's eyes, he couldn't believe it. The love of his life was by his side once again. It was really her. Unbelievably, she was here with him, in the flesh, it seemed. He could feel her warm touch and smell the sweet fragrance of her hair. With her long blonde hair and clear blue eyes, she was even more beautiful than he remembered.

Overwhelmed with emotion, he couldn't help but tell her, "I've missed you so much!" She smiled back at him, her eyes reflecting the love he felt.

Despite the lateness of the hour, the sun seemed to shine brightly. They strolled hand in hand through the forest, feeling the cool breeze brush against their skin. Ellie and Ty, also present, ran ahead of them on the trail, their giggling laughter echoing through the woods. The sunlight filtered through the leaves and branches, casting a warm glow over the forest floor. It was a moment of pure joy and happiness, a perfect family outing that could have come straight out of a Hallmark movie. Carter caressed Vivian's hand with his thumb, feeling a deep sense of gratitude and love for his family.

After a few seconds, he lost sight of the kids as they ran ahead on the trail. When they reached a bend, Vivian turned to him and said, "I can't continue with you after this point."

Perplexed, he asked her, "Why not?"

She gazed at him with tenderness and smiled. Placing her hand gently on his cool cheek, she whispered. "You can't see *them*, but *they* can see you. You can't see them, but you have to be there for them. They need your strength. They need your faith. So, be strong. Be brave." Pausing for a moment, she continued, "Carter, there is a cross to bridge the divide between you and *them*. Remember, God loves you, and so do I."

As she disappeared into the trees behind her, he felt a sense of loss wash over him once again. In an instant, she was gone, leaving him standing alone in the forest. As he looked around, he noticed that the setting had changed. The sun was no longer shining, and the once bright and colorful woods had become darker and foreboding.

He sensed the grip of worry take a hold of him as he remembered the kids. He wondered if they were lost or injured. "I have to find them," he thought, a feeling of urgency gripping him. Hastening his pace, he started jogging along the trail, scanning left and right, feeling his heart rate quicken. Though he couldn't see them, he could sense their presence, their energy. They seemed close, yet out of sight. Suddenly, their voices rang out through the forest. "Daddy! Daddy! We're over here! Hurry!"

At last, he arrived at a spacious opening at the end of the trail. Across the way, he spotted Ellie and Ty, apparently unharmed, yet something seemed off. They appeared frightened, shouting out his name, "Daddy!

Daddy!" While they appeared physically well, they didn't move an inch closer to him. He wondered why. In front of them, there was an uncharacteristic mound of dark earth and withered leaves, rising to about three feet high.

As he drew closer to them, he noticed the mound was not as harmless as it appeared. It started to shift and rise slowly, eventually towering over him. To his astonishment, a colossal Bigfoot, covered in dark soil and leaves, had emerged from the mound and now stood before him. It had been camouflaged, blending in perfectly with its surroundings. Though the creature had no distinguishable features, he knew exactly what it was: a massive Sasquatch. With one swift motion, the creature extended its muscular arm, clutching Carter's throat and lifting him off the ground to meet its gaze.

As he gasped for air, he found himself trapped in the powerful grip of the monstrous Bigfoot. The creature's lifeless black eyes bore into his own as it growled, revealing large yellow teeth. With its jaws wide open, it was clear that he was about to be devoured. In a desperate attempt to save himself, he let out a blood-curdling scream.

Carter awoke from his nightmare, his scream still echoing in his ears. Gasping for breath, shaking, and drenched in sweat, he sat up in bed, trembling, trying to calm his racing heart. Confused and disoriented, he struggled to shake off the remnants of the terrifying dream that had just plagued him.

What—in the hell—was that all about?! He muttered to himself. *Worse nightmare ever*, he thought.

Indeed, even the ones he had been having about the accident, which had plagued him for months, paled in comparison.

With his heart rate barely decelerating, he realized he was still very shaken. So scared, in fact, that he thought the creature might lurk somewhere in the house—waiting in a dark corner. He opened the lamp on his night table, just to make sure.

Nope. Nothing. He thought. Well, nothing in his bedroom at least. *Better check on the kids.*

He got out of bed to check on Ellie and Ty and found them sleeping peacefully. *They look like angels;* he thought to himself. Relieved that his screams didn't wake them up, he then went to the bathroom to freshen up, wiping his face with a facecloth. As he looked at himself in the mirror, he was still shaken and in disbelief. The eerie feeling he experienced during his nightmare lingered. He grabbed a clean and dry t-shirt from his drawer, along with his gun, and investigated the rest of the house.

After thoroughly inspecting the house, he breathed a sigh of relief that everything seemed undisturbed. There were no signs of forced entry or any indication of a break-in. As he descended the stairs, he kept the lights off to avoid attracting any unwanted attention. Once in the kitchen, he opened the patio door and stepped out onto the deck, hoping to listen for any unusual sounds or movements.

Once outside, in the cool of night, he cautiously surveyed his surroundings, scanning ahead and to his left and right, his grip on the pistol firm. He then stood still, outside in the darkness of the crescent-moon-lit night, straining to hear any sign of the elusive creatures. He listened intently for howls, screams, chatter, or wood knocks. But for over 45 minutes, all he heard was the pure sound of unadulterated silence, except for the occasional chirps of small creatures.

Throughout his vigil, his mind kept returning to the vivid dream and Vivian's words. Somehow; it *was* really her. He was sure of that and couldn't shake the feeling. He also was certain there was meaning behind her words, but he couldn't quite figure it out.

What did she mean by "You can't see them, but they can see you? You can't see them, but you have to be there for them. They need your strength. They need your faith?" Obviously, she was referring to the kids in that second part. But what about the first part? She must have been referring to the creatures. Or was she? Who are 'them'? he pondered, puzzled by his own dream and its cryptic meaning.

As the clock now showed 4:00 am, Carter, sleepy but relieved by the quiet state of his property, opted to go back inside and back to bed.

Maybe I can catch a few more Zs before the kids get up. He thought.

He was wrong.

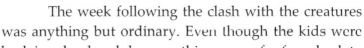

The week following the clash with the creatures was anything but ordinary. Even though the kids were back in school and daycare, things were far from back to normal. Ellie, in particular, seemed to have a tough time. She was feeling sad, frustrated, and complained all week about having a "boring nerd-man" as her substitute teacher.

Work-wise, things were slow. With only a couple of odd jobs during the week, Carter worried about his future as a plumber in Simeon Heights. Was the town simply too small? Was there too much competition from established and trusted plumbers in the area? Maybe he needed to do more market research to see what he was up against. Or, he thought... *Maybe I just need to ask Ellie for more marketing advice*, he reasoned, smiling yet again at his daughter's unusual business savvy.

But, all that aside, there was a thick silver lining... today was Friday. And tonight was *the* night.

Although Alex's invitation for dinner didn't quite qualify as a genuine or official date, he found it was still pretty special. With her dad present, that meant he was formally welcomed into her inner circle. And the same could be said of himself. She invited *his whole family*. She was going to meet Tyler for the first time.

Going through his limited wardrobe and hesitating for over five minutes, Carter realized once again just how much Alex meant to him. After all, he never hesitated about what to wear—even for weddings or funerals. It never took him more than, say, three minutes—max.

The Mitchell family, with Carter at its head, arrived at Alex's house at 4 o'clock sharp, just as instructed.

"Miss Alexandra has a nice house. Don't you think, dad?" said Ellie, standing on the porch.

Trying not to imply that he had been there before, he replied casually, "Yeah. It's a lovely place, sweetie."

Alex opened the door, beaming, "Hey! It's so good to see all of you!"

Carter's heart skipped a beat as she greeted him and his two children warmly.

Looking down, she saw Tyler and caringly said, "You must be Tyler. Your dad told me *so much* about you!"

Tyler paused, looked at her, furrowed his brow, and asked, "Are *you* my sister's teacher?"

Alex gave Ellie a quick glance and replied, "Yes, I am. I also teach 27 other students in my class."

He stared at her for a few seconds and then asked, "Can I be in your class, too?"

Carter smiled, knowing this meant his boy liked her.

Alex bent down to Tyler's eye level and said, "You know what... you're not old enough yet, but in a few years, maybe you will be in my class. Would you like that?"

Tyler nodded enthusiastically and smiled. Then, he clutched his gorilla toy, which he had brought with him, showed it to her and said, "This is my gorilla. He looks just like the monkey-men that come in our yard at night."

Alex looked up at Carter, trying to hold back a laugh with her lips pursed into a sly smile. He looked back at her, feeling slightly embarrassed. With a helpless shrug, he brushed it off and said, "All right, buddy. You can talk to Alexandra inside… about *other stuff*, okay?"

Once inside, they settled down in the living room. As Alex fixed them some drinks, James, relaxing in a spacious armchair, welcomed Carter and his kids.

"Daddy, who's that?" Ty asked, looking at the elderly man sitting in the corner, puzzled.

Before Carter could answer, James replied, "I'm James Walker the Great. I'm Alexandra's father, and your father's… *forest guide*."

Puzzled, Ellie turned to her dad and asked, "Is that true, dad? Is he really your *forest guide*?"

Carter replied, "Only on weekends," as both men exchanged a knowing smile.

Ellie looked at them and said, "You guys are *weird*."

James laughed and said, "Young lady, you have no idea!"

Despite his eccentricities, the kids were both fascinated by Alexandra's dad. They sat with him and bombarded him with questions, mostly about his cast and how he got it. James showed a tender side that Carter didn't know existed. He answered their questions with wit and humor, never hinting how he had injured his ankle.

Unlike his first time at Alex's, which was more of a work opportunity and a friendly lunch, Carter was careful to look around everywhere. He now looked at her home with fresh eyes, noticing the decor, colors on the walls, and the arrangement of the furniture. *These are the fingerprints of her soul*, he reflected deeply, captivated. For the first time, he appreciated all the minute details and saw things from a different perspective. He was impressed and felt drawn to her style.

Alexandra also impressed him with her ability to be an organized and gracious host, especially given the fact that her dad was wearing a cast. Although James did his best to help out and not be a burden, Carter still found it commendable how well she managed everything.

As he considered her household further, he couldn't help but appreciate the country charm and warmth that surrounded him. The decor was tasteful and elegant, with a touch of vintage flair that gave the space a cozy feel. He noted the attention to detail that she put into every aspect of the house, from the beautifully framed forest scenery in the living room to the decorative plates featuring delicate flower motifs adorning the kitchen walls. He realized she had a knack for creating a comfortable and inviting atmosphere that made everyone feel right at home.

"Your home is beautifully decorated. It's warm and inviting. I really like the cozy feel to it," Carter remarked, feeling a sense of nostalgia stirring up in him. Indeed, the familiar elements of country charm reminded him of his parents' home and the fond memories he had of growing up there.

Alexandra smiled from the kitchen, where she was busy preparing Caesar dressing. "Thank you," she called back. "I've always had a thing for the country look. It just feels homey and comfortable, you know?" she said, pausing for a moment to glance over her shoulder at Carter.

As he continued his slow stroll around her living room, he noticed an engraved wooden plaque set on the wall of her front entrance. It was a scripture verse from Jeremiah 29:11. It read, "For I know the plans I have for you," declares the Lord, "plans to prosper you and not to harm you, plans to give you hope and a future."

Carter paused, drawn in by the message of the plaque, and felt a warmth spread through his chest as the words resonated within, bringing a soft smile to his face. *She also shares her father's strong faith*, he thought to himself, now seeing this as a good thing.

As he strolled around further, something else caught his attention. He noticed Alexandra appeared slightly nervous, just like him.

As they spent the late afternoon together, he found himself drawn to her and couldn't help but steal glances in her direction. It seemed like she felt the same way, as she frequently met his gaze with a smile. Even Ellie noticed the chemistry between the two adults, despite their attempts at subtlety. She watched as they talked and laughed together, and couldn't help but think that they made a magnificent pair.

Ellie was highly intuitive and could pick up on subtle hints. She missed her mom, sure. But, more than anything, she wanted to see her dad happy. Besides, she liked the match. After all, hadn't *she* hinted at the beginning of the school year that her new teacher was beautiful, trying to get her dad interested somehow?

As for Tyler, James kept him entertained with a series of silly card tricks, accompanied by old-fashioned jokes and sleight of hand. The boy was mesmerized by the older man's humor and fascinated by his large mustache. James relished every moment. Alex watched her dad with a smile, her heart filling with warmth at the sight of his readiness to be a grandpa.

While Carter had initially experienced trouble deciding what to wear for the evening, he had finally settled for a pair of beige Dockers and his favorite blue plaid flannel shirt. He ran his fingers through his wind-tousled hair, taming it to a ruggedly natural look. Though he skipped shaving, he had added two drops of cologne to his outfit. Alex couldn't help but notice how he seemed to have put in some extra effort for the evening.

As for her, she had switched her glasses for her contacts. Besides that, she wore a lovely light blue jean dress with four pockets on the front and straight down buttons. The snug fit of the country dress highlighted her silhouette in all the right ways. To further enhance her classic facial features, she had applied slightly more make-up than usual, with a focus on her mascara.

Her eyes are even more striking, Carter thought, as he complimented her on her appearance.

When they sat down to eat, everything was perfect. Alex had cooked up an Italian-themed feast composed of homemade garlic bread, Caesar salad, and a simply amazing-looking lasagna.

Taking the lead, James said, "Let's all thank God for this meal." And he said grace.

As the meal progressed, Carter savored every bite of the lasagna, thoroughly impressed by its deliciousness.

Echoing his thoughts, Ellie exclaimed, "Dad, this lasagna is *sooo* much better than yours!"

At this, he raised an eyebrow. "Ha-ha, very funny Ellie. Just eat, will you?" he replied, pretending to be annoyed.

Intrigued, Alex asked, "Why is she saying that? What do *you* put in yours?"

Carter sighed and smirked, glancing at Ellie, and then at Alex. "Well... *nothing*. I put nothing in it. I just... buy it frozen," he confessed, looking sheepish.

The room erupted in laughter. James chimed in, "Hey, there's no shame in that. Alex grew up on that frozen stuff, and she turned out okay. Frozen food is the way of the single dad."

"I'll drink to that!" expressed Carter, raising his glass eagerly.

Alex replied with a smile, "Well, I don't know about that. There's definitely a reason I became obsessed with *fresh ingredients* later in life." She stated, looking at her dad with a mix of humor and defiance.

During the meal, James, with a thoughtful look, directed his attention towards Carter and said, "Son, can I ask you a favor?"

"Sure. What's on your mind?" Carter answered, taking a sip of his red wine.

"Well, to be honest, my truck, trailer, and my *one remaining four-wheeler* are on my mind. They've been sitting in your driveway, and…" He trailed off, offering a slightly uncomfortable look, "Well, I was wondering if you could drive them back to my place this weekend. Alex would go with you and drive you back home afterward. Right sweetie?" he said, turning to his daughter and putting his rugged hand on her forearm.

"Sure," she answered, looking back at Carter expectantly.

"That's no problem. Absolutely," assured Carter, smiling back at both of them. "I was actually thinking about the same thing this week, after I informed you about, um, your other four-wheeler." He added with an apologetic look.

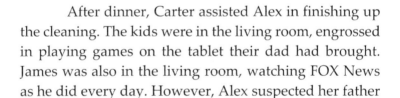

After dinner, Carter assisted Alex in finishing up the cleaning. The kids were in the living room, engrossed in playing games on the tablet their dad had brought. James was also in the living room, watching FOX News as he did every day. However, Alex suspected her father would soon doze off as his pain medication took effect.

Both Carter and Alex had longed for some privacy to engage in a more intimate conversation. Although her house was lovely, it was small. So, they had to find a suitable spot. Fortunately, her office was on the same floor, so they retreated there to chat. As they entered the room, they pushed the door back, almost closing it shut.

186

Carter spoke first. "You know, Ellie was right. Your lasagna was *delicious*, and I had a great time tonight."

"I'm glad you enjoyed it. I had a great time, too. And I'm really glad you came over," she said, adding, "And your kids are really sweet and funny."

He looked at her, his eyes longingly telling her more than they should have. This made her feel weak in the knees. As for him, he could feel butterflies stirring in his stomach, like a love-struck teenager.

"I've been thinking about you... *a lot*," he whispered.

"Me too," she admitted, before adding, "I..." she hesitated. Looking up at him, she then asked, "Can I be *honest* with you?"

"Of course. What is it?" he inquired, curious.

"Here's the thing..." she said, as she gathered her thoughts. "I've been waiting for someone like you for a while, but..."

With his hands gently settled on her waist, he leaned closer to her, but noticed her hesitation. "But what?" he pressed.

"Look," she said, "Truth is, I'm *ready for this*. I have been for some time. Nothing's holding me back." She paused before continuing, "But that's just the thing." After another brief pause, she continued, "What about you? I mean, I just have some concerns because of what you've been through—your past, your baggage, you know? Are you *sure* that you're... *ready*? Are you *serious* about me, about us, about taking this further? Is it too soon for you?"

He smiled tenderly at her and said, "Hey, Alex, let me put your mind at ease…" Gazing deeply in her eyes, he said, "I haven't been this serious in a long time. *I am* ready for this—*ready for you*. And I don't play games. That's just not my style."

Putting his muscular arms around her, he gently pressed her against him. Unable to hold himself any longer, he leaned into her. She let him, abandoning herself to his strong lead and the moment itself. Their lips collided as they passionately embraced, melting into each other, forgetting everything around them.

Suddenly, he had no children here, and she had no father in the next room.

The kiss heightened all of their senses at once, as both their hearts now beat in unison, leading them to a passionate crescendo of nearly unbridled affection. He kept going, caressing her delicate neck with his lips and breathing heavily. She shakily whispered, "We--we can't."

He whispered back, "Yeah… I know," while continuing to run his fingers through her long, dark brown hair and gazing at her piercingly, inebriated by the subtle perfume of her hair and pheromones. With great difficulty, however, they wisely refrained from moving past first base. Then, looking deeply into each other's eyes once more, they passionately kissed again.

As they again engaged in the same dance, they both heard Ellie calling out from the kitchen, looking for her father, "Da-ad, the tablet has a glitch. The game logged me out!"

With that, they both knew it was game over for them as well.

Looking at Alex, he whispered, "Well, I guess it's time for us to go."

"Yep," she replied, amused by his fatherly responsibilities. "Oh, and about dad's truck, I can't do it tomorrow. I have an appointment at the hairdresser and some shopping to do. Can I come over on Sunday morning instead, around 10:00 am? Would that work for you?"

"Yup, Sunday works for me. But don't you have to be in church or something?" he teased.

"Well," she teased back, "If you prefer I go to church, we can always do it *next weekend.*"

"Nope, Sunday works," he replied promptly, not wanting to waste an opportunity to see her shortly.

Lying in bed the day following his dinner at Alex's, Carter, lost in thought, closed his book, allowing the fresh words and wisdom of Sun Tzu to permeate his consciousness:

"Engage people with what they expect; it is what they are able to discern and confirms their projections. It settles them into predictable patterns of response, occupying their minds while you wait for the extraordinary moment—that which they cannot anticipate."

He reflected on the instructions of the Chinese general, finding resonance in the profound advice. With a sense of contemplation, he placed the book back on his night table, alongside his recently dusted-off Bible. The respect he now gave these two very different books stood as tangible evidence of his renewed interest in ancient wisdom literature and history. His newly gained reverence for these writings was also a testament to his insistent quest to understand his present circumstances, and to make sense of his life.

Since the move and the overwhelming stress he had endured, Carter discovered that reading before bedtime was a remarkably effective way to unwind and relieve tension. It had become a ritual that aided him in achieving a more restful sleep. What surprised him most was the growing fondness he had developed for reading; a notion he found rather amusing. He had, after all, always regarded himself as a rather likeable jock-type, a manual guy, never envisioning himself as someone who would take much pleasure in intellectual pursuits.

That said, tonight exceptionally, the words of the Chinese general echoed in his mind, leaving a lingering impact that was far from calming.

Ever since James had warned him about the Sasquatch being known for holding grudges and retaliating, he'd been on edge. He had also read stories in blogs and listened to many Bigfoot encounters in podcasts, both of which didn't help to ease his mind. *Am I becoming obsessed? Like he used to be?* He questioned himself.

While there were no visible or audible signs of the creatures anywhere near or around his property at this time, Carter still wasn't sure he was out of the woods yet, both literally and figuratively.

Is that what they're doing? He thought. *Are they waiting for me to settle into a predictable pattern so that they can strike back when I least expect it? Are they even that smart? Or am I just wrestling with PTSD?*

Sure, he reasoned, he had the guns, hunting experience, outdoorsy know-how, the floodlights, the trail cams, and a trusted partner and experienced advisor in James. But whenever he thought about the creatures, he found no peace.

Furthermore, there was that peculiar and vivid dream he had experienced just a few nights ago, which seemed to cling to him insistently. The unsettling emotions it evoked lingered, gripping his very soul and refusing to be dismissed.

X

Family Matters

Sunday, October 9, 7:55 a.m.

On that Sunday morning, when Carter awoke, the sun shone brightly through his room-darkening drapes, bringing a warm light that filled the bedroom. However, the sight of perspiration-like droplets glistening on the windowpane served as an obvious reminder that summer had ended. Fall had gracefully descended upon Oregon, painting the landscape of Simeon Heights in a breathtaking palette of gold, yellow, orange, and red. The trees and forests stood adorned in their resplendent autumn attire, a testament to nature's ever-changing beauty.

He felt surprisingly refreshed; a rare occurrence for him. In the past year, he could easily count the number of truly restful nights he had experienced on one hand. Glancing at his alarm clock, he noted the time: 7:55

am. *Kids must be up,* he thought as he rose from bed, stretched his limbs, and slipped into his favorite jogging attire. Descending the stairs, he discovered his two cherished mini-humans engrossed in quiet television watching, their presence bringing a smile to his face.

"Hey Daddy," said Ellie cheerily. "I hope we didn't wake you."

"No worries, sweetie. You didn't. You were both very quiet," he said, adding, "So, how did *you guys* sleep?"

"Good," they both replied, with Ty not even looking at his dad, hypnotized by the cartoons on TV.

"Are you hungry?" he asked them.

"Yeah!" they both exclaimed.

That last part really got their attention. It never failed to.

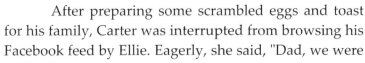

After preparing some scrambled eggs and toast for his family, Carter was interrupted from browsing his Facebook feed by Ellie. Eagerly, she said, "Dad, we were cooped up all week inside. And it's really sunny outside… and beautiful, and—"

He looked up at her and sighed, understanding her request before she even finished her sentence. "… and you'd like to go play outside a bit with Ty?" he said, reading her mind and completing her sentence.

Grinning, she nodded expectantly, "Uh-huh."

Still uncertain, he glanced briefly outside. She had a point. And he had been closely monitoring the situation all week—day and night. There were no more signs of the Bigfoots around the property. Moreover, he didn't want his children living in fear. However, still cautious and recognizing the importance of taking precautions, he said to his ten-year-old daughter, "All right, but on a few conditions."

"What?" she asked, intrigued by her father's requirements.

"Go get Ty, and I'll tell you," he replied, gesturing for her to fetch her brother.

As the two kids stood before him, he adopted a stern expression and began laying down his rules.

"First of all, I really want to finish my coffee in peace. But later, I have some work to do in the workshop, so I'll be outside with you two for a while. How does that sound?" he asked, seeking their agreement.

"Yay!" they both shouted, expressing their excitement.

"Finally, some normalcy and fresh air," ingeniously added Ellie, as if to reinforce her stance.

Carter smiled at them and continued, "*Secondly*, you are not allowed to go further than the workshop. I need to keep a close eye on you. Can you both follow that rule?"

"Yes," they both answered in unison.

"And Ellie," said Carter, "I want you to keep a close watch on Ty," he added, pointing towards the boy.

"Sure, Dad," she replied confidently.

"When I'm done with my work, I'll call you both in, and that will be it for today. Does that sound good?" he asked, seeking their agreement.

Ellie looked at her dad, her expression somewhat disappointed, and reluctantly said, "Yeah."

However, she didn't budge an inch.

Carter's improvised playing perimeter effectively limited their activities to a mere fraction of their expansive yard. They were now confined to an area comprising the deck and a small patch of grass surrounding the workshop. This significant reduction in their usual play space left them with barely a few square feet to explore.

Patiently standing beside her father, she now wore a disappointed expression as she voiced her question, "Dad?"

"Hmmm?" he responded, taking a sip of his coffee and attempting to refocus on browsing his phone.

"How long are we going to be stuck like this?" she inquired, her tone laced with a hint of sadness, longing for the freedom they once enjoyed.

Recognizing the underlying concern in her question, Carter paused his browsing, set aside his phone and directed his full attention towards her.

Her burdened demeanor tugged at his heartstrings. *If only she knew about everything that happened*, he thought. But she had been through enough already. He knew he couldn't divulge the truth about the recent events that unfolded in those woods.

"Sweetie," he began, his voice filled with reassurance, "you're aware of those creatures, the monkey-men, just as much as I am."

"They're called Sasquatches, dad. I'm not five, you know," she interjected, her annoyance clear as she corrected him.

"Huh, right, of course," he acknowledged, feeling a twinge of embarrassment. "Well, I've taken many precautions to ensure the safety of our property. But until I'm absolutely *certain*, I can't take any risks—for the sake of everyone. You understand that, don't you?"

"Yeah, I do. But—" she hesitated, her expression revealing a mix of resignation and frustration.

He gently placed his hand on her shoulder, planting a soft kiss on her forehead. "I know, sweetie. I know. It's difficult, right?"

"Absolutely," she replied with conviction.

"And I understand. But remember, it's only temporary. You just have to trust me, okay?" he implored, his smile aimed at reassuring her.

She let out a sigh, a tinge of annoyance lingering in her voice as she responded, "You *always* say that."

"That's because you *always* need to trust me," he countered, his smile widening as he met her gaze.

Having been brought up on a farm, Carter understood the importance of autumn being a season of preparation. He vividly remembered watching his father meticulously organize and store belongings, attending to neglected tasks along the way. The transition from summer to winter brought forth a flurry of activity on their expansive farm. It was a time when there seemed to be an endless list of chores and responsibilities to tackle before the arrival of the colder months.

During his time living in a condo in Portland, however, Carter's experience of fall took on a much different tone. With fewer responsibilities and obligations, he had grown accustomed to a relatively relaxed autumn routine. His chief concern had revolved around ensuring the timely installation of his winter tires. But, deep within, he couldn't help but feel a sense of longing for the intricacies of country living and the unique challenges that came with owning a home.

Now, as he embraced life in their fresh setting, he faced a myriad of tasks in the upcoming weeks. Cleaning, decluttering, and organizing various items became pressing matters, but above all, he was eager to install the sizable wooden shelves he had purchased a month earlier. These shelves promised to provide additional storage in his workshop and contribute to a sense of cleanliness. This made them the top priority on his agenda for the day.

From the vantage point outside the workshop's expansive garage door, Carter had a clear view of the back deck and could even catch glimpses of the kitchen through the glass door. As for the kids, their joy was palpable as they shrieked, ran, and engaged in a lively game of tag around the spacious 18' x 40' workshop. Though there were some areas where his line of sight was obstructed, their exuberant voices reverberated through the air, reaching his ears with unmistakable clarity.

Engrossed in his task of taking precise measurements for the shelving project, an unsettling sound abruptly pierced the peaceful ambiance. The sound seemed to stretch out, echoing through the atmosphere in slow motion, causing a knot of dread to form in Carter's stomach. It was a scream. A nightmarish scream unlike anything he had ever heard before. It was the type of piercing scream that sends shivers down the spines of parents everywhere.

One thought was on his mind: *Ellie!*

In an instant, the measuring tape slipped from his grasp as he bolted outside. There, by the side of the workshop, he found her. She was in a state of sheer terror, crouched with her head between her knees, shaking uncontrollably and as pale as a ghost. Her gaze was fixed upon the trees that stood ominously behind the workshop, sending chills down his spine.

"What's wrong?!" he exclaimed; with alarm clear in his voice. As his eyes scanned the surroundings, he noticed the absence of Ty, and a wave of panic surged within him. Desperately, he added to his urgent inquiry, "Ellie, where's your brother?!"

It was the words that escaped her quivering lips next that plunged him into his worst nightmare.

With a voice filled with fear, she stammered, "It… it… it took him."

Despite his growing shock and terror, he couldn't help but ask, hoping against hope that there might be some alternative explanation, "*What* took him?"

199

Her response only confirmed his worst fears. "The... the Bigfoot," she whispered, her voice trembling.

Gripping her arms tightly, he pressed for more information. "*Where?* Where did it come from? Where did it take Ty?"

She pointed shakily towards the back of the workshop, where a narrow trail cut through the dense line of trees. "It--it, he came from those trees," she stammered, her eyes wide with fright. "It came out so fast, took Ty, and disappeared back into the woods. It was *humongous*."

His first instinct was to charge into those woods in pursuit of the creature and his son, but a flash of lucidity won him over. He knew he had to think before acting, especially as a single parent. With a heavy heart, he restrained himself from rushing blindly into the unknown.

I can't leave Ellie—especially in that state. Besides, what would I do? This creature is bigger, stronger, faster, and I'm unarmed.

As panic threatened to consume him, he forced himself to take a deep breath and clear his mind. *Think Carter,* he said to himself. *Think dammit!*

He had to approach the situation logically and strategically if he had any hope of finding his son. Every second mattered, and he couldn't afford to waste precious time. His mind raced, searching for a plan of action amidst the chaos. He also knew that the more time passed, the harder it would be to find Tyler in those woods.

A spark of hope flickered within as he realized the significance of the day. *It's Sunday!* He remembered. *Alex is coming over.* His heart skipped a beat as he glanced at his watch, noting the time: 10:02. *She should arrive soon,* he reassured himself.

However, a nagging doubt crept into his mind.

She should have been here by now. Why is she late? Is she not coming? He thought.

Frustration surged through him as he reached for his phone, hoping to find a missed call from her. Disappointment overtook him as he discovered no incoming calls. With a mix of anxiety and determination, he dialed her number, his fingers trembling slightly. One ring. Two rings. Three rings. Four rings... and the dreaded sound of her voicemail greeting filled his ear. He let out a frustrated sigh and ended the call.

"Dammit!" he yelled, his exasperation reverberating through the air. The weight of the situation and the uncertainty of Alex's whereabouts intensified his emotions. It was a moment of utter helplessness, the culmination of mounting fear and desperation.

His mind raced with countless possibilities, each one more worrisome than the last. Why hadn't she answered? Was she okay? Was she still coming? Doubts and fears swirled within him, threatening to engulf his thoughts.

Taking a deep breath once more, he knew he had to stay composed and think clearly. He couldn't afford to lose hope or succumb to despair. As he looked down, his eyes settled on his daughter, who just stood there at his feet.

Clasping Ellie's trembling hand, his eyes darted anxiously in every direction. With a sense of urgency, he propelled them both inside the house, sliding and locking the patio door behind them. The atmosphere inside was charged with fear and distress. Hastily, he guided Ellie to the couch, her tear-streaked face a reflection of her anguish. Time seemed to slip away, slipping through their fingers like sand.

"It's going to be okay, sweetie," he reassured her, his voice laced with resilience and strength despite the chaos raging within. "Ty's going to be just fine." With those words, he dashed upstairs to his bedroom, with resolution propelling his every step.

In a matter of minutes, he re-emerged, transformed. Now clad in his trusted camo hunting outfit, the attire that had proven its worth against the creatures recently, he exuded a determined aura. Each piece of equipment he carried had been meticulously chosen, evidence to his unwavering resolve.

Just as his heart pounded with trepidation, the doorbell rang, its chime piercing the air and offering a tinge of much needed hope.

* * *

As she stood at the door, Alex's anticipation danced in her eyes. Her newly styled hair and meticulously manicured nails bore witness to her effort to look her best. Donning a carefully curated fall ensemble, she had selected a pair of flattering blue jeans, complemented by a cozy beige and blue wool sweater that enveloped her in warmth. The final touch came in the form of chic faux-suede ankle boots, an embodiment of her desire to merge the allure of the city with the rugged charm of the countryside.

While her practical purpose for being here was undeniable, which was to drive her dad's truck back to his place, she couldn't help but hold on to the hope of a leisurely weekend car drive with Carter and the kids, cherishing the fleeting moments of carefree togetherness.

However, the instant he swung open the front door, reality came crashing down, shattering her aspiration into countless fragments.

Her initial words tumbled out in a rush, her smile wavering, "Hey, did you just try to call me? I missed it because I was… almost… here…" The lightheartedness in her voice evaporated as she took in the scene before her.

Something was clearly amiss, and her concern grew.

Carter stood in front of her, his somber presence accentuated by the camo hunting outfit and gear he wore. The familiarity of his attire sent a shiver down her spine, reminding her of the distressing night they had spent at the hospital when her father was injured.

His complexion was visibly drained, his distress obvious in his troubled expression. And there, behind him, sat Ellie on the sofa, her tear-streaked face and trembling form revealing depths of anguish.

Moving closer, Alex's voice dropped to a hushed tone, filled with worry. "What's happened? What's going on?" Her words quivered with the weight of the unknown, mirroring the anguish in Carter's eyes.

"Carter... *tell me*, what's going on?" she pleaded once more, her voice filled with urgency.

With his lips trembling, he mustered the words, his voice filled with desperation, "I really need your help."

"Of course. What's going on?" she asked once more, her voice now brimming with worry.

Slowly, painfully, he spilled out the words, his voice heavy with sorrow, "It... he took Tyler."

"What? Who? Who took Tyler? Good Lord! ..." Her voice trailed off, dreading what she was about to hear.

"The--the Bigfoot. It took Tyler, right from under my nose, and ran back into the woods with him. Ellie saw everything. It... just happened... just now. That's why I called you. I'm going nuts here," he confessed, his voice filled with agony.

Distraught, she glanced at Ellie, then back at Carter. "Oh, my gosh! Of course. What do you want me to do? Did you call the police?"

"No. No. No cops. Not right now," he responded, his tone resolute. "By the time they show up, ask their questions, and write their useless report, Tyler could be gone forever!"

"Carter—" she began, her voice laced with concern.

But he anticipated her plea and spoke before she could continue. "Look, I really need you now. Could you *please* stay with Ellie while I go into those woods and get my boy back?" he implored, his voice trembling yet resolute.

"What?! Carter, *this is crazy!* I mean… I do want to help you, and *sure,* I can stay with her. But you need to call for help *first,*" she insisted.

"I said NO cops for now," he retorted, gritting his teeth with an edge in his voice.

She realized he meant business, so she nodded, acquiescing.

In a hurry, he then led her towards his walk-in armory, located across from the den, and quickly unlocked the door using the code. Returning with a sense of urgency, he handed her a high-powered rifle, a 375 Ruger Hawkeye Alaskan, along with an extra box of ammunition.

"It's already loaded," he informed her. "You told me you knew how to use these, right?"

"Um, yeah, sure. This one's good for bears—or, well, Bigfoots. But what do you think *you're* going to do? Do you have any idea? Do you have a plan? Something?" she questioned; her words tinged with concern.

"Look, I told you; I'm going after that creature. It took my boy. What else am I supposed to do?" he replied, his voice resolute.

"Carter, I think you're acting recklessly here. Surely, you could still call the authorities and file a report. They have resources, dogs, and—" she said, attempting to reason with him.

"Forget about that," he interjected, cutting her off. "I've seen firsthand what these things can do to dogs. And besides, what do you want me to tell them? *Bigfoot* took my son?"

She knew he had a valid point. Her gaze fell downward, feeling disenchanted and puzzled, realizing the complexities of the situation they were facing.

He continued, his voice filled with determination, "Look, I've read a lot of blog posts, and you know this from your dad, too. We both know how that usually goes, right?"

Observing her dejected demeanor, he paused, sighed, and meeting her gaze; he spoke as calmly as possible, "Look, if I'm not back here in two hours…"

"Two hours!" she jumped, cutting him mid-sentence. "No way, I'm not waiting that long, Carter. If you're not back here in an hour… I'm calling the authorities… for both your sake and Tyler's."

He earnestly looked at her, and asked tentatively, "An hour and a half?"

Meeting his gaze, she stared back, considering his counter offer. "Okay, *fine*. One hour and a half… but not a minute longer!" she said worriedly.

He nodded, feeling a sense of understanding and agreement between them. While he took a moment to double-check his gear and securely tuck his gun inside his vest holster, she noticed his familiar silver cross pendant resting on the kitchen counter. Acting on instinct, she grabbed it and handed it to him, gently folding her hands over his in the process.

"Make sure you wear this before heading out," she said.

As he accepted the silver cross and placed it around his neck, he looked at her said, "You're a lot like your dad, you know that, don't you?"

Smiling knowingly, she responded, "You mean, full of faith, helpful, and persistent?"

Clearing his throat, he replied, "Um, yeah. That too." The moment of lightheartedness provided a glimmer of strength amidst the uncertainty of the situation.

Then, she nudged her head, nodding it toward Ellie, who was sitting on the couch this whole time, visibly still in shock.

Understanding the unspoken message, Carter approached his beloved daughter, his heart aching for her. Though she had ceased crying, her fear and shock were still evident.

Lowering himself to her eye level, he spoke in a tender voice, "Hey, um, Ellie, sweetie, I'm gonna... I'm gonna go into that forest and bring Tyler back."

Seeing her unmoved, he urged himself inwardly. *Come on... talk to her, you dork. She needs you now. Be a real dad!*

Summoning inner strength, he made another attempt, his voice filled with love and reassurance, "Ellie, look at me, sweetie."

With a mix of sadness and fear reflecting in her innocent blue eyes, she turned her gaze towards him, seeking solace in her father's words.

"I'm going to come back with your little brother. Do you believe me?" he asked, his voice quivering with emotion.

"Daddy, I don't know. I--I'm *so scared*. And... I'm so sorry," she responded, tears streaming down her face once again.

Pulling her closer, Carter embraced her, offering comfort and support. "Hey, hey, don't be sorry. This isn't your fault, sweetie. None of it is. There's nothing you could have done. Look, I promise you, I'll do everything to find Tyler and bring him back safely. We'll be together again—*soon*."

His encouraging words were aimed at easing her undue guilt and provide a glimmer of hope amid despair.

"Now... look at me," he said, gently cupping her tear-stained face in his hands.

With her attention fully focused on him, Ellie listened intently to her father's words.

"You're scared. I get it. You know why?" he asked, his voice filled with empathy.

Curious, she responded, "No. Why?"

Taking a deep breath, he replied, "Because I'm scared, too." Pausing briefly, he continued, "But we've gotta have faith. We have to believe that..." he paused, surprised by his own words, "Sweetie, we *have to believe* that *God* will take care of Tyler, and me too, as I go into those woods to find him and bring him back."

Pointing towards Alex, he assured Ellie, "Alexandra is going to stay here with you. You're going to be okay. You're safe here."

Their eyes locked in a moment of understanding, and she felt a sense of calm wash over her. She embraced her father tightly, whispering, "Oh, daddy! I love you so much! I'll be praying for you."

With trembling lips, he returned her embrace, declaring, "That's all I ask for. And I love you too. I'll be back soon."

Standing up with a determined gaze, he turned to Alex and sternly instructed, "Lock those doors. Stay away from windows. And please... keep her safe. I left the armory unlocked. Take anything you need."

Alex nodded in agreement, understanding the gravity of the situation.

"Sure." She said. Then she added, "Carter... *ninety minutes*. And if you're not back after then I'm calling the—"

But before she could finish her sentence, he interrupted her with a steadfast tone, "Look, Alex... like I said, that won't be necessary. Mark my words... I'm coming back with my boy."

She nodded, admiring his determination.

As he prepared to leave, Alex followed him into the kitchen and then outside onto the deck, closing the sliding door behind her. They stood face to face, clinging to each other's hands, with a combination of affection and worry in their eyes. In a tender moment, she gently kissed him on the lips and pleaded, "I'll be praying for the both of you. Please... be careful. Find him and come back with him, okay?"

With a nod, he replied, "Look, um, if anything happens to me out there, I just want you to know..."

Silencing his words with her index finger on his lips, she interrupted softly, "Shhh. You can tell me when you and Tyler get back safe and sound, okay?"

A warm smile formed on his face as his heart filled with appreciation. "Sure," he whispered.

With a final lingering gaze, she watched him disappear around the corner of his workshop, embarking on the narrow trail that led into the depths of the forest. Her eyes remained fixed on the spot where he vanished, as she offered a silent prayer for his protection and safe return.

XI

Simian Showdown

Sunday, October 9, 10:29 a.m.

Staring apprehensively at the edge of the dense wood line, Carter took a deep breath, steeling himself for what lay ahead. Gripping his trusty and powerful handgun tightly, he entered the same path where the dreaded Bigfoot had disappeared into, carrying his precious five-year-old boy in its grasp.

The once sunny sky had transformed into a somber gray, signaling the imminent arrival of rain. Dark clouds loomed overhead, casting a shadow over his journey and amplifying his own dismal mood.

Walking along the narrow trail, he called out his son's name repeatedly, his voice echoing through the rain-soaked forest. Each raindrop added to the melancholic symphony as it gently landed on the leaves of the towering trees.

There were fewer tracks than he had hoped for on the trail, making the tracking process more challenging than expected. However, the few footprints he came across were massive, confirming the direction of the elusive creature he pursued.

If this is the one that took Ty, it's probably the alpha. These are at least 20 inches long, he thought.

Straight up ahead on the trail, something both familiar and troubling caught his eye. Standing in the middle of the narrow trail, covered in mud, with its arms outstretched and looking menacing, was….

Ty's gorilla toy! Carter leapt within, encouraged by the find. *Good. I'm on the right track.*

Seizing it, he clutched it in his hand and held it near his chest for a few seconds before putting it away in his large jacket pocket.

———————◦●◦●◦●———————

"So, Ellie, tell me, how have things been in class while I've been away?" Alex asked, hoping to shift the conversation and provide a momentary break from the ongoing drama.

"Okay, I guess," Ellie replied. "Mr. Bradford is nice enough, but he's kinda boring. I think… I think we all miss you."

"Aww, that's sweet. Well, you saw my dad, right? I need to make sure he's all better. And once he is, I'll be back to finish the year with you guys."

"Yeah, I know," said the ten-year-old. "By the way... I saw you with my dad outside, you know, *kissing* him."

Alex vacillated, embarrassed, and searching for the right words. "Oh, um, well, I—"

"Don't worry." Ellie interjected, "I know you guys are more than just friends," she added. "I'm okay with it, you know."

"Really?!" Alex responded, feeling a sense of relief.

"Yeah. He's been different in the last few weeks. Happier, I guess. I'm pretty sure it's because of you," Ellie said, her smile growing.

"That's... good to know," said Alex, rejoicing at the thought. "And you know what?"

"What?"

"I've been happier too, since I've met your dad." She confided, smiling.

Ellie smiled back, appreciating the sentiment.

Alex then gently took Ellie's hand in hers and said, "You mentioned earlier that you'd pray for him and your little brother. How about if we do it now—*together*?"

Ellie beamed at the suggestion. "Yeah. I'd like that."

"Tyler! Tyyyler!" Carter called out repeatedly, feeling the weight of solitude on his trek. He sure could have used a partner right now; someone like James or even Ajax, to accompany him in this challenging and fearsome undertaking.

As he had ventured about half a mile from his house, a sound caught his attention. He called out once more, and to his relief, a faint voice responded, "Daddy? Daddy!"

Recognizing his son's voice, Carter sprinted as fast as he could up the trail in the sound's direction. His earnestness led him to a wide clearing, spanning nearly 30 yards, but there was no sign of the boy.

Perplexed, he called out again, and sure enough, the voice echoed back, "Daddy! Daddy!"

Curiously, the voice seemed to come from... above.

Lifting his eyes, he found his boy perched 12 feet up on a tree branch, tightly gripping the trunk and another branch in front of him, keeping balanced.

"Ty! Thank goodness! Are you okay? Are you hurt?" he anxiously inquired, his worry fading as the child shook his head, indicating that he was unharmed. However, Tyler was drenched, covered in dirt, and clearly shivered from the cold. Carter's immediate instinct was to get him down and leave the area as quickly as possible.

Upon closer observation, however, he realized that there were no lower branches on the tree. It was now clear that Ty couldn't have climbed up there on his own. *The Bigfoot put him up there;* he grasped, furthering his mounting apprehension.

Cautiously, Carter retrieved his gun, his gaze sweeping the entire clearing. He couldn't shake the feeling that this was a lure, a clever trap set by an intelligent adversary. Thoughts raced through his mind as he focused on the safety of his son. Meanwhile, Tyler's sobs grew louder. "Daddy! I wanna come down! Daddyyy!" his desperate cries, echoing through the clearing.

Not perceiving any immediate threat, Carter's tension eased slightly. He carefully un-cocked his gun and returned it to the holster inside his jacket. Gazing up at Tyler, he spoke reassuringly, "All right, Tyler. Daddy's going to come up and take you down now, okay?"

Relieved by his father's words, Ty trustingly nodded in agreement.

Although the distance wasn't significant, navigating the branchless and slippery trunk proved to be a challenge for Carter. As he neared the desired height, a chilling scream pierced the air, instantly recognizable as the distinctive yowl of a large Sasquatch.

Tyler, seemingly unbothered, casually remarked, "That's the monkey-man, daddy. He's coming back."

Understanding the imminent danger, Carter looked up at his son with a mixture of sorrow and determination. Rightly judging the boy might be safer up the tree for now, he pursed his lips remorsefully and said, "Listen, Tyler, I promise I'll get you down from here. But we have to wait a little longer. So, for now, just hold on as tight as you can, okay?"

"Okay, Daddy," responded Tyler, displaying a surprising sense of calmness amidst the chaotic situation.

Priming himself, Carter couldn't help but think, *Thank God he doesn't fully get the situation we're in. Ignorance truly is bliss.*

As they knelt together in front of the sofa on the living room floor, Alex gently asked Ellie, "Would you like to pray first, or should I?"

"You go first," Ellie replied.

"Okay," Alex nodded. As they both held hands and joined their hearts in agreement, she prayed…

"Father God, we come to you on behalf of Carter and Tyler, who are out there in the forest right now. We care for them deeply, but we know you care for them even more. So, we ask you to look after them. Father… please protect them from all evil and all harm. We ask that you send mighty angels to surround them and guide them right now in their time of great need. Guide Carter so that he can quickly find Tyler and bring him back safely. In Jesus's name we ask, *Amen.*"

After concluding, she turned to Ellie, smiled, and said, "All right, your turn."

No sooner did she utter those words, that a nine-inch across rock came crashing violently through the kitchen patio window and crash-landed loudly on the wooden floor a mere foot behind them.

Carter could hear the thunderous footsteps of the Bigfoot as he carefully slid down the tree trunk. Once on the ground, he steadied himself near the base of the tree, gripping his gun tightly with both hands. His gaze and aim remained fixed on the rustling branches a mere 20 yards away, fully aware that he had walked right into an ambush.

As the trees parted, a single Sasquatch emerged from the wood line. It wasn't a group or clan of Bigfoots, but a solitary creature. Yet, from its appearance, it became clear to Carter that this lone creature was more than enough to pose a formidable threat.

Towered at a staggering height of well over nine feet, the imposing figure before him was none other than the alpha male Sasquatch. There he stood, the same elusive creature that had so stealthily evaded them only a few days earlier. Now beholding it in broad daylight, Carter was confronted with its awe-inspiring presence.

Indeed, the Bigfoot was a sight to behold. His massive frame and distinct features were unlike anything he had ever encountered, and left him in utter astonishment. A wave of fear engulfed him as he realized the sheer magnitude of the beast before him. *This thing is colossal!* He thought, his disbelief mingled with shock and apprehension.

Adorned in a cloak of long, matted, dark brown hair that shimmered under the gentle touch of rain, the Sasquatch intimidatingly stood its ground. Its chest and shoulders were reminiscent of a massive barrel, spanning well over four feet in width. Its legs, akin to large and sturdy tree trunks, exuded raw power. The creature's sheer muscularity and appearance were enough to render any man's nerves shaky. And sure enough, Carter felt his stomach queasy and his bladder on the verge of surrender.

The intimidating creature had a chiseled six-pack and arms that were bigger than those of a professional bodybuilder, and there was no doubt he could easily tear even the strongest of men apart. And so the alpha stood, emitting an aura of incredible strength and dominance. The silvered strands that peppered its face spoke volumes of wisdom and experience, acquired only through the passage of time. With its chest rising and falling with heavy breaths, the creature fixed its menacing gaze upon Carter and his gripped firearm.

For Carter, encountering this Bigfoot in daylight presented an entirely new level of intensity. Though he maintained a tight grip on his firearm, his trembling hands struggled to steady it. His entire body now quivered, his limbs threatening to give way. In that moment, he realized that the grip of fear he felt surpassed any case of buck fever he had ever experienced. His nerves were completely shattered by this sight that defied all rational explanations.

However, it was the creature's eyes that truly unsettled and haunted him. They were a deep shade of brown, so dark they bordered on black, and held a profound expressiveness. Within those depths, he discerned an undeniable intelligence, a wellspring of emotion, and perhaps, could it be possible—the glimmer of a soul?

The notion of those eyes being almost… *human* sent a chill down his spine, leaving him contemplating the inexplicable depths of what stood before him.

A torrent of thoughts flooded his mind as he grappled with the enigma before him. Deep down, he knew this creature transcended the classification of a mere North American wood-ape or oversized primate. Had the encounter taken place under the cover of darkness, he might have already discharged his weapon in defense. Yet, in the brightness of daylight, an internal struggle prevented him from summoning the resolve needed to pull the trigger.

Locked in a gaze with the alpha, disbelief mingled with confusion within Carter's psyche. The question arose, unfathomable yet persistent: Could this being possess even a trace of humanity? The notion seemed preposterous, defying all rationality and challenging the boundaries of his understanding.

As rain cascaded down, each droplet obscuring his vision, Carter squinted, determined to regain clarity amidst the persisting blur. The water went in his eyes, momentarily arresting his vision. As his trembling hands reacted instinctively to the discomfort, they descended ever so slightly, causing the once-aimed gun to lower toward the sodden forest floor.

That's when the alpha seized its chance.

"Aiiieeeeeee!" Ellie shrieked, terrified by the crashing large rock that had just landed behind her and Alex—miraculously missing them by inches.

Served by her quick wit and knowledge of Bigfoot behavior, Alex put two-and-two together and almost instinctively knew what to do.

"Ellie, sweetie, listen to me... I want you to run upstairs and find a safe place to hide—*away from any windows*. Do you understand me?"

"Y--yes" stammered the girl, her obedience immediate as she swiftly ascended the stairs, seeking refuge out of sight.

Following her own advice, Alex cautiously maneuvered away from the nearest windows, making her way to the hallway, where the rifle leaned casually against the wall. As she grabbed the weapon, the chilling taunts of a Bigfoot reverberated through the yard, amplifying the urgency of the situation.

Filled with anxiety, Alex now found herself speaking in a hushed voice, more to herself than anyone else. "This was supposed to be a *relaxing* Sunday morning drive, *dammit!* A *fun* time! I got my hair done for the first time in what? *Six months*? I bought this new cutesy outfit, and for crying out loud... I *never* get my nails done! All this for a guy who... who's *just like my dad! Ugh!*"

Frustration and disappointment colored her words as she vented away in self-talk. Taking a deep breath, she crouched behind the wall, the rifle pointed upward, her mind racing. In a moment of composure, she prayed once more.

"Okay, Lord, I'm sorry. *I'm sorry*. I'm complaining again." She paused, collecting her thoughts and refocusing her plea. "God, I'm the one who needs you now… so, please protect me, Ellie, and this house, in Jesus' name…"

With a resolute "Amen" spoken aloud, she rose to her feet and made her way to the smaller kitchen window above the sink, seeking a better vantage point to observe the formidable adversary outside.

Taking a cautious position behind the counter, Alex carefully elevated herself to the lower part of the window, ensuring she had a clear view of the outside while remaining hidden from sight. As she peered out with her senses heightened, she was greeted by the thunderous crash of yet another rock. This one collided with the house's exterior wall. The proximity of the impact sent her heart racing at an accelerated pace as she scurried back behind the kitchen counter.

"Dammit!" she exclaimed, frustrated with her own startled reaction. Determined to regain her composure, she gradually steadied herself, rising slowly, preparing to face the situation head-on. Remaining inconspicuous and motionless, she observed the Bigfoot in the yard—swaying from side to side and emitting primal sounds. The creature stood approximately 35 yards away from the house, a formidable female towering at seven feet in height.

Overwhelmed by fear, Alex instinctively recoiled, quickly retreating behind the counter once more and assuming a crouched position. The sense of dread gripped her, making her acutely aware of the danger lurking outside. "Oh Crap! Crappety-crap-crap!" she said in a low, almost whispery tone, shaking.

This marked her first personal encounter with the legendary creature. Her knowledge and familiarity with these elusive beings were merely second hand, acquired vicariously through the experiences and tales of her army vet-turned-Bigfoot-hunter father.

Summoning her resolve, she took a moment to steady herself, before mustering every ounce of her past training and bravery. With resolve in her eyes, she rose once more to face the imminent threat. "Forgive me, Carter," she whispered, her voice tinged with remorse as she swiftly employed the rifle's stock to shatter the kitchen window, creating an opening that afforded her maneuverability and a clear line of fire.

"All right, Patty," she stated with a resolute tone, her words carrying a blend of defiance and determination. "Let's see you dodge *this!*" Her proclamation rang out as she leveled her sights, took aim, and fired mercilessly at the creature.

Summoning its awe-inspiring speed and strength, the monstrous Bigfoot launched itself ferociously at

Carter, bridging the distance between them in a mere fraction of a second. Using its massive bulk, power, and weight, the beast ran into him like a cement truck. The force of the collision sent Carter hurtling backward through the air for nearly twenty feet before crashing into the dense cluster of small trees behind him. The jarring impact crushed his cell phone lodged in his chest pocket, knocked the wind out of him, and the chaos of it all also caused his pistol to slip from his grasp.

It was in that moment that the gravity of his predicament struck with a chilling realization. Struggling to rise on all fours, Carter experienced a searing pain radiating from his left shoulder. The incapacitating agony rendered his left arm completely immobile, leaving him at the mercy of his labored breathing and the intense pressure now weighing upon his chest. It was clear that he had suffered more than just a few broken ribs.

Brought to a squatting position on bended knees, he found himself reduced to a subservient posture before his colossal assailant, head bowed in submission. The sheer magnitude of the creature's size became palpable as Carter beheld its titanic feet, which measured an astonishing 21 inches.

Before he could even contemplate mounting a countermove, an uncannily large hand ensnared his right arm and shoulder, hoisting his 210-pound frame off the ground with effortless ease. Suspended in mid-air, he now found himself pinned against a towering tree a full ten feet above the forest floor.

Throughout the harrowing ordeal, Carter's ears were assailed by the anguished cries and heartfelt pleas of his young son, Tyler, who remained perched in the tree above him. Innocently, the boy implored the towering creature, "Let my daddy go! Please, Mr. Monkey-man!" He said, begging it over and over to relinquish its hold on his helpless father, his voice trembling with desperation and fear.

Carter was dazed and barely conscious, his body immobilized and his mouth filled with the taste of his own blood. The creature responsible for his family's torment now stood before him vengefully. He flailed and kicked at the alpha, but even his sturdy hiking boots made no impact on the beast's rock-hard chest and stomach.

He remembered the flash grenade in his right pocket, but his right arm was immobilized by the Bigfoot's relentless grip, making it a non-option. Even his trusty bowie knife on his left hip was out of reach, as his injured left arm was also useless. With the realization that he was now facing certain death, the single father's thoughts raced a hundred miles an hour.

It's true, he thought, slowly falling back on accepting his harrowing fate. *Your life really does flash before your eyes.*

Visions of Vivian and the haunting memories of the accident played out in his mind once more, intermingling with images of his cherished children, his sister, his dad, and all the loved ones who had shaped his life. The rush of recollections included his recent exploits and treasured connections in Simeon Heights. It was a whirlwind of emotions and memories condensed into a fleeting moment.

Still gripping Carter tightly by his right arm and shoulder, the Bigfoot locked eyes with him and unleashed a thunderous roar, shaking his very core. The primal scream reverberated through his entire being, causing him to go even more limp, teetering on the brink of unconsciousness.

Meanwhile, Tyler's cries grew louder, filling the air with raw emotion. "Please, let my daddy go!" He begged the creature, his warm tears mixing in with the rain.

Though weakened, Carter fought against the encroaching darkness. He couldn't succumb to unconsciousness, not even for a second, not when his son needed him. The sound of his child's desperate tears served as a lifeline, a reminder of his purpose and the strength he had to summon to protect his family.

As the rifle pointed menacingly at her through the shattered window, the female Sasquatch instinctively sensed the imminent danger and dropped to all fours, sprinting across the yard with astonishing agility, making a beeline for the safety of the distant tree line.

Caught off guard by the Bigfoot's quick reaction, Alex refused to let the opportunity slip away. She swiftly reloaded, determined to take another shot before the creature disappeared into the woods. However, the female Sasquatch proved to be a cunning adversary, darting with remarkable speed and employing a zig-zag pattern to confound Alex's aim.

Despite her best aimed efforts, Alex missed two more times as the elusive female Sasquatch retreated deeper into the forest. Frustration welled up within her, and she couldn't help but berate herself for her lack of accuracy. "Urgh! Unbelievable!" she exclaimed, realizing that her skills had dulled over time.

Anger simmered within her, directed not only at the situation but mostly at her own missed shots. In a last act of defiance, she fired one last shot towards the edge of the tree line, her voice piercing the air as she screamed at the retreating creature, "Yeah! You better run! There's plenty more where that came from, you b****!"

Taking cover once again behind the counter, Alex gripped the rifle tightly in her hands, while a mix of frustration and realization settled upon her. In her heightened state of anxiety and fervor, she had squandered every round in the weapon, rendering her threat to the creature utterly meaningless. A wave of disappointment washed over her as she reflected on her impulsive actions.

Well, at least she's gone now, thought Alex. *She won't come back—I hope. Gotta go check on poor Ellie. She must be terrified. But I should reload first, just in—*

Before she could complete her own thought, a thunderous boom reverberated through the house as an immense force collided with the front door. The impact was so strong that the entire structure trembled on its hinges, billowing clouds of plaster dust into the air.

Alex's heart found its way to her throat as she instinctively rose to her feet, her body flooded with adrenaline. Yet, despite the surge of energy coursing through her veins, she found herself momentarily frozen in shock. The magnitude of the assault on the door left her momentarily stunned, her mind struggling to process the surreal turn of events unfolding before her.

Before the echoes of the first strike could fade away, another colossal boom resounded, breaking down the door off its hinges and sending it thundering onto the living room floor, just inches behind the sofa. Through the dust-filled haze, a figure emerged from the shattered doorway, taking form as yet another imposing Bigfoot.

The sight before her was both terrifying and awe-inspiring. The massive creature stood there, commanding attention with its formidable and towering stature. Alex felt a surge of mixed emotions—fear, wonder, and a deep-rooted instinct to protect herself and Ellie.

Standing before her was a male Bigfoot, seven and a half feet in height, mirroring the size of the large female she had just confronted. Its auburn hair, unkempt and matted, clung to its towering frame. But, unlike the female, this creature revealed a face only a mother could love. Its visage would have easily haunted the darkest nightmares. Its features, distorted and asymmetrical, contorted into a ghastly grimace that sent shivers down her spine. The beast also displayed what appeared to be a painful and puss-filled injury on its left shoulder. It was as if the embodiment of pure horror had materialized before her very eyes. Adding to the macabre scene, a putrid stench emanated from the Bigfoot, assaulting her senses with its overpowering foulness.

Transfixed by the monstrous presence before her, time seemed to grind to a halt for Alex. The sheer terror of the situation overwhelmed her, causing her body to tremble uncontrollably. In that moment, the grip on her rifle slackened, and it slipped from her trembling fingers, clattering onto the hardwood floor. The adrenaline coursing through her veins was no match for the terror that gripped her, and she could feel her bladder betraying her as fear took hold.

The tension in the house was palpable as both Alex and the Bigfoot locked eyes, frozen in a stalemate akin to an old western standoff. Time seemed to stretch as they measured each other's resolve, awaiting the decisive moment.

With her back pressed against the counter, Alex's gaze darted across the room, landing on the glint of kitchen knives. She knew she couldn't afford to prolong this silent confrontation any further. Determination ignited within her, urging her to swiftly make her move and secure the largest knife within her reach. But fear paralyzed her. If she could only grasp it before the creature advanced even a single step, it might provide her with a slim chance at survival.

However, the Bigfoot's immense size and strength meant that a single stride could bring it within striking distance.

In the encompassing darkness of her bedroom closet, Ellie found solace amidst her fear. The usual ominous nature of the darkness had transformed into a comforting shield, enclosing her with temporary safety. She sought refuge in this small space, barely six feet by three, finding a peculiar comfort in the presence of the hanging clothes that hung above her head. From within her hidden sanctuary, she could hear the cacophony unfolding downstairs — the earlier cracks of gunshots and the resounding crash of the front door being breached. Her ears told the truth; the intrusion of the creature into their home was undeniable.

Conflicting thoughts raced through Ellie's mind, grappling with her overwhelming terror and concern for Alexandra's well-being. The tremors in her body refused to subside as anxiety coursed through her veins. She yearned to know if Alexandra was unharmed, yet dread accompanied the mere thought of venturing outside her bedroom closet. Should she remain concealed, awaiting the resolution of this nightmarish ordeal? Or should she summon the courage to venture out, driven by her deep-seated worry and desire to help? The weight of this decision pressed upon her, a profound struggle between personal safety and her growing bond with Alexandra.

Who am I kidding? What can I do? And why didn't Dad want us to call the police? She thought, perplexed.

After seconds had elapsed, she made the gut-wrenching decision to stay put; and she prayed once more, *Oh God, please, please, please, make it go away. Save Alex... and Dad, and Ty... and me. Amen.*

Trapped in the immense clutches of the towering beast, Carter's mind sought solace in a distant memory — the lessons from James and the tale of David and Goliath. This dire situation mirrored the epic struggle of young David against the formidable nine-foot-tall giant. Layered in his memory were also James' words, which echoed in his thoughts, reminding him of the creature's intelligence and alleged reverence for a higher power.

"They fear God more than they fear man." James had told him with a seemingly unshakeable conviction.

The phrase reverberated within Carter's hazy consciousness, resonating repeatedly with inexplicable meaning and depth.

His mind also retraced the biblical account of David's encounter with Goliath, recalling the bold words spoken by the young shepherd:

"You come to me with a sword, with a spear, and with a javelin. But I come to you in the name of the LORD of hosts, the God of the armies of Israel, whom you have defied."

As time stood still and the creature withheld the fatal blow, a question gnawed at Carter's thoughts. Why did it delay? Why hadn't the decisive strike been unleashed upon him? The answer eluded him, buried within the enigmatic motivations of his immense adversary.

As the weight of the moment pressed upon him, an epiphany dawned on him. The answer to the enigma of the creature's hesitation became increasingly apparent—*because it fears God more than it fears man*, he reflected.

After a brief pause, his train of thought resumed on this faint glimmer of insight that now illuminated his mind....

... Because it fears God more than it fears man...

And man, despite all of his flaws, is made in the image of God.

Could this be it? He contemplated, sensing a guiding presence beyond the natural. Could this realization hold the key to his seemingly impossible circumstance?

So, summoning his remaining strength and embracing his budding faith, Carter resorted to the last weapon in his arsenal. Just like the young David of old, he spoke to his giant.

Restricted by the powerful grip of the creature's muscular arms, with its penetrating gaze fixed upon him, as if awaiting an apology, and Tyler's tearful pleas resounding in his ears, Carter mustered the courage to address the Bigfoot. His words, delivered with uncertainty about their comprehension, carried a raw and heartfelt plea.

"I'm... *hmmmf*, not sure if you can understand me," he stammered, the weight of his angst palpable, and peppering his speech with groans. "My wife died months ago. I'm all this boy has left. And these kids... they-- they're all I have left."

Carter's voice hung in the air, a vulnerable plea laced with grief and desperation. He wondered if his words would resonate; if the depths of his pain could penetrate the creature's consciousness, bridging the divide between their worlds. In this precarious moment, he entrusted his sorrows and the fate of his family to the enigmatic beast, while praying for a glimmer of understanding, mercy, and favor.

Struggling to catch his breath, a taste of blood lingering in his mouth, he summoned the remnants of his strength to forge ahead. With determined yet trembling words, he continued his address to the colossal creature before him, his voice laced with resolve, despite his precarious bargaining posture.

"*Hmmf...* if--if there is any core of goodness or compassion in you... In the name of all that is holy in this world... *hmmmf,* I'm asking you, in the name of the LORD of hosts, the God of all, and in the name of His Son... Jesus Christ..." he paused, groaning and trying to catch his breath, and then, boldly and loudly ended with, "Let me and the boy go *now...* and leave my family alone."

After this commanding plea, time seemed to stand still.

Ever so slowly, however, the alpha's facial expression shifted from an angry frown to a more solemn one. Its eyes remained fixated on Carter's, darting back and forth between them and the man's chest.

Perceiving the creature's shifting gaze from his eyes to his chest, Carter thought, *That's it... He's about to rip my heart out*, as he braced himself.

With one hand still clenching Carter, the creature's other massive hand reached towards his neck. Using its index finger, it delicately lifted the silver chain adorning the man's neck. Slowly, the finger traced down

232

the chain until it reached the silver cross resting on Carter's chest.

In a surprising gesture, the giant Sasquatch gently clasped the cross between its two carrot-sized fingers. It held the gleaming silver pendant, displaying a mix of fascination and curiosity.

And then, in a moment of sheer shock, something extraordinary happened. Still holding the silver cross, and looking Carter straight in the eye, the creature... *spoke*.

Pointing his hand and finger upwards, toward the sky, the large alpha male unmistakably uttered the word, "Galaka." And for good measure, as if to make sure this would not be mistaken for anything else, and to Carter's sheer astonishment, he spoke the word *again*, "Galaka."

Then, to his surprise, the creature loosened his grip and gently lowered him down to the forest floor. Back on the ground, Carter struggled to maintain his balance on his shaky legs as he stood before the massive creature. The 34-year-old father remained frozen, unsure of what would happen next, as the alpha male continued to stare at him. The Sasquatch held his gaze, briefly glancing towards Tyler before returning his attention to Carter, holding the stare for a few more seconds.

After a brief moment, the Sasquatch calmly turned around and began walking slowly away, disappearing into the thick underbrush.

Carter and Tyler were now left behind, in stunned silence, unable to comprehend the events that had just unfolded before them.

His body battered, his mind hazy, and his nerves shot; Carter wearily sank to his knees, his gaze fixed on the spot where the creature had vanished into the trees. Rain continued to cascade over him, drenching his clothes and mingling with the turmoil in his mind. Amidst the haze, a distant memory resurfaced, as whispered by his late wife, Vivian, in his recent and disconcerting dream.

"Carter, there is a cross to bridge the divide between you and them. Remember, God loves you, and so do I."

The words echoed in his thoughts, their meaning gradually taking hold. "A cross… to bridge the divide… between you and them." Carter's hand instinctively found the silver pendant hanging from his neck, and he cradled it in his palm, its weight a comforting presence and confirmation.

In that moment, he closed his eyes, his grip tightening around the cross. A surge of faith and gratitude washed over him, an acknowledgement of the extraordinary turn of events he had just witnessed. This was no ordinary encounter; it was a miracle. It was an undeniable sign of divine intervention and favor. He knew it.

Overwhelmed by the weight of his experience, he surrendered to his emotions. Unrestrained sobs wracked his weary frame, each tear an outlet for the pain he had endured. Despite the ache it caused his battered body, he allowed himself this release.

With each heaving breath, his injured upper body rose and fell, as if carrying the burden of his anguish. The floodgates of his emotions had burst wide open, and he no longer tried to stem the flow.

It had been too long. It had been too much.

The tears streamed down his face, their salty trails marking the culmination of too many hardships endured by this single father of two.

In the midst of his unrestrained weeping, a profound relief washed over him. The tears became a cathartic balm, cleansing his soul of the emotional turmoil, depression, and stress that had plagued him throughout the past year. As the drops mingled with the forest floor, it was as though he released the weight of his burdens, watching them dissolve like dirty water draining from a bathtub.

Halfway through the transformative moment of spiritual and emotional renewal, a small voice pierced through the air, drawing Carter's attention upward. It was a gentle voice that reminded him of his purpose. The voice said, "Daddy, the monkey-man is gone. Can I come down now?"

Carter looked up to see his son perched quietly in the tree, and despite his tears, a smile graced his face. "Oh! Of course, Ty! I'm sorry, buddy," he replied, using the sleeve of his damp jacket to wipe away his tears. "Let's get you down now."

In his battered state, the task proved challenging. Carter couldn't climb the tree, making it difficult to convince Ty to jump into his one good arm. After a few minutes of negotiation, they managed, though it was an awkward descent.

As they reunited on the forest floor, Carter enveloped his son in a tight embrace, as if extending fatherly love for the first time. "I'm so glad you're okay. I love you so much, buddy," he expressed, planting tender kisses on Ty's forehead amidst the gentle rain.

"I love you, Daddy," Ty replied, holding on tightly, pouring all his strength into the embrace.

Despite the pain, the physical demands, and the slow pace dictated by his physical state and his child, Carter mustered his best efforts to hasten their journey back home. He had a deep yearning to ensure everything was in order on the home front, and so they pressed forward, their steps propelled by determination to reunite with Ellie and Alex.

In the Old-West showdowns of legend, the one who possessed unwavering confidence and quick reflexes often seized the initiative, ensuring their survival and preserving their tale in the process.

However, when the pitting involved a wounded and enraged seven-foot Bigfoot against a terrified woman standing at a mere 5'6", the outcome appeared painfully clear from the outset.

Without hesitation, the creature made its move, launching itself forward with a sudden lunge. Its outstretched arm reached for Alex's leg, closing the daunting twelve-foot gap between them in a mere instant.

Still reeling from the shock and struggling to comprehend the horrifying reality before her, Alex faltered in her response. The massive beast proved too agile, too swift for her to counter.

Regret pierced her thoughts like a shard of glass. *Shoot! Should have gone for that knife*, she silently lamented as the creature clamped its grasp around her left leg, forcefully yanking it upwards.

Thrown off balance, she landed forcefully on her back as the creature relentlessly yanked her towards it. She grunted, desperately clinging to the wall that divided the kitchen from the hallway, but her efforts proved futile, only amplifying her agony. With its monstrous strength, the beast persisted in pulling her leg, stretching her body to its limits.

Relinquishing her grip on the dividing wall, she instinctively switched to a strategy of making herself into tough prey. With a surge of adrenaline, she attempted to kick the creature's arm, all the while unleashing piercing screams. "Let me go, you ugly son-of-a-b****!" Her kicks and screams, however, proved ineffective in rattling the monster. Undeterred, despite her thrashing on the floor, she strained and extended her reach, successfully retrieving the rifle she had previously dropped, even though it remained unloaded.

Laying on her back, she mustered the strength to raise her upper body in a seated position, aiming the barrel of the rifle directly at the creature. Employing a clever bluff, she unleashed a commanding yell, "Let me go or I'll blow your ugly friggin' face off!"

The sheer authority in her own voice astonished her—and the creature. At that moment, it appeared to have an effect. The Bigfoot, taken aback by her brashness, ceased pulling, appearing to contemplate the potential threat. However, his response was unexpected. Fixing his gaze upon her, he countered her bluff with an unsettling smile, as if challenging her to follow through.

Bewildered by the beast's reaction, her only thought was, *He knows it's empty. But how?!*

Maintaining a firm grip on her ankle, the creature rose from its crouched position and callously turned its back to her, dragging her across the floor. The monster pulled her by the leg over the remains of the broken-down door, her shirt becoming torn and her skin scraped and cut by the rough edges of the splintered wood. Each agonizing moment intensified her cries of anguish.

He was now heading back from whence he came—with her in tow. In that moment, Alex's realization struck hard: he *was* taking prisoners. She was being taken captive. Her thoughts raced, desperately searching for any viable options. *Should I shout for Ellie?* She thought. *No. He'd probably turn on her. Can't have that.*

Her thoughts then shifted to the further realization that she had left her phone behind on the kitchen table, right next to the spare box of ammo. She desperately wished she had either with her, knowing it could have been her lifeline.

But in a sudden twist of fate, the creature came to an abrupt halt, freezing in its tracks. Something unexpected erupted from the woods, shattering the tense atmosphere.

It was a howl. But not just any howl or yowl.

It began as a low rumble, gradually building in intensity until it reached an earth-shaking crescendo. The sheer volume of the sound was awe-inspiring. It would have struck fear into the hearts of even the bravest souls. Reverberating through the trees, it shattered the silence with a thunderous resonance that echoed for miles around. The voice carried a commanding presence, resonating with an indescribable authority that required the attention of all who heard it. With primal reverberation, it stirred the very essence of the natural world. Birds ceased their songs, and even the wind seemed to hush, as if in reverence to the power and authority embodied in the menacing vocalization. Its power and range defied human comprehension and shook the very core of all living beings in range.

Carter and Ty were halfway home when they heard the primal yowl echoing across the woods nearby. Concerned, Carter picked up the pace even more as Ty asked, "What was *that*, daddy?"

Ellie was still hiding in her closet, crying and ever so still, her trembling form desperate for safety. The moment she caught wind of the echoing sound, her fear magnified, causing her to freeze completely.

Alex, in the greatest peril of her life, was being dragged away to a more-than-likely grisly fate when she heard it, only adding to her rising anguish.

Each iteration of the haunting yowl lasted well over 15 seconds, only to fade momentarily before resuming its eerie refrain.

None of them had ever heard anything like it before.

For Carter, Alex, Ty, and Ellie, the sound was entirely unfamiliar, an enigma that defied explanation. It possessed an otherworldly quality, reminiscent of scenes from the dense jungles of distant lands, or the most chilling moments of a suspenseful horror movie.

But for the others; for *them*, it was different.

For *them*, it carried familiarity; it was an instinctive recognition. The resonant echoes held a profound meaning that stirred their primal senses. It was a call, a rallying cry that reached the depths of their beings. They knew it to be the commanding voice of their alpha, the undisputed leader of their clan who guided their every move.

It was an order, a directive that commanded their obedience. The alpha's call echoed with authority, embodying the essence of their collective strength and unity. It was a summoning, a declaration that stirred their hearts and propelled them into action.

With unwavering loyalty, they responded.

Among them was the Bigfoot that had been dragging Alex. In a sudden shift, he turned his gaze towards her, maintaining his grip on her ankle for an extra fleeting moment. Then, to her astonishment and overwhelming relief, he relinquished his hold. And with a swift motion, he darted away, emitting a triumphant whoop that reverberated through the air as he hastily departed the scene.

Alex, bewildered and shaken, just sat there on the floor for a minute. Staring outside the front door, she slouched on the floor and began sobbing with relief, realizing how close she had been to dying. Her nervous tears heaved her body and stirred up her nauseous stomach. She threw up.

Before she could regain her composure and painfully pick herself up, she reassured herself, *it's over. It's--they're... gone.* She then wobbled onto her shaky legs.

Grimacing from the searing pain of the scratches etched across her back, she took a moment to assess herself for any further injuries. With a surge of relief, her thought was one of heartfelt gratitude. *Thank God! Nothing broken.* Yet, a nagging concern lingered in her mind.

"Ellie!" she cried out, her voice resounding through the tense silence.

In response, she heard nothing—at first. But after a moment, she heard faint footsteps cautiously descending the stairs.

As Alex walked towards the bottom of the staircase, their eyes met. With a tear of relief tracing a path down her reddened cheek, she gazed up at Ellie, her now favorite student. Concern etched across her face, she asked, her voice trembling with a mixture of worry and care, "Ellie, are you all right?"

Ellie nodded silently, her demeanor hinting at a state of shock that enveloped her fragile being.

Understanding the weight of the ordeal they had just endured; Alex couldn't help but empathize with Ellie's overwhelming emotions and state of shock.

She then spoke gently to her, "It's okay, Ellie. They're... it--it's gone. They left. You can come down now."

As the girl descended, their arms intertwined in a tight embrace, seeking comfort and reassurance. Ellie's eyes, filled with worry and uncertainty, locked with Alex's gaze, and she implored, her voice trembling, "What about my dad? And Ty? Have you heard anything?"

With a determined expression, Alex pursed her lips and replied, "Let me go check once more." She walked over to her phone on the table, desperately hoping for any news that would ease their growing anxiety. As she glanced over at the screen, a sinking feeling washed over her. She sighed, looked over at Ellie, her voice heavy with disappointment. "No, still nothing. I'm sorry."

Although it had only been an hour and ten minutes since Carter left for the woods, it had seemed like an eternity. Alex felt a mix of frustration and helplessness, lowering her gaze and shaking her head in disbelief.

Breaking the oppressive silence, she said with resolve, "I've had enough of this craziness. If they don't show up in the next five minutes, I'm calling the police."

Ellie's facial expression showed a mixture of resignation and hope. She nodded in silent agreement.

242

Sensing the weight of responsibility, Alex gently placed her hand on Ellie's shoulder, offering reassurance. Not wanting to be caught off-guard again, she said, "Ellie, I'm going to go reload the rifle, just in case. You just sit tight, okay?"

Once again, Ellie nodded, acknowledging her teacher's instructions with a mix of obedience and gratitude.

As Carter negotiated the final stretch of the trail, anticipation and dread clenched his heart. He treaded cautiously, skirting along the edge of his workshop, his eyes fixed on the familiar sight of his deck, patio, and the view into his kitchen. A wave of despair washed over him as he beheld the shattered glass patio door. *Oh, no! Please, no… not this*, he thought.

Turning to Tyler, his voice strained with concern, he instructed, "Ty, listen… you stay right behind me, son. And if you see anything strange—like a monkey man—you *scream*, all right?"

Without hesitation, Tyler nodded, trusting his father's guidance implicitly.

Resolute and alert, Carter retrieved his gun once more, his trembling fingers cocking the weapon as he ascended the three steps to the deck, his gaze piercing into the interior of his dilapidated home.

Meanwhile, Alex, attuned to the sounds of footsteps and labored breathing, stood poised with a freshly loaded rifle. Positioned strategically behind the kitchen wall in the hallway, she steeled herself for whatever lay ahead. A mix of adrenaline and determination coursed through her veins as she braced for the next encounter.

And then, amidst the tense stillness, she heard it...

"Hello? ... Ellie? Alex?" Carter's voice rang out, traversing the broken glass, his ears yearning for the familiar sound of a female response.

"Carter!" Alex exclaimed, a rush of relief washing over her as she lowered her rifle and hurried toward the boundary between the kitchen and hallway, making herself visible.

Simultaneously, another voice erupted from the stairs, filled with a mixture of disbelief and joy. "Dad? Dad! Is that you?!" Ellie's words spilled out in an eager and emotional stream.

Carter stood there, surrounded by the remnants of his dilapidated kitchen, his heart swelling with emotion at the sight of his beloved Ellie running towards him. Tears welled up in his eyes as he embraced her, savoring the warmth and safety of their reunion.

In that moment, a silent understanding passed between Carter and Alex as he kept glancing over at her invitingly. With a nod, she approached them, joining in the group embrace, her heart filled with both comfort and concern. As she touched Carter, he winced, his physical state clearly reflecting the challenges he had endured.

Stepping back slightly from the family huddle, Alex cast an assessing gaze up and down at Carter's disheveled appearance. With a mix of relief and playful concern, she couldn't help but speak her mind. "Believe me, I'm relieved to see you, but, honestly, you look like crap," she remarked, her voice laced with both tenderness and a touch of humor.

Carter, wincing slightly at the soreness in his body, replied, "Well, you should see the other guy," his voice strained yet filled with a hint of bravado.

A smile tugged at the corners of Alex's lips as she nodded in understanding. "Oh, I can imagine." She replied. "I had the displeasure of meeting his brother," she quipped back, acknowledging the shared ordeal they had endured.

XII

Tender Loving Care

Sunday, October 9, 1:04 p.m.

Carter found himself about to embark on an
ambulance for the first time, an experience he
never thought he'd feel like he was missing out
on, but here he was, about to be hoisted in the back of the
emergency vehicle.

Before dialing 9-1-1, he and Alex had carefully
agreed on a precise narrative and course of action that
they would stick to, no matter what unfolded. To avoid
any complications, unwanted attention, or third-party
intrusions, they were determined to remain unwavering
in their plan and story.

As the two paramedics attended to Carter, one of
them proved to be more talkative than the other. The
cheerful and tall African American man in his late
twenties securing him onto the gurney couldn't help but

make some observations. "Falling off a cliff did this to you?! Man, that must've been one heck of a cliff!" He shook his head in disbelief.

Momentarily disregarding the paramedic's remark, Carter turned to Alex, who stood next to him just outside the ambulance, and nervously restated his wishes regarding the kids.

She just smiled in response and quipped. "Yes, I got you the first three times." However, seeing he really needed the reassurance, she whispered, "Don't worry, I've got it covered. You just focus on getting better, okay? We'll come and see you in a bit."

The chatty paramedic continued sharing his confusion. "I just don't get it. Why do you white folks keep venturing out into the wild like this? Do you have *any idea* how many hunting and hiking accidents like yours we see in a year? Take it from me, y'all need to stay indoors. Play video games or watch TV or something, you know?"

Carter, seizing the opportunity to inject some humor, replied in a playful tone, "But, *hfnn*, then I wouldn't have had the pleasure of meeting you, buddy."

The paramedic chuckled and responded, "Ah, true dat, my man. True dat!" He flashed a wide grin and added, "And you know what? Because of that comment, I'm gonna keep you company and ride in the back with you. How's that sound?"

Carter, adopting a sarcastic tone, quipped, "Do I have a choice?"

The tall paramedic grinned even more and replied, "Nope, you don't." They shared a lighthearted laugh as the ambulance, sirens blaring, sped toward Simeon Heights General Hospital.

As Carter lay in the hospital bed, a man in his mid-fifties entered the room, holding a pad and pen. He had a slim build, neatly combed graying hair, glasses, and an overall uptight and intellectual appearance.

"So, um… What's up, doc?" Carter joked, attempting his best Bugs Bunny impression to lighten the mood.

Unamused, the doctor simply smiled at the witticism. "Well, Mr. Mitchell, it appears you have quite a bit of recovery ahead of you," he said.

"Yeah, I gathered as much," replied Carter. "Go ahead, doc. What's the verdict? I'm all ears… *hfnn*, if not much else." He continued with another jest.

The doctor smiled before delivering his diagnosis. "Well, you see, in your fall, you've sustained multiple contusions, four broken ribs on the right side, and your upper left arm has a closed fracture," he explained, presenting Carter with x-rays and test results.

"Okay. So, how long will it be until my arm is healed?" He inquired.

"Well, that might take some time. The ribs could heal in about six weeks, but the arm… You see, fractures like this typically require anywhere between 10 to 12 weeks to heal properly, depending on the individual, of course."

Crap! was the only word that came to mind as he absorbed the news.

Before leaving, the doctor paused and said, "Mr. Mitchell…"

"Yes?"

"You know, this town is called Simeon Heights for a reason…" the doctor said, adding a weighty and suspenseful pause.

Does he know about the town's name origin too? Carter fretted. But he exercised verbal restraint and asked the medic, "What's the reason?"

"Well, we live in an area surrounded by mountains, cliffs, and precipices. Hence the name *Simeon Heights*," the doctor explained matter-of-factly.

"Heights, ah, yes. *Got it*," Carter acknowledged, with a mix of amusement and relief.

The medic continued, adopting a stoic tone. "Knowing *this*, you need to be more careful when venturing into nature for hiking, fishing, or hunting. Your fall could have been much worse," he advised, before exiting the room.

<hr />

"Hey, Daddy," a soft and concerned voice broke through the haze. Carter groggily opened his eyes, realizing he had been asleep for a while under the effects of pain medication. Standing by his side were Ellie, Tyler, and Alex.

"Um, hey, guys. What's up?" he greeted them, a smile stretching over his sleepy face.

"The doctor said you'll be all right," Ellie said, with obvious relief in her voice.

"Yeah, but it's going to take some time," Carter replied, looking at his children with regret.

"We know. We'll pray for you to heal faster, right Ty?" Ellie said, turning to her little brother, who simply nodded. "And also, we're excited to go stay at grandma and grandpa's!" she added.

"Yeah," Carter said, "It'll be like a vacation for you guys, right?"

"Oh, yes!" they both exclaimed, their smiles reaching from ear to ear.

Carter returned the smile, then looked at Alex and asked, "So… when did they say they'd pick them up?"

"They said tomorrow, around noon," she answered.

"We can't wait!" Ellie chimed in enthusiastically.

Carter grinned, "I bet you can't," he said, turning his attention back to Alex. "This is good. I'm glad they agreed to take them. I don't know what I would've done if they'd said no."

"Hey, no worries, I would've done it for you," Alex reassured him. "Even if it meant extending my leave from school."

"Trust me," he said, gently taking hold of her hand. "You've already done *more than enough*. I'm grateful. Besides, you do have bills to pay, right?"

"Yeah, how can I forget?" she replied, rolling her eyes.

"So, um, how's your back?" Carter asked with a sympathetic grimace, concerned, and recalling her nasty scratches.

"Well, pretty tender, to be honest. But Dad took care of it. He disinfected the wounds and patched me up real good. I'll be okay."

"Was he... *upset*?" He asked apprehensively.

"Well, I am his *baby girl*; so, yeah." She said, chuckling. Noticing his nervous look however, she added, "But he understood the situation. Don't worry. He's not mad at you. He even said he would have done the same in your situation. He was just happy to know you'd be okay."

"Oh. Good." he said, relieved.

"Oh, I almost forgot," added Alex, "your in-laws were quite concerned when they heard the news. So, they mentioned they'd stop by the hospital before picking up the kids tomorrow, just so you know."

"Okay. Duly noted," he acknowledged, adding, "Oh, and Alex..."

"What?"

"Next time you come to visit, could you bring me... a Bible?"

Upon hearing this, she leaned down towards his night table, opened the drawer, and retrieved a New Testament. Waving it at him with a smile, she gently placed it on his lap.

"Well, will you look at that!" he exclaimed, slightly embarrassed. "I guess I have a lot to learn, huh?"

She chuckled at his lightheartedness. "Yes, you do. But that's okay. I can help you with that. I'm a teacher," she teased, before planting a gentle kiss on his cheek. With that, she bid farewell and left with the kids.

To inform his sister of his ordeal, Carter chose to do a video call. As anticipated, she was alarmed when she heard about his physical state and situation. He also informed Sadie about the temporary arrangement for the kids and the expected duration of his recovery.

Mindful of her tendency to worry excessively, however, he wisely stuck to his adopted narrative and withheld everything pertaining to the creatures. He rightly judged that his easily disquieted older sister wouldn't be able to handle the truth of what had transpired in those woods and the trials the kids had endured.

And when she offered to visit him at the hospital, he kindly told her to wait until he was discharged and settled back home before making the trip.

"Are you sure?" she asked, showing her eagerness. "It's not that far. I can come and visit."

With a reassuring tone, he replied, "Look, I appreciate your willingness, but trust me, I'll be out of here in a few days. I'm doing okay. Really. Plus, I can keep you updated through video messages, like now. I have everything I need right now. However..."

Interestedly, Sadie followed through. "Yes, I'm listening."

"Well, considering the holidays are just around the corner, and I won't be able to do much for a while, I thought it would be *real nice* if you and Marty would come over for Thanksgiving. And then maybe you could help, you know, prepare our traditional family feast, just like mom used to make. *Please*?" He pleaded, flashing his most endearing grin.

She responded with a chuckle, agreeing. "Oh, of course! I'd love to! That sounds fantastic!"

Happy, he added, "Plus, Thanksgiving falls on Ellie's birthday this year. I know she'd be thrilled to see you again for the occasion."

"Oh, how exciting!" she exclaimed. "Oh, and I have something *very special* planned for her 11th birthday. I promise I'll prepare a feast that you'll never forget!"

"I have no doubt about that. That's precisely why I asked," he said teasingly. "By the way, what's the surprise for Ellie?"

"Ha! I'm not telling *you*. It'll be a surprise for you and Ty as well," she replied in a mischievous tone. "But you know, Thanksgiving is still a month away. I'll come over before then. Once you're out of the hospital, I'll visit your place on weekends to cook and clean for you."

"Hmm, that sounds great, sis, but um... I already have someone helping me with that," he admitted.

"Really? Did you hire a maid?" she asked, bursting into laughter.

He joined in, laughing, and replied, "I wish. Actually, I kind of met someone."

"Whoa, wait... really? Well..." she paused, as if contemplating her own thoughts on the matter.

He half-expected a reproof, knowing her tendency to give him lectures. But her reaction surprised him.

"Ha! Well, wow! I'm really glad to hear this! You know, having a good woman by your side can make a world of difference!" she exclaimed. But just for good measure, she asked, "She *is* a good woman, right?"

"Oh, absolutely. *Of course* she is. I really think you'll like her," he reassured her.

"Well, what matters is that *you* like her," she said, pausing for a moment. "You know, I thought I had detected something different in your voice; a change in your tone. You genuinely seem... happier," she observed. "So, tell me everything! What's her name? What does she look like? Come on, spill the beans!" She teased playfully.

Gladly, he obliged her.

It felt liberating for Carter to share his feelings about the woman who made his heart beat once again. He hadn't had the opportunity to do so until now. So, he poured out his thoughts to his supportive older sister, cherishing her support.

As he spoke, his heart swelled with anticipation of what lay ahead this coming Thanksgiving. *Despite everything, I have a lot to be thankful for. So much can happen in a year,* he thought, reflecting on the transformative journey he had been on.

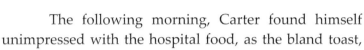

The following morning, Carter found himself unimpressed with the hospital food, as the bland toast, flavorless oatmeal, and pale scrambled eggs lived up to their infamous reputation.

Flipping through the cable TV channels, he couldn't find anything that caught his interest either. "I can't stand Cable News Network," he muttered as he switched off the TV and laid the remote next to him.

Suddenly, a gentle voice broke through his state of boredom. "Hello, Carter. Can we come in?" He recognized the voice of his ex-mother-in-law, Esther Adams. She and John stood at the doorway, hesitating to be invited in.

"Hey, of course. Yes, come in!" Carter welcomed them, genuinely happy to see them both.

After sharing the news of his diagnosis, discussing the potential length of his recovery, and engaging in light conversation, he provided them with more details about the children.

"Ellie's teacher, um, Alexandra, she's currently taking care of the kids," he explained. "She'll be tutoring Ellie three times a week over video calls to ensure she keeps up with her schoolwork."

"Yes, we know. That's what she told us over the phone, too. You don't need to worry. We've got this,"

Esther reassured with a warm smile as she laid her hand on his right arm. "Listen," she continued, "we just want you to know *two things*."

"Sure, what are those?" Carter responded.

"Well, first, we want to thank you for the trust you're showing us to take care of the children while you recover. And second, we want to reassure you that everything will be okay... with them... and with you," she explained.

"Um, gee, thanks," Carter replied, a hint of uncertainty in his voice.

Noticing his apparent confusion, John chimed in, "Look, Carter, we felt *terrible* when we heard the news of your accident, and... well, what she's trying to say is... we've got your back. We, um... we assumed you probably didn't have the proper insurance yet, so... we took care of your hospital bill. I hope that's okay."

Carter's eyes widened at the news. "I... *wow*. For sure, *yeah*, it's okay. Definitely. I... don't know what to say. I—"

"Look, it's the least we could do. Really." John said, cutting in and placing a sympathetic hand on Carter's shoulder. "After all, you're the father of our grandkids," he added.

"Thank you... thank you both so much. This... really means a lot," Carter expressed, moved by their kindness and generosity.

John then turned to Esther and asked her if he could have a word, "man-to-man" with Carter. She agreed and left the room.

What's on his mind? Thought Carter, feeling a tinge of apprehension.

"Look, Carter, um, here's the thing…" John began, pausing momentarily to gather his thoughts. "I've worked in the lumber industry for a significant part of my life, you know?"

Understanding this was a rhetorical question, Carter simply nodded.

John continued, "We used to cut down trees in many areas across the state to sustain our supply chain. And years ago, we've done some work in your area too, around Simeon Heights."

"Oh, I didn't know that," Carter said.

"Well, yeah, we did. And here's something not many people know because I never told them," John said, lowering his tone and pausing cautiously as if ensuring he disclosed nothing he shouldn't.

"Occasionally, we've encountered… *things* in the woods of Oregon, especially around here. We witnessed some… *unexplained* things."

Carter's heart skipped a beat, feeling a sense of unease.

"There was even a time when something, a creature, attacked our logging camp at night. Something *big*," the older man continued, his gaze unwavering as he looked directly into Carter's eyes. "Anyway, the next morning, we discovered footprints all over the place. These footprints were about 18 or 19 inches long, and they looked… human."

Carter couldn't help but feel a mix of curiosity and unease at this point.

"Look... you must be wondering why I'm telling you all this, right?" John asked.

"Well, yeah. I kinda am," Carter admitted, his curiosity piqued.

"Here's the thing... When you arranged for us to take care of the kids yesterday, we talked to them over the phone. And your friend, um, Alexa?" John said, searching for the correct name.

"Alexandra," Carter corrected.

"Yeah, right, *Alexandra*. Well, she passed the phone to us so we could have a conversation with them," John explained.

At this point, Carter found himself unsure of where this was heading, so he simply nodded and focused.

"So, we spoke with both of them. And Tyler... well, he kept talking about some *monkey-men* appearing in your backyard and telling us some wild tales," John revealed.

"Oh, I see..." Carter paused, mimicking a confident smile and mulling over his next words carefully, "Well, you know... kids, right? At his age, they have vivid imaginations," he responded, attempting to dismiss any concerns and hide the truth.

But John replied earnestly, "Carter, son, *please*. I know we've had our differences in the past, but... you can trust me with this."

After a loaded pause, the older man continued, "Now, Esther understood nothing Ty said. She just doesn't know anything about *Bigfoots* or anything like that. But as for me, well..." John paused once more, his gaze filled with sympathy as he seemingly peered inside Carter's soul. "Let's just say that my experience tells me you didn't just fall off a cliff."

Carter, taken aback, was rendered speechless.

Here stood a man he had known for well over a decade; someone who had mentioned *nothing* about his own encounters with Bigfoot. The revelation was both surprising and intriguing.

Sensing his ex son-in-law's reluctance to share his own experiences, John respectfully bade him farewell, expressing his well wishes before preparing to leave. However, before he departed, he turned to Carter one last time, a compassionate expression on his face. "I just wanted you to know. I guess... I wanted you to know, and I wanted to assure you that if you ever need to talk about it, I won't dismiss you as crazy or anything."

Carter, feeling a mix of gratitude and uncertainty, stammered, "Um, well, I--I thank you, John. I--I appreciate it."

The older man simply nodded, understanding the weight of the situation. As he stood in the doorway, ready to leave, Carter called out to him, "John..."

Turning around, John faced him once more, awaiting his inquiry.

Carter asked with a hint of vulnerability, "Did... did people call you crazy?"

"No." He answered, in a somber tone.

"Oh," Carter responded, his voice filled with a mixture of relief and curiosity.

"That's because I never told anyone but you," John said quietly, his words carrying the weight of a powerful hidden truth.

The man turned his back once more and silently left the room, leaving Carter to contemplate the significance of their shared knowledge.

XIII

Home Sweet Home

Saturday, October 15, 12:04 p.m.

It was a relief to finally be released from the confines of the hospital and return to the comfort of home. As he sat in the car, his arm in a plaster and sling, Carter couldn't help but appreciate the familiar sights along the road. *We notice things differently when we're not driving,* he mused.

Alex and James had graciously offered to drive him home. Carter found it surprising that James had actually insisted on accompanying them. The war vet just sat in the back of the vehicle and kept to himself for much of the way.

Is he trying to chaperone us? Carter speculated, finding his behavior odd. Nevertheless, as always, he welcomed the man's practical and no-nonsense company.

In his attempt to break his mentor's silence during the short drive, he asked, "So, how's the ankle now?"

James, with a quick wit and grin, simply replied, "Better than your ribs."

Carter chuckled, shrugging off the comment, and turned to Alex, who was focused on the road. She was smirking, clearly accustomed to her father's dry humor.

The atmosphere in the car was easygoing, easing his transition from the hospital to home. He was grateful for their presence and the familiar and friendly banter that brought a sense of normalcy to the ride.

As the car turned onto his driveway, he couldn't help but notice a familiar dark blue Ford pickup truck parked there. And sure enough, it was occupied by his neighbors, Glenda and Henry. As they parked, the couple stepped out of the cab to greet them eagerly. Carter observed an unusual spring in Henry's step. Opening the car door to get out, he was met with a warm smile from the old man, who extended his bony hand to help him and shook it vigorously.

"Welcome back, Carter!" Henry exclaimed with enthusiasm; his energy palpable in the handshake.

"Um, thanks, Henry," Carter replied, slightly taken aback by his elderly neighbor's uncharacteristic exuberance. He glanced at Glenda, expecting her to offer some explanation for her husband's behavior, but she simply smiled kindly and said, "Welcome back, dear."

Carter couldn't help but feel a sense of curiosity and intrigue about the sudden change in Henry's demeanor. The Twilight Zone analogy crossed his mind, wondering if there was something he had missed on the time-line continuum while at the hospital. He nonetheless appreciated the warm welcome from his neighbors, even if it left him puzzled.

Henry then extended his open hand, revealing a set of keys, and declared, "These, dear sir, are *your keys*."

Puzzled, Carter responded, "My... *keys*? I don't understand. I already have—"

Interrupting him, Henry pointed toward the house and explained, "For your *new* front door and back patio door."

Carter's confusion quickly turned to realization as he took in the state of his house. The memory of its dilapidated condition upon leaving for the hospital had momentarily slipped his mind, and he hadn't noticed the new doors yet.

With a hint of pride, Henry revealed, "After you called and asked me to nail plywood boards to your front and back doors, I thought I could do you one better. Didn't I ever tell you I worked as a contractor for fifteen years?"

Carter, teary-eyed, let out a chuckle. "Well, as a matter of fact, *no*, you never mentioned that," he said gratefully.

James chimed in, reassuringly, "Don't worry about it, son. We all pitched in."

Glenda added, "Yes, we did."

Henry then explained further, "I have connections in the construction industry, and we secured some great bargains. We even fixed that broken window in your kitchen. Everything is as good as new… for you and your kids."

The elderly neighbor beamed with a broad smile, proud of their collective effort to restore the house.

They all stood there, smiles lighting up their faces. Obviously, they had eagerly awaited this moment. Carter turned to Alex, his eyes wide with surprise, and asked, "You knew about this?"

Alex laughed gleefully and replied, "Are you kidding? *Of course, I did!* And I couldn't wait to see your reaction."

Glenda chimed in, "We also took care of cleaning up everything inside."

Overwhelmed with gratitude and emotion, he shook his head in disbelief. His lips trembled as he said. "Geez. This is too much, guys. Thank you, Henry. Thank you *all* so much!"

Glenda gently placed her warm hand on his arm, offering comfort. She smiled and softly assured him, "This is your home, Carter Mitchell. You and your kids are part of our community now—like family. You've more than earned it. And in Simeon Heights, we take pride in taking care of our own."

Carter, putting his hand atop of hers, couldn't help but wonder how much they knew about his journey, but he felt a deep sense of trust towards these people who had shown him such kindness.

"Come on," Alex interjected, taking his bag and guiding him up the stairs onto the porch. "Let's get you settled inside."

They spent an additional hour together, offering warm welcomes, keeping him company, and ensuring he'd be okay for his healing journey. Before parting ways, they gave him a tour of his fully stocked fridge and freezer, filled with Glenda's meticulously prepared meals.

As the evening set in, casting a twilight hue over the surroundings, Carter decided to make his way to his backyard and retrieve all the trail cameras. He had been thinking about those and was curious to review their footage. Realistically, however, he didn't expect capturing much. If there was one thing he had learned, it was that Bigfoots were masters of evading detection.

Seated in front of his PC, he methodically clicked through their footage, but one particular clip grabbed his attention and refused to let go. He paused it and replayed it—for the tenth time. His disbelief grew with each viewing.

Indeed, the trail camera installed on the side of the workshop had captured something truly ominous. It was dated from October 5th; the infamous day of Ty's abduction.

In the brief span of about seven seconds, the video revealed a dark, hairy figure, clearly bipedal, moving past the camera. Then, in a chilling twist, it returned, this time cradling his terrified son as it disappeared into the depths of the forest. It was the unmistakable alpha.

To Carter's shock, it seemed as if the creature had been aware of the camera, even looking right at it as it went past.

The trail-cam had captured not just the sight of his son being taken, but also the face of the creature responsible. It was a reminder that the entire nightmare had unfolded mere feet away from him, right under his nose. He was overwhelmed by the memory, realizing how close he had come to never seeing his son again that day.

They're safe now. Thank God, he thought, with a sense of relief. He briefly entertained the idea of having them stay with his stepparents permanently, but swiftly dismissed the thought. Deep down, what he dreaded was the notion of bringing them back here, with no assurance of safety.

Running his weary hand over his face, he took a step back from the PC, attempting to fend off the torrent of anxious thoughts inundating his tired mind. With the kids away for a few weeks, he now found himself with much free time. He reasoned it could be a blessing or a curse, depending how he chose to use it.

It's a lot of free time, he thought, recalling his father's admonition that idle hands were the Devil's playground. He resolved to make the most of this period — to heal, certainly, but also to restore a sense of peace and normalcy to their home and lives. He wondered if it was even possible, considering the trauma they had all experienced in this very house.

His thoughts returned to the harrowing trail camera footage, which, although extraordinary, had left him deeply disturbed. The clip had a dual quality to it. Not only was it highly personal, but it was also evidence—very compelling evidence. If it were to find its way online or into the hands of the Bigfoot community, it could serve as undeniable proof of the legendary creature's existence.

Taking precautions, he made three careful backups of the trail camera memory card—one on his laptop, another on a USB key he put in his safe, and a third sent to his own email. He also emailed the clip to James, confident that his mentor would handle it with utmost discretion.

Despite the footage's potential to bring him instant fame and validate the existence of Bigfoot, he made the deliberate choice to keep it private. Its sensitive nature and deeply personal impact outweighed any desire for recognition and notoriety at this point.

"Ha! Ca-Li-ma! *Caution Live Animals*. I Love it!" exclaimed Carter, as he cuddled Alex tightly on his living room couch. Cozied up together; they enjoyed every second of the movie.

During his recovery, one thing Carter had wanted to prioritize was deepening his relationship with Alex. He had invited her over for dinner on the weekend, but with his arm still in a sling, she had generously taken charge of most of the cooking. And as promised, she had also finally joined him in watching the 2001 version of *Planet of the Apes*.

"You know what?" he said, as the movie reached its harrowing conclusion.

"What?" she asked.

"It was *all right*, but I still prefer the classic 60's version with Charlton Heston."

"Really?! I was sure you'd prefer the 2001 version with Alexandra Walker," she quipped, a mischievous smile on her face.

He looked at her for a moment, clueless about the joke at first, until it clicked in his mind.

"Oh! Okay, *ha-ha*. Very funny. And yes, since you put it that way…"

He leaned in for a gentle kiss, which she happily reciprocated. However, tonight would not be a night for any fooling around, nor would it be for a while. Concerned about his recovery and true to her convictions, she had made that clear early on, *and* before coming over. As the end credits rolled on the screen, accompanied by eerie music, Alex rose from her seat to gather some dishes and bring them to the kitchen counter.

The clock had struck 9:00 pm, and the chilly rain tapped against the bay window in the living room, while gusts of wind swirled the dead leaves in Carter's front yard.

"I really *do* have to get going. Even if tomorrow is Sunday, I have a lot of corrections to do, so I have to get up early." She said.

"Oh, are you sure you need to leave now? It's still early. Can't you stay longer?" He said as endearingly as possible.

She sighed, restraining herself from falling under his charm. But she stuck to her guns. After all, she had been to his place a lot lately, making sure he was okay. This was her fourth time this week alone.

Deep down, he knew he needed to ease up on her heartstrings and her apron strings as well. On the other hand, he just couldn't get enough of her.

Looking at her, he smiled and said, "Okay. You know what? You're right. You do have *a lot* on your plate. I'll let you go… *for now*."

"Oh, thank you, warden!" she said facetiously, relieved he understood.

Now it was his turn to sigh.

He looked at her, paused, and then said, "You know, you've been taking care of me *a lot* ever since we met—and especially since my injuries." He paused again, and this time gently brushed his right hand against her left cheek, adding, "Mark my words, Alex. I'm going to get better soon; and then I promise… it will be *my turn* to take care of you."

A gentle smile spread across her face; her heart melting at those words. Now she really didn't want to go. She nonetheless gathered her courage and left the cozy warmth of his house, stepping away from his soothing embrace to confront the cold, wet, and muggy autumn weather outside.

Accompanying her to the front porch, he maintained a vigilant stance, gripping his handgun tightly while she traversed the 30-foot distance to her car. Alex and Carter both scanned their surroundings, their minds still haunted by recent memories and still healing from past ordeals.

Barely five minutes after her departure, Carter busied himself with tidying up the remnants of their lovely evening, when he caught the sound of an engine outside, accompanied by the glare of headlights shining through his living room window, nearly blinding him.

A surge of anticipation rushed through him as he entertained the thought that perhaps she had changed her mind and had returned. *Lucky me!* He thought, eager to welcome her back.

However, as he approached the front door, peering outside, it became apparent that the vehicle parked there did not belong to Alex. The reality sank in, dispelling his hopeful assumption. No, this was not Alex. Not even remotely close.

The door, once opened, revealed two ominous men dressed in black suits who now stood on his dimly lit porch. One of them, a towering figure of Mediterranean descent, appeared to be around his age. He stood at an intimidating 6'5" height. With his slicked-back black hair, well-groomed beard, and an imposing expression, he exuded an aura of intimidation. Weighing in at about 265 lbs, it was obvious that he served as the duo's muscle. The other man was older, balding, with a more affable demeanor. He addressed him, asking, "Carter Mitchell?" to which he nodded in confirmation.

After presenting their badges, which bore the inscription "Department of the Interior - U.S. Fish and

Wildlife Service - Special Agent," the older man introduced himself as *Special Agent Miller* while pointing to his partner as *Special Agent De Luca.* Agent Miller then expressed their intention to ask him a few questions as he inquired, "May we come in?"

"Um, yeah, sure," Carter replied, attempting to hide his rising anxiety.

As they proceeded towards the living room, Carter, trying to ease the tension, added a touch of sarcasm, saying, "I didn't realize fish and wildlife agents worked late nights and weekends. You guys do know it's Saturday, right? Do you get overtime pay for these visits?"

Agent Miller simply smiled at the gibe and responded, "We work around the clock, Mr. Mitchell. Nature never sleeps."

Carter gave a nod, put on an uncomfortable smile, then pointed them towards the large living room, allowing them to take a seat on the couch, while he stood facing them in a singular chair.

"Mr. Mitchell," Agent Miller began, "it has come to our attention that you've had some *unusual wildlife encounters* on your property lately."

"Um, yeah, I have. How...?" Carter paused, contemplating where they might have gotten this information. "Did you learn about this from the hospital?"

"We'll be asking the questions, Mr. Mitchell, if you don't mind." Agent Miller firmly replied.

"Huh, sure," Carter agreed reluctantly.

"So, would you care to tell us how your wildlife encounters took place?" asked Agent Miller.

"Well, the thing is, I've had many incidents of… *bears…* coming around on our property ever since I moved here some months ago. I have two kids, you know; a boy and a girl. They're not here now, but I can tell you it can be quite unnerving to have *bears* around when you're a parent of small kids. I've managed to…"

"Bears?" interrupted agent Miller, quickly glancing over at his counterpart, who remained stoically mute and still the entire length of their visit.

"So…" he continued, "these *bears*; have they engaged in any unusual behavior? Have they caused any *property damage?* Did you engage with them in any way? Did you shoot them? Have you noticed any *projectiles* thrown in your direction?"

"Woah! Slow down a bit. Well, yeah. I mean, they have caused some pretty nasty messes and some damage to my trash containers outside. I have to keep them under lock now. And… *projectiles*, you say? I don't understand. Can bears throw stuff?" He chuckled, almost tauntingly.

Agent Miller smiled reassuringly, before adding, "Of course not. We're just trying to be as thorough as possible in our investigation."

Carter remembered from his conversations with James that the government would never admit to the existence of Bigfoot. He also knew that they almost always substituted the word "Bigfoot" for "bear" in their reports. So, he cleverly attempted to stay under their radar for the length of the conversation—using their own lingo against them and feigning ignorance.

It worked. Almost.

They continued prodding him with their questions. Carter played the innocence card the whole time—staying on the subject of black bears. Before leaving, agent Miller said, "Well, Mr. Mitchell, we thank you for your cooperation in this investigation. Now, word to the wise... Do not engage with the... *bears*... in any way. Steer clear from them. This entire area is subject to a lot of activity and investigation. We'll deal with the rogue bears."

"Okay. I understand. Hey, thanks for coming by. Really." He said, accompanied by a slightly cocky smile.

As they were being escorted out, agent Miller turned to Carter and said, "Mr. Mitchell, one last thing..."

"What's that?" said Carter, recognizing the burgeoning intimidation tactic and expecting what would likely follow.

Agent Miller maintained a serious expression as he delivered his final admonition. "We know and understand what you saw and your interactions with *them*. Be advised that this place, your property, has a sordid history with these "bears", and this whole area is teeming with our monitoring and surveillance. It has been for years. Nothing escapes us. So, make sure that no matter what, you stick to your story—whether in person, on the phone, or online. Remember, if you deviate from *this story*, we will know. And our next visit may not be as agreeable. Is that understood?"

Carter tried to maintain his composure, simply nodding in response. He swallowed nervously and reluctantly replied, "Sure, I understand."

Finally, Agent De Luca, who had been silent until now, spoke up. He looked down at Carter's left arm and his cast, offering a sly smile. "Take care of that arm. Bears can be real bruisers."

With that, the agents stepped off the porch, casually strolled back to their black SUV, and departed from the premises, leaving Carter alone with his thoughts as he stared into the dark night through his rain-speckled window.

XIV

Thankful

Wednesday, November 23rd, 11:15 a.m.

As the silver Mercedes pulled up in his driveway, a mixture of nerves and excitement coursed through Carter's veins. It was the eve of Thanksgiving, and John had graciously driven the kids home to be reunited with their father on this special occasion.

"Daddy! Daddy!" Ellie's exuberant screams pierced the air. Bursting out of her grandfather's car, she wasted no time and dashed towards her father, her outstretched arms a beacon of love and joy.

"Daddy, daddy, daddy!" Tyler echoed, joining his sister in the heartwarming sprint.

It had been a long month, despite their many video calls. Carter's arm was still in a cast, but he felt much better overall. So, when they came charging, he embraced their fervor, absorbing the shock of their affectionate whirlwind of hugs and kisses.

He reciprocated their affection, holding them in a tender embrace. "I missed you both *sooo* much!" he whispered; his words filled with longing. Time seemed to stand still as they clung to each other, cherishing every precious second of their reunion.

John observed the heartwarming scene before him, a gentle smile gracing his lips.

Turning to him, Carter said, "I'm so glad you brought them over! Thanks!"

John dismissed the notion with a wave of his hand. "Don't be silly," he replied. "They're *your* kids—and they missed you *a lot*." His eyes shifted to Carter's injured arm, and he inquired, concern lacing his voice, "So… how are *you* feeling?"

"Better every day. Thanks for asking." Said Carter, as he added, "The arm still has a way to go. But I don't feel pain anywhere else. Ribs are fine; which is good. With any luck, I'll be able to resume work as soon as the cast is off. The doctor said that should be the week before Christmas."

John nodded, a supportive expression on his face. "That's good to hear," he acknowledged.

A brief moment of silence hung in the air before Carter steered the conversation in a new direction. "John, um, I was wondering, what are you and Esther doing for Thanksgiving? Any plans?"

John leaned back, considering the question. "Nah," he replied with a casual tone. "We're keeping it simple. We're doing our own quiet little thing."

Carter's eyes lit up as he spoke earnestly, "Well, the reason I'm asking is that we're having a nice gathering here tomorrow, for Thanksgiving—and you guys *are family*. You'd be more than welcome to join us."

Eavesdropping on the conversation, Ellie couldn't contain her excitement and chimed in, "Yeah, grandpa! That would be great! You and grandma should definitely come. My aunt Sadie will be cooking a feast... and she's the *best cook ever*. Plus, it's going to be my birthday celebration, too."

Her grandfather grinned mischievously, playing along, "Oooh, that sounds *important*," he teased, feigning surprise.

Determined, she insisted, "It is!"

Tyler joined in, echoing his sister's gusto, "Yeah, grandpa. We're gonna eat turkey, cakes, and all kinds of good stuff. You and grandma just gotta be here!"

Lowering himself to their eye level, John looked at both of them, his eyes twinkling with affection. A warm smile crossed his face as he responded, "Well now... that sounds like an offer I just *can't* refuse. I'll have to talk to grandma about it. Do you guys think I can convince her?" He then glanced up at Carter, exchanging a knowing wink.

Ellie and Tyler exchanged excited glances, nodding emphatically. "Oh, I'm sure you can, grandpa! She won't say no once she hears about all the delicious food," Ellie declared confidently.

That same afternoon, Ellie and Ty eagerly awaited the arrival of their Aunt Sadie and cousin Marty. The scene stirred a sense of déjà vu within Carter.

Ellie, in particular, was bursting with excitement. Not only would the celebration encompass Thanksgiving, but the prospect of receiving birthday gifts added an extra layer of gratitude to her anticipation.

Carter, too, looked forward to his sister and nephew's *second visit*, remembering all too well how the first one had gone. This felt like a fresh start for him in Simeon Heights—a second chance to rewrite his story here. He believed that this time would be different. After all, he was no longer weighed down by depression, and the Bigfoot situation seemed resolved. The absence of any recent activity gave him a newfound sense of ease and security. There was nothing to conceal this time around. Despite his still-healing arm, he felt content and at peace.

Inviting his ex-in-laws for Thanksgiving had also seemed like a wonderful idea to him. Well, initially anyway. He couldn't deny the awkwardness that would surely arise from Vivian's absence. But he reassured himself that, in time, they would all adjust and find a new rhythm. The presence of Alexandra undeniably also added a layer of complexity to the gathering, making him realize it too might feel strange at first. Truthfully, he hadn't fully considered the implications before inviting John and Esther. Yet, given the positive turn his relationships had taken recently, he held onto the belief that everything would work out just fine.

Life goes on, he reflected, looking back on the last year and acknowledging what lay ahead.

Just months earlier, he never could have imagined that he'd have a new love interest, new friends, and that he'd be reconciled with his step family. He had experienced loss, challenges, and growth; and now he stood at a new juncture filled with hope and possibilities. With a calm resolve, he embraced the future, ready to create new and lasting memories along with loved ones.

As the doorbell chimed, Ellie dashed downstairs, her enthusiasm lighting up her face as she swung the door open to be greeted by an exuberant Sadie, her arms outstretched in excitement.

"Hiii! Ellie! Ty!" she exclaimed with unmistakable joy.

"Aunt Sadie!" they both exclaimed in unison, wrapping their arms tightly around her in a warm embrace.

Sadie turned her gaze towards her brother and exclaimed, "Come here, you!" She hugged him carefully, expressing, "I've missed you all so much. We're going to have such a fantastic time!"

Standing behind her was Marty. Carter looked at his nephew, a smile stretched across his face. Extending his powerful hand, he greeted him warmly, "Hey Marty, buddy. How's my favorite nephew doing?"

Marty, somewhat uncomfortable at seeing his uncle with a broken arm, smiled shyly and responded, "Um, I'm good. Thanks." Then, turning to his mom, he eagerly asked, "Can we bring them over to the car, Mom? Can we do it *now*?"

Sadie looked up at them, paused her gaze on Ellie, and said, "Your cousin is excited because I have a gift for you in the car, *and it can't wait*. I can't give it to you in two days. It has to be *now*."

Ellie's eyes widened like saucers, and she clasped her hands together in front of her face, bouncing up and down with anticipation. "Really!"

"But," Sadie added, "this gift will also be a gift for your dad and brother. You'll have to share it."

At this, Tyler extended his grin ear to ear.

Ellie's excitement slightly dampened at the mention of sharing, and her jumping subsided, a visible reaction that made her aunt laugh.

"Oh, come now, girl! When have I ever disappointed you?" Sadie teased. Then, addressing everyone, she exclaimed, "Come on, follow us!"

As they approached the car, their curiosity grew as they noticed movement in the back seat. Carter, puzzled by the suspense, couldn't help but wonder if his sister had perhaps brought a surprise guest.

Pointing to the car, she revealed, "Your gift is in the back seat, Ellie."

With anticipation, they all peered inside the vehicle, and in a moment of collective amazement, they realized...

"It's a *puppy!*"

"Oh, my gosh! It's a puppy!" Ellie exclaimed once more, overwhelmed with joy.

Carter, taken aback, needed a moment to catch his breath.

Tyler joined in the excitement, cheering, "Yay! We have a new doggy! Yay!"

Sadie opened the car door and carefully picked up the pudgy, dark faced and brownish-gold puppy, passing it over to Ellie. Tears of joy streamed down the girl's red cheeks as she embraced the precious gift from her aunt.

Carter looked at his sister, shaking his head in disbelief. Concerned, he asked her one simple question, "What *breed* is it?"

"Leonberger," she replied, without missing a beat. Then she added, "and it's a male."

Carter pursed his lips, exchanging a meaningful glance with her. He then turned his attention back to the kids, and then the pup, then simply nodded and said, "Huh-uh."

The heavy pause between them spoke volumes.

"That's going to be a *BIG dog*," he said.

Sadie, keeping her gaze fixed on the heartwarming bond gradually forming between the kids and the puppy, calmly responded, "Yep, a BIG dog. Huge." She then added, "Oh, and I also bought you a bag of dog food. It's in the trunk."

"Um, thanks… sis," Carter acknowledged.

"You're welcome… bro," she said, smiling and still staring at the exuberant scene.

Aunt Sadie had made her mark. And with her determination unwavering, she wouldn't be denied. So, as the Mitchell children gladly welcomed their new furry member, Carter knew that this addition to his family was non-negotiable.

───────────── ◦●◦●◦ ─────────────

The kitchen at 426 Simeon Road overflowed with an abundance of food, joy, and celebration.

The long wooden table groaned under the weight of delectable dishes: creamy mashed potatoes, sweet potato casserole with a golden marshmallow topping, velvety gravy, a medley of marinades, vibrant green beans, sweet corn, warm golden dinner rolls, and tangy ruby-red cranberry sauce. But the centerpiece of this gastronomic spectacle was none other than the majestic turkey, roasted to near-perfection and brimming with flavorful stuffing, eagerly awaiting the skilled hands of a carver.

Seated around the table, a symphony of laughter and conversation filled the air. Ellie, Tyler, Alexandra, James, Sadie, Marty, John, and Esther each claimed their spot, their faces beaming with anticipation and gratitude.

At the head of the table, presiding over the festive gathering, sat Carter. A sense of fulfillment radiated from him as he embraced the warmth of their presence.

He stood up, and as his gaze swept across the faces gathered around the table, his voice filled with sincerity, "Today is Thanksgiving, and I want to do just that. I want to *give thanks*."

He had their undivided attention, so he cleared his throat and continued.

"For the longest time, I used to take this holiday for granted. I really did. I would just go through the motions. I would just, y'know, stuff myself silly, and then sit on my ass to watch football." He said with a grin.

They all laughed, imagining the scene.

He confessed further, "I just didn't get it," his voice now filled with a mix of humility and awe.

The attentive faces around him conveyed their curiosity and support, as they waited eagerly for his next words.

He continued, "In all honesty, this last year has been the *craziest* of my life, but also one of the most blessed."

He was a bit choked up by the emotion, so he paused once more, gathering his thoughts.

"This past year has been an absolute *blessing* because I finally realized how much God is watching over me and my family. He watches over me through some amazing folks and despite very tough times," he said, giving everyone a grateful glance. "I've truly understood the depths of His love for me. But let me tell you, this year has also been a blessing because of all of you right here at this table. I can literally count my blessings just by looking around at each one of you. I have a unique bond with everyone here that I cherish. Each in your own special ways, you've all been exceptional to me throughout this year. So, what I really want to say is that... I want to give *thanks* to each one of you. I also want to express my gratitude for my health, my life, my children, and this delicious feast. Oh, and Sadie, let's raise our glasses to *you* for whipping up this incredible meal." He said, turning to her at the last.

And a mere second later he added, "... and for skillfully carving that turkey, especially considering my arm," lifting his glass and letting out a chuckle.

"Woo-hoo!" Shouted James, who added jokingly, "Carter Mitchell for president!"

They all burst into laughter, clapping and cheering along.

"Hey, dad," Ellie called out playfully, "You totally forgot to give thanks for Bruno!"

Carter looked at her, a hint of confusion etched on his face. "Bruno? Who's *Bruno*?"

Ellie rolled her eyes and replied with a hint of annoyance, pointing to the lively pup playing with a squeaky toy in the living room. "He's *our new puppy,* silly!"

"Oh, yeah. My bad. So, Bruno it is, huh?" he whispered to her, nodding in understanding.

"Yeah, that's his name," Ellie proudly confirmed.

"Well, it's a good name. I like it," he said with a smile.

Taking a spoon, he gently tapped his glass to get everyone's attention once more. "Listen up, everyone. Ellie is absolutely right. I almost forgot to express our gratitude for our new family member: Bruno the Leonberger."

They all chimed in, agreeing the name was well chosen for the feisty pup.

"He did *what*?!" Alex gasped, nearly choking on her cranberry spritzer.

Sadie couldn't contain her laughter, her eyes teary from the amusement. "Oh, yes! Yes, he did! Let me tell you, he wasn't exactly an angel growing up."

"I can believe that!" Alex exclaimed, surprised by what she had just heard.

Overhearing their conversation, Carter's curiosity and apprehension got the better of him, so he approached them.

"All right, you two. So, what did she tell you, Alex?" he asked, a hint of nervousness in his voice.

"Oh, no you don't," Sadie interjected playfully. "This is between *me* and *Alexandra*. There are some things she just needs to know about your younger years. And since you won't spill the beans, it's *my duty* to enlighten her," she teased.

Carter looked at Alex, his worry obvious. She pursed her lips, trying to stifle a laugh.

"Please tell me she didn't tell you about the time I got drunk and crashed my dad's tractor," Carter pleaded.

"As a matter of fact, *no*, she didn't," Alex replied, her eyes widening in surprise. "But now that you mention it, I'm dying to hear *that* story!" She turned back to Sadie, who erupted into laughter.

"Oh, *yes!* You absolutely have to hear this one!" Sadie exclaimed, clearly enjoying herself.

Slightly annoyed by their complicit banter, Carter shook his head as he left the conversation. Deep down, however, he was glad to know that these two important women in his life were getting to know each other, and getting along, even if it came at his expense.

Next, he shifted his focus towards John and Esther, who had made the decision to leave the party early in order to embark on the hour-long drive back to Portland. Expressing his good wishes, he warmly embraced both of them. And the kids, who had also gathered to bid farewell to their grandparents, joined in for heartfelt hugs.

Meanwhile, quietly sitting in the living room, observing Bruno playing with his chew toy, was Carter's older partner in crime, James. Unassumingly, Carter joined him on the couch.

Keeping his gaze fixed on the dog, James remarked, "You know, this pup is going to make *one fine dog* for your family."

"Yeah, he's something special, isn't he?" Agreed Carter.

James simply nodded in agreement, understanding the sentiment.

They sat there in silence for a minute until Carter spoke up. "A couple of weeks ago, I had a visit from some government agents."

Turning to Carter, with a raised eyebrow, James suggested, "Let's grab our coats and go for a walk."

A couple of minutes later, they made their way to the workshop at the back of the house. It was evening, and darkness enveloped the surroundings, prompting Carter to switch on the lights.

James peered outside through the open garage door and asked, "So, who paid you a visit? Cops? FBI?"

"Fish and wildlife. Special agents," Carter replied.

"Hmm, they wasted no time, huh?" James remarked, nodding slightly. "So, what did you tell them?"

"I told them it was bears," Carter answered.

"Good," James nodded. "That's what they would have said too, if you had gone to them. Trust me, they're just tryin' to scare you."

There was a pause, and then James inquired, "Did they scare you?"

"Well, yeah, somewhat. One of them was huge, and he looked nasty," Carter admitted.

"Yeah, I know. They came to see me at my place as well," James revealed.

"What?! Why didn't you tell me?" Carter exclaimed.

"Hey, isn't that what I just did?" James replied with a smirk.

Carter sighed and shook his head. But he had grown accustomed to James' unique way of conversing by now.

"So, what did *you* tell them?" Carter pressed.

"The same thing as you. Bears," James calmly replied.

"So… what's our next move?" Carter asked.

"We lay low for a while. Don't worry, you'll be fine. Trust me," James said reassuringly.

The old soldier paused, then added, "By the way… that clip you sent me, it was the best damn clip I've ever seen from *any* trail cam. And believe me, I've seen a lot of clips you won't find anywhere."

"Um, yeah, about that... Can I ask you something?" Carter inquired.

"Sure."

"Were you ever tempted to, like, use footage or other stuff to, like, get rich or famous?" Carter asked.

"Of course I was. I may not look it, but I'm as human as the next man," joked the old soldier, quickly adding in a more serious tone, "But I never did—for security reasons. And neither should you. And now, I'd like to tell you somethin'," he said.

"Sure. What's that?"

"Well, I know your entire story because, out of necessity, you shared it with me. I'm thankful for that. Now, through these encounters and battles you've been through with these creatures, you might not realize it, but you've been given a gift," he said.

"Oh. What's that? My broken arm or my broken ribs?" Carter said in jest.

James chuckled and gathered his thoughts before expounding, "Son, I've been through war and situations that would frazzle most men. I've lived through them and learned to keep my cool under fire. I've become hardened and seasoned. But it took me years to get there. I had to learn it."

After a heavy pause, he sighed and continued, "When we were in that firefight together, and all hell was breaking loose, I gotta tell you... I had never before seen a guy keep his cool as well as you did—except for some marines. I tell ya, what you did, and the way you did it— it took balls of steel."

Knowing James only gave compliments sparingly, Carter said, "Um, thanks, I guess. But my motivation was different. I was fighting for my home and my kids. I'm pretty sure a lot of guys would have shown the same guts under those circumstances."

"Maybe so... but I have a point to all this," replied James.

"Oh, okay. Go on," said Carter.

"Even if I'm healing, the truth is... I'm getting older. I'll probably stay with a limp, too. And what you don't know is that..."

He paused, and then continued, "Throughout the years, for every *one* landowner that I've helped with their Bigfoot problem, I probably had to refuse three more. I just couldn't afford the time, resources, and energy to help all those people who were referred to me."

"Wait, are you suggesting...?"

James cut him off before he could finish. It was hard to get him to talk, but when he got started, he always had lots to say. "Now hear me out. What *I am suggesting* is this... you were given a gift from the Lord—if kicking Bigfoot's ass can be called that."

Carter chuckled at the man's colorful words.

"So, here's what I am saying, son. I believe our talents are God's gifts to us, and what we do with them is our gift back to God. Now, with my resources, my know-how, my coaching, and your youthful nerves of steel, we could start doing what I could never do alone. We could help more people than ever find freedom from fear on their own property." Said the older man, confidently gazing at Carter.

"Um, okay. That's a cheery little speech. It's Cute. It really is. But there's something you seem to be forgetting," said Carter, looking James in the eye.

"What's that?" inquired James.

"Seriously?! I have to spell it out for you?!" said Carter, clearly annoyed. "You *do realize* we almost *died* out there, right?! I mean... look at your ankle! Look at my arm for crying out loud! Plus, I've got government spooks after me, and my house was torn apart; not to mention I almost lost my son!"

James remained quiet, and he nodded understandingly. After a loaded pause, he said, "Look, Carter, I know. And you're right, too. There was a hefty price tag—no doubt about it. I'm not saying you should go all gung-ho with this either. Not at all. I'm just saying that maybe you should consider it. That's all."

Bordering exasperation, Carter sighed and said, "No way! It would be crazy! And, with all due respect, *sir*..." he said pointedly, "you're forgetting Alex in all of this. Are you forgetting she got attacked, too? And how many times did she fear losing her dad because *you* had chosen to do this crazy stuff? I mean, after all, it was *this lifestyle* that killed your marriage, *wasn't it?*"

James sighed, acquiescing and remembering all those times. His gaze fell downward. "You're right." He said pensively. "I have done some *crazy things* that I'm not proud of throughout the years. Made some poor decisions. I definitely took too many risks. But..." He raised his gaze to meet Carter's once more, "If I remember correctly, it was for this '*crazy stuff*' that you asked for *my help*. And *help* I did. You can't deny that, can you?" He said, defiantly staring at his younger counterpart.

The two men had never argued this way before. And this last remark stung. James knew it. He liked Carter, almost like a son, so he relented. "Look, I don't want to get on your bad side. I know what you've been through. I--I'm just asking you to think about it. That's all." He said calmly.

To which Carter replied directly, "And there's *nothing* to think about. I care too much about my kids, and about your daughter, to even consider it. So, no. Not gonna happen. Case closed."

"Fair enough." Said James, nodding. "Now, I just want you to know… that I respect your decision."

"Really?" asked Carter, surprised.

"Nah. I don't. I'm too dang old to change my mind. I'm just trying to sound agreeable." Wittily retorted the army vet.

Carter chuckled and, changing the subject, said, "Hey, it's pretty brisk out here. How 'bout we get back inside and catch the rest of the football game? I'll make a fire."

"Sure. Sounds good. Who's playing again?" asked James, as they walked back towards the house.

"Arizona vs. Washington." Answered Carter.

Their conversation grew faint as they turned off the lights, exited the workshop, and returned to the bustling atmosphere indoors. Once there, they sought the comfort of the celebration and engaged in more casual discussions.

The vibrant sounds, revealing lights, animated voices, bustling gathering, and the unusual level of activity on the property had, once again, captured the interest of an unseen presence. Unbeknownst to both men and the oblivious revelers indoors, there had been a silent spectator, scrutinizing their every move from a distance, concealed in the woods—just beyond the tree line.

Epilogue

Sunday, May 21, 4:08 p.m.

After a long, peaceful, and rewarding winter, Spring had finally sprung in Simeon Heights. True to their reputation, April showers had paved the way for an enchanting display of May flowers, filling the air with their delightful fragrances.

Not wanting to let a beautiful Sunday afternoon go to waste, Carter, accompanied by Alex, the kids, and Bruno, had decided to indulge in a pleasant family bout of baseball in the backyard.

America's favorite pastime had once been Carter's passion. In high school, he possessed natural athleticism, determination, and had even earned accolades from his coaches, paving the way to a potential career in the major leagues. For varying reasons, however, not the least of which were injuries; he had redirected his path towards the more pragmatic and secular pursuit of residential plumbing. He excelled at the trade, too, becoming highly skilled and even enjoying it. So, for him, baseball, although not a possibility professionally, never had the sting of a broken dream. Rather, it signified a different chapter in his life, a distinct season that evoked many cherished memories. Even to this day, playing it brought him immense joy.

Throughout the previous colder months, Carter had diligently built a name for himself as one of the finest plumbers in town. Combining clever marketing, hard work, fair pricing, and positive word-of-mouth, his business now thrived beyond his wildest expectations. The influx of customers was such that he now contemplated the idea of expanding his operations by bringing in additional help.

Meanwhile, Ellie and Ty were nearing the end of their first academic year in Simeon Heights. Ellie, in particular, had made notable progress. Her grades were good, and with the help of the school psychologist, Mrs. Cole, her therapy sessions had proven immensely beneficial.

As for Alex, she now proudly and deservedly sported a gorgeous diamond ring on her left hand. Carter had eagerly proposed over the Christmas break, and she had been more than happy to oblige. Prior to popping the question, he had even mustered the courage to ask her father for her hand in marriage. How she wished she had been a fly on the wall for that conversation. But she knew that her dad, despite his hardened exterior, really liked Carter. *These two have been through a lot together*, she thought, as she heard the crack of the bat hitting her best fastball.

"Yay! Go Daddy!" yelled Tyler enthusiastically, clearly revealing where his loyalties lay.

Carter looked over at Alex and beamed as the baseball sailed high above the trees and far away into the forest, making it impossible to retrieve.

"Well, that's the fourth ball we've lost today. I think we should call it a day. This is getting expensive," he said.

"Aww, come on!" said Ellie. "It's not fair to us. Can't we have one more turn at bat?"

"Oh, all right. Just one more round," said her dad, reluctantly giving in to her plea.

As the joyful clamor and excitement of their family ball game eventually subsided, they tidied up and retreated indoors for dinner.

Once they departed, an eerie stillness settled over the backyard.

The gentle breeze rustled the budding branches, creating a faint whisper. But beyond that, a deep quiet blanketed the area. No birds sang, no bees buzzed, no crickets chirped; there was nothing but complete stillness.

And then it happened.

With no witnesses or audience to observe, it descended from the sky and landed in the heart of the yard. Emerging from the depths of the woods, high above the tree line, it bounced three times and rolled effortlessly until it reached the center of the open space and attained motionlessness.

There it now stood, amid the green grass...

One solitary baseball.

In the forest they remain, skillfully blending into the shadows, concealed from sight. There exists something formidable within those woods—colossal beings.

There, they lie in wait, observing, monitoring, their presence obscured by silence and stealth.

In the forest, no one ever truly stands alone. Hikers, hunters, and nature enthusiasts may not perceive their presence, but they are always watching, always vigilant.

Across the vast expanse of Oregon's woodlands and beyond, they have been observing us for centuries. Deep within America's national parks, states, provinces, and spanning the entire North American continent, they have thrived, existing both nearby and far away, often overlooked to this very day.

Only a select few, the likes of Carter Mitchell or James Walker, have glimpsed fragments of their mysteries. Yet, in contrast, they have been privy to our many secrets for centuries.

Within our forests, they thrive, lurking, observing, and patiently awaiting their time. They decide when to be seen.

And make no mistake—they see you. Every. Single. Time.

"Be extremely subtle, even to the point of formlessness. Be extremely mysterious even to the point of soundlessness. Thereby you can be the director of your opponent's fate."
~Sun Tzu, The Art of War

THE END

ABOUT THE AUTHOR

Kyle Steel was born in 1974 and currently lives in Eastern Canada with his wife, Elisabeth, and their three children: Jason, Marissa, and Katelyn. They share life with their beloved miniature poodle, Teddy.

Kyle's insatiable curiosity about cryptids, conspiracy theories, and ancient history has shaped his unique perspective on the world. A former blue-collar worker, he embarked on a transformative journey to become an author and preacher, channeling his passion into captivating storytelling.

When he is not immersed in his writing, Kyle can be found exploring the great outdoors or cherishing quality time with his family. He is an ardent fan of life-changing books and movies, drawing inspiration from the realms of mystery, the supernatural, or science fiction. He is passionate about the comfort of pub-style food, and has proven to be a decent cook in his spare time.

Through his writing, Kyle loves to offer readers thrilling adventures that challenge their perceptions and ignite their sense of wonder. His unique blend of gripping storytelling and thought-provoking themes captivates audiences, leaving them yearning for more.

With an innate desire to explore the unknown and share profound insights, Kyle Steel's work has established him as a distinguished voice in the cryptid fiction world.

Made in United States
North Haven, CT
16 January 2025

64514306R00186